The Talk of the Town

The Brazen Burrells, Book 3

By
Lynne Connolly

DRAGONBLADE
PUBLISHING, INC.

ARE YOU SIGNED UP FOR DRAGONBLADE'S BLOG?

You'll get the latest news and information on exclusive giveaways, exclusive excerpts, coming releases, sales, free books, cover reveals and more.

Check out our complete list of authors, too!

No spam, no junk. That's a promise!

Sign Up Here

www.dragonbladepublishing.com

Dearest Reader;

Thank you for your support of a small press. At Dragonblade Publishing, we strive to bring you the highest quality Historical Romance from some of the best authors in the business. Without your support, there is no 'us', so we sincerely hope you adore these stories and find some new favorite authors along the way.

Happy Reading!

CEO, Dragonblade Publishing

Additional Dragonblade books by Author Lynne Connolly

The Lyon's Den Series
Lyon Eyes

The Brazen Burrells Series
The Only Honest Man in London (Book 1)
An Unusual Courtship (Book 2)
The Talk of the Town (Book 3)
On Christmas Day in the Morning (Novella)
The Lair of the Burrells (Novella)

The Daring Dersinghams Series
A Touch of Silver
A Hint of Starlight
A Trace of Roses
A Bunch of Mistletoe
A Whisper of Treason
Past, Present, Future (Novella)

Chapter One

June 1818

DESPITE THE RAIN, Alexander Fraser enjoyed his ride to work. Once he arrived, the usual press of activity awaited him. After handing his horse's reins to the groom in charge of the stables, he went inside, enduring the "Good morning, sir," from the overseers and foremen who could spare the time to greet him. As he walked through the door, the sound of engines chugging and shuttles flying greeted him. Home. He might have a perfectly comfortable house in the country, but this was where he belonged.

"And to think," he muttered sardonically as he finally gained the sanctuary of his office, "I could have been wasting time in the ballrooms of London." He would never regret turning his back on all that.

He'd grown up running around the factory, being scolded by the foremen. He'd never forget the strictures he received from his father when he'd joined a boy under one of the machines. The lad had to grab the loose wool before it clogged the machine, and Alexander had regarded it as a game. It wasn't. Children were killed.

When Alex had learned about the danger, he'd worked obsessively until he'd developed something that did the job with less peril to human life. His father had said it would take too long, but Alex insisted, and they'd put the extended broom into practice. Other factories still used children because it was faster, but Alex never begrudged the bale or two that it cost him. But then, he could afford it.

He nodded to the people who found the time to look up. The drone and churn of the looms, the clang and the constant chug-chug of the engines that drove them would have deafened most people, but Alex wasn't most people. He'd grown up here, learning the business, getting into mischief. The noise was so loud the women only mouthed to each other when they wanted to speak. Alex could do that, too. He could have avoided the factory, gone in the main entrance, the one used by important visitors, but he preferred to survey his kingdom before he took his place in the throne room.

The series of offices held clerks and managers, who glanced up and nodded. Alex preferred not to stand on ceremony. As he expected, his manager scurried in after he'd perched his hat and coat on the iron stand by the door and taken his seat behind the desk. Despite the drizzle that promised to keep up all day, Alex was looking forward to getting to work.

"Morning, master," the little man said, dropping a pile of correspondence on his desk. "Not much, sir, but a few requests to see you."

"About what?"

"This 'n' that." Acaster scratched his bald pate, avoiding the fringe of hair that ringed it like a halo. His angelic appearance belied a sharp mind and an ambition for himself and for Fraser's. "The machine on the third floor nearest the door is broken again."

"It might be easier to get rid of it and buy a new one."

"It might," Acaster said. "We can use the old 'un for spares."

Alex looked up, meeting his manager's eyes. "You counted the cost." It wasn't a question.

Silently, Acaster dropped a sheet of paper on the desk. "I did."

"I'll look at it." And probably approve it. They were low on spares. Scrapping a problem machine was usually cheaper than continually trying to mend it.

As if begrudging the words, Acaster said, "There's a man waitin' to see you. I put him in the small waiting room."

"Yes?" Alex leaned back and gave Acaster his whole attention. "Does this man have a name?"

Acaster waited for the space of a blink, as if he was trying to recall the name. "Villiers," he said. Fumbling in his pocket, he dropped a card on the table. The right-hand corner was folded down. Not a convention used in these parts, but Alex knew it. It meant the man was waiting for an answer in person. Society used it. If he spent his time at home receiving visitors, no doubt one of them would use it.

He picked up the card. Thick, pricey pasteboard. He read it. *Charles Villiers, attorney at law, land steward.*

"Wonder who he's working for as a land steward?" he said, but he thought he knew. "Wonder if I should see him," he continued.

"Your father's people?" Acaster said.

"Probably. Can you send him away?"

"Might be quicker to see him," Acaster answered, going to the door. "You can listen to him and get rid of him rather than him taking up space."

"You don't approve."

"Not my place." Acaster sniffed. "But for what it's worth, no."

Alex trusted his manager's judgment. So he would see this Villiers and send him on his way. The man might hang around all day otherwise. He had a fleeting vision of finding him in twenty years, a shriveled skeleton in a small room that everybody had forgotten. He smiled. Not in this place, where every inch of space was put to use.

"All right, send him in. I didn't see anything in the stables."

"Left his chaise outside the front door. If you'd used that you'd have seen him."

Well, he hadn't. Alex waved at Acaster, who went out.

He returned in five minutes, with the visitor in tow. That gave Alex time to retrieve his coat and shrug into it. But good though his clothes were, he could not compete with this vision of magnificence.

Charles Villiers was a tall man, not to say lanky, and the way he stuck his nose in the air made him seem taller. He could hardly help it, though, because of the height of his shirt points, which stuck into his cheeks as if pointing the way to his brain. He wore a coat of blue superfine that looked as if Weston had a hand in its making, but Alex's critical eye spotted the way it didn't quite fit in places, as if it had belonged to someone else, or that the owner had lost weight and breadth of shoulder.

He rose from his chair, hand outstretched. But Villiers executed a graceful bow.

"Mr. Fraser," Villiers said, as if addressing a public meeting. Not in pitch, but in the careful enunciation of each syllable. Almost reverently.

Alex went on alert. He didn't have to hear any more to know the person this man served. But he listened anyway and concocted a rough plan.

"Shall I get some tea, Mr. Fraser?" Acaster asked, his accent a little broader than usual.

Alex followed his lead. "Aye. The best china, I'm thinking." He used the long *a* instead of *I*, drawing it out more than even the locals did.

Villiers's finely plucked brows rose slightly. "I have come from Stonyhurst Park, at the behest of my master, the Marquess of Stonyhurst."

So the old devil had deigned to talk to him, had he? Alex had received another letter from his uncle a week or so ago. Come to think of it, it was more like two weeks. He hadn't opened them yet. He had no reason to do so, and he was considering tossing them on the fire rather than letting them gather dust on the mantelpiece in his bedroom. But now the old man had sent someone. He must be rattled about something. Perhaps he wanted money, although the marquess had been well cushioned when he'd last looked. How long ago? Must be, oh, five years.

Alex leaned back and indicated the chair in front of his desk with an airy wave. "Sit."

The man examined the chair, pulled out a monogrammed handkerchief and dusted the shining wood before he lifted his coat tails and delicately sat. He kept his back straight, his knees together and his hands lightly resting on them. "Sir. Mr. Fraser," he began, and cleared his throat. "You bear an honorable name."

"Thank you. Fraser's is a gradely business. Built from a little mill right up to this." He let his chest puff up with pride and watched Villiers try not to wince. The wicked spirit that had taken hold of him rejoiced.

Villiers failed miserably. His wince could have been seen on the factory floor if the walls were glass. "I was not referring to . . . this." He waved a hand, dismissing Alex's life's work. Alex didn't take offense. Why should he, when the opinion of this man meant nothing to him? This factory was only one of the concerns Alex owned, and a mere part of his investment. "I understand that your father and his father were . . . estranged."

Alex's grandfather had made it very clear to his father what "going into trade" meant when he was still a young man. In short, Alex's father had "betrayed his birthright" and was no longer welcome in aristocratic circles. But he'd had a family to feed, and he'd already proved his worth trading fabrics in India. He had made his money and some useful contacts then come home and continued his career. And made a huge success of it. What was aristocratic society next to that?

"You thought right," Alex said grimly. "His father didn't approve of my mother. But 'e was only the third son, so it didn't matter. Plenty of folk between 'im and the title." He only remembered to drop the h at the last second. Maybe that was going a little too far. But he didn't want this man getting ideas. He might bear the name, but his heart and spirit were all with his mother's side of the family. If they thought he was common and vulgar, they were less likely to bother him.

A guilty pang struck Alex when he thought of his sisters, and what he could offer them if he bowed to the wishes of his uncle. But would they care? They tended to go their own way. Independent women weren't popular in aristocratic circles. They'd turned down presentation at court once, so why would they accept it now?

"Matters have changed," Villiers continued, bearing the attitude of a man talking down to a child. "I presume you know of the recent family misfortunes?"

Alex shook his head. He had no idea, and why would he care, in any case?

Villiers folded his gloved hands in his lap. "You must know of the tragedy that took your cousin Lord Youngman five years ago."

"Yes, I do. Smallpox, I heard. I was reet sorry to hear it."

"Indeed. A sad business." Villiers heaved a great sigh. "The family tragedy has only increased in recent years. You are of course aware that the Frasers have a long history of military prowess? Sadly, that has cost the family dear."

"That is a shame." He had not kept in touch with his father's family, so he had not been aware of any tragedy.

"We lost Lord Frederick and his two sons at Waterloo. A sad business."

Alex vaguely remembered an array of swords and muskets laid in pretty patterns on the walls of the Great Hall of Stonyhurst on his one and only visit there. His father had gone to record Alex's birth in the family annals, at the urging of Alex's mother, who had pointed out they owed him that courtesy at least. Alex had been seven. It had taken that long for his father to agree to his mother's demands. They'd arrived and left on the same day. His oldest uncle, who had inherited the title by then, glanced at him once and never looked his way again. Only uttered the choice insults that had caused his father to turn his back on his brother and vow never to return. When he'd arrived back home, he'd had his courtesy title removed from every piece of stationery he used. "I want no more to do with that family," he'd said, and he meant it. While officially he still held the title, he chose to never use it again.

But the news of his second uncle's death startled Alex. The recent war had cost a lot of families dear, including his own, apparently. "What, all of them?"

Villiers heaved a sigh. "I am surprised you did not hear of it. You and your cousins from your younger uncle are all that are left."

"A tragedy," Alex murmured.

Alex's grandfather, the fifth marquess, had married twice. Once for duty, which had produced two sons, and ten years later, for love, producing another two. After the old man had died, his younger two sons went their own way.

The first son had inherited the title and estate, becoming the sixth marquess, while the second son, Frederick, joined the army. Smallpox had taken the sixth marquess's heir, but Frederick had produced two more sons. Nobody counted the daughters, Alex recalled with a wry smile. But the title was safe and that was all that had mattered.

Alex's father was the third son. He and his wife produced Alex and five daughters. While the title did not acknowledge girls, Alex certainly did. He wouldn't be without them.

But now Frederick's death, and his two sons with him, meant that Alex and his two neglected cousins—the sons of his father's younger brother—were now the only heirs left. They were not close, but at least he knew them.

There had to be a way out of this.

Alex sat very still. Events had brought him dangerously close to the title. He might have to meet the old man after all. But he refused to make it easy. Or to make any decision without discussing it with his family.

His two oldest uncles had despised the younger two, constantly referring to them as "low" and "common." Perhaps Alex could use that to deter the powers-that-be from bestowing the title on him. Was that how it worked? He wasn't sure, but he'd take that path. It couldn't hurt.

Villiers went on. "In short, as matters stand, you are the heir to the marquessate."

Not if he could help it. "Let one of t'others have the title. I've no interest in it." It seemed easy enough to him. Simply leave it to the person most suited to run the enterprise.

Villiers brightened, he shifted in his chair, no doubt trying to find some comfort. Not in that chair he wouldn't. Nobody who knew that chair sat in it twice. A silver pin in his lapel, where a man of fashion might wear a nosegay, glinted. It had a distinctive shape. Did all the marquess's minions wear a silver coat of arms on his lapel? "His lordship has recently remarried, and he expects good news."

"Then you don't need me. My best wishes to 'im."

That was a relief. What use was a title and a bunch of gracious, expensive houses to him? "I don't want the title. I don't want nothing to do with it." After the egregious insults offered by his uncle to his father, especially after his marriage, Alex had done with his father's family.

"Interested or not, the title will be yours, Mr. Fraser, if her ladyship should fail in her efforts."

"What could I do with it? What good is it to me?" Inside, Alex was as tense as a coiled spring. What did his uncle want, after ignoring him all these years? If he wanted somebody at his beck and call, he could whistle for it. Surely he could be left out of the succession. When Alex died, his property would go to his mother and sisters, if he had no child of his own. He was always meticulous in matters of property. He was surprised that his uncle had not made a similar will.

Villiers drew another deep breath, as if groping for patience. "His lordship wishes you to attend Stonyhurst to discuss the matter."

"No." Why waste words? He had no intention of going anywhere at his uncle's command.

After Alex's father had left the family he was born into, he did not concern himself with them, or any other of his previous acquaintances. They had made a new life and were the better for it. From time to time, invitations had arrived, elaborate raised print on cream paper or card. His father had always torn them in two and thrown them away. Whenever Alex had questioned him on it, his father had always answered brusquely. "They're nothing to do with us now. We don't need them."

Villiers heaved another sigh. He was very good at those. "His lordship wishes to discuss several important matters with you."

Ah. As far as he was concerned, they had nothing to discuss. "I'm not minded to go."

"His lordship insists, sir."

Like an order from a being on high? With supreme self-control he kept completely still and wiped any annoyance from his face. He had too much going on. He couldn't up sticks and go to some bedeviled country house on the whim of an old man who had naught to do with him.

"Don't count on my coming."

"My lord expects you," Villiers said as if that explained everything. He got to his feet and bowed. "I look forward to seeing you at Stonyhurst, sir. Good day to you."

"Aye, well . . ." Alex grumbled as the man let himself out.

He would have ignored the entire incident had Acaster not mentioned Villiers again when he brought the midday post through. "Yon gent said you'd be visiting your uncle, sir. I'll need your dates so I can cancel any appointments and such."

His ears were all but flapping. Alex looked up from his calculations and grimaced. "Did he now? I've no mind to go."

Acaster paused, met Alex's eyes. Said nothing. Alex nodded to the chair—the comfortable one Villiers had disdained. Acaster sat.

"What?"

"May I speak plainly, sir?"

Alex had known Acaster for ten years, and he'd never put a foot wrong. He put down his pen and leaned back. "Go on." He relied on the honesty of those he employed. If Acaster needed to say something, then he should do it.

"It strikes me, sir, that you're very—guarded where your father's relatives are concerned."

Alex folded his arms. "I've reason."

"You've been working like a dog the past year or so, especially on the model village. Now you have to leave the work to the men, you said so yourself."

Alex had been working to build cottages for his workers, and the project had expanded of late. Now he was building a model village. He could attract the best workers that way and give them somewhere decent to live. The project had obsessed him, but Acaster was right. The plans were done, the architects had agreed on the design, the workers were on site.

"Did you know my soldier uncle led his sons into battle? They all died at Waterloo. Seems a shame."

"Aye, sir." Sadness tinged his voice. "It was a great tragedy."

"I thought generals didn't take the field?"

"This one did."

"And the marquess's own son died a while back."

Acaster nodded. "Five years, I believe. I understand the tragedy of losing his brother and nephews was why his lordship married again. A very young woman, but well born."

"A love match?" He thought of his grandfather, who married late in life for love.

Acaster snorted. "I doubt it. Not on her part, anyway." He shrugged. "But you never know."

"You've been keeping up on my family's affairs." Which was more than he had done. As soon as he saw the name Stonyhurst in the newspapers, Alex skipped that part.

"Somebody had to." Acaster clasped his hands. "Sir, you've been working too hard right now. You could do with a rest and some fresh air."

Alex snorted. "I ride over here every day. I get enough fresh air then."

"You snapped at young Taylor last week. That's not like you, sir."

It wasn't, Alex had to admit. He'd apologized to the clerk later, because the fault lay squarely with Alex, but the loss of self-control bothered him. Perhaps he could do with a break from work for a while.

"You could go and pay your respects," Acaster suggested tentatively.

"I could." Alex stroked his chin.

Yes, he did need to discuss matters with his uncle, much though he might hate that side of the family, even if it was to make clear that his uncle was on his own, as his father had been. It might be a good idea to clear the air.

Alex had another reason for making himself scarce. He wanted to see how Acaster managed on his own. He had other concerns, and having a manager he could trust would be invaluable. Like old Harvey when he'd first come into the business. Harvey had taught him the ropes, and then, a year after the death of Alex's father, he retired before, as he said, he dropped dead on the factory floor. Acaster was as capable, but Alex had never left him alone for long, and then he'd left him with detailed instructions. Even last year, when he'd visited London he'd rushed back after attending the Prince Regent's party at Clarence House. When he went to London on occasional business he never went for more than a week.

How far was Stonyhurst? Thirty miles? He could do that in a day.

Acaster was ready, he was sure of it. He was five years older than Alex and reliable. Time he put that to the test.

"All right," he said with a sigh. "I'll go. You're in charge."

THE DUCHESS OF Whiston sat at the breakfast table. With a practiced gesture, she flicked back the lace at the end of her wrapper sleeves so it wouldn't get stained with coffee or marked with butter. The wrapper dated from her extravagant days, when she thought nothing of having intimate garments trimmed with expensive lace. These days she couldn't afford to replace it.

"Good morning, Mama," she said, shaking open her napkin.

Her mother looked up from her morning paper. "Good morning, Bianca. Do you have any plans for today?"

"No." She never had plans. The quiet life she'd yearned for after her husband died was now growing tedious. She'd left off deep mourning six months ago and now she was out of half-mourning, too. Not that she hadn't loved her husband, but he wouldn't have approved of such sobriety. She could still hear his voice. "Dash it, Bianca, can't you wear something more becoming? We have a position to keep up, you know!"

He'd married her for her beauty, at least he'd said so at the time. But truthfully, he'd married her because her sister's husband gave him little choice. He was supposed to marry an heiress, but compromising Bianca had ended that.

"We could go shopping. Or Mrs. MacNee is having an At Home this afternoon. She has a soprano coming."

"Did you say we'd go?" Bianca looked up from buttering her toast.

"I said I would. She said you'd be welcome."

Edinburgh society could be as gossipy as London. Bianca wished her looks weren't quite so spectacular, or she weren't so tall. There was no chance of her passing unnoticed, even if people didn't know who she was. That sounded like sour grapes, and perhaps it was, but recently there'd been times she wished she could slink past people.

She couldn't, and that was that.

She went to the sideboard and helped herself to a plateful of food. A side of ham stood by, but she contented herself with scrambled eggs, kidneys and toast. And a slice or two of bacon.

Would she go to Mrs. MacNee's? She supposed she should. "Perhaps this soprano will be good. The last one wasn't."

Her mother shuddered. "No, she wasn't. But Mrs. MacNee means well. She considers herself a connoisseur of music."

The door opened and the maid put the silver salver holding the post on the table. "Anything else I can do for you, ma'am?"

Mrs. Burrell checked the teapot. "No, thank you, Scott. We're fine."

"Aye," the maid said, and left the room. Scott had been with them in London, but she was originally from Edinburgh, so she'd witnessed all Bianca's adventures. And the scandals she'd made.

Mrs. Burrell glanced through the post and handed Bianca one. "Oh! A letter from Juliet!" Bianca's sister had gone to America with her husband, so a letter from her was a great event.

A surge of happiness went through her. "Is she well?" She tucked away a helping of her breakfast.

Her mother ripped through the seal. The outside of the letter was stained and tattered, but inside, the contents fell out untouched. Juliet generally enclosed her letter with a carefully and tightly wrapped outer letter. It was a wonder they received any at all. She glanced through it. "There's six pages of it. We can read it in detail later. She's well, so is Langston. Their son is thriving." Her eyes swam with tears as she looked up. "And they're coming home."

"Oh, how wonderful!"

"The treaty with the United States is signed, and their baby is strong enough to travel. Langston's been called home." She studied the paper. "She crossed the last page. They're setting out—I can't make it out. But she definitely says they'll be home for Christmas."

"That's marvelous!"

She put the folded papers down and laid her hands over it. "Who's your letter from?"

"Why are you interested?"

Her mother nodded at the small packet Bianca had barely

noticed. She turned it over, studied the seal on the back. She didn't recognize the coat of arms although her mother probably would. "Fancy," she commented. She didn't receive many sealed packets these days. Still . . . she picked up a knife letter opener and loosened the seal, letting it weigh the paper as she unfolded the missive.

"An invitation," she read in wonder. "From the Marquess of Stonyhurst, to a house party. Why on earth would he ask me?" The name rang a bell, though she couldn't place it.

"Maria," her mother said softly.

Bianca's head jerked up. "Of course!"

Maria, a friend of Bianca's sister Juliet, had fallen in love with a man her mother deemed unsuitable. After the Burrells had helped her escape her mother's clutches, she'd cravenly gone home and agreed to marry the Marquess of Stonyhurst. Since the marquess had agreed she could bring her lover with her, she probably thought she had the best of everything.

"We left her to her own devices. We could have ruined our own reputations, especially after her mother accused us of leading her astray."

Her mother's mouth flattened. "I remember. But that was more the fault of Lady Rotherham than her daughter."

She shook the letter and something fell out. Another note. She opened it. "Maria says she wants to make amends. She is truly happy these days and she would love to see us again. She adds that her mother will not be present." She glanced up at her mother. "Do you think she means it?"

Mrs. Burrell shrugged. "She might. She was a biddable girl. But, Bianca, it's a house party at Stonyhurst. People long for invitations there. The marquess is an old curmudgeon but his house is wonderful, and he always invites the best of guests. Interesting mixtures, for the most part. Despite the presence of Maria, I think it's a good place for you to start your re-entry into society."

"Really?" Bianca couldn't admit she had avoided the prospect.

"You should. We're visiting Viola later in August. You could go from Stonyhurst to Viola's. Stonyhurst is in north Derbyshire, so you'll have traveled halfway there."

Until now, she'd been content in Edinburgh. But yes, it could be a way back. She could do that.

"You could come with me."

"No," Mrs. Burrell said instantly, reaching for the teapot. Her capacity for tea was bottomless. "You should take this step alone, not have your mother trailing along with you. She did not specifically invite me, did she?"

Bianca shook her head. "She did not, but I could write and say I'm bringing you."

"No," her mother repeated.

"So I'm to go on my own?"

"You should get your feet wet again," her mother added. "It's time, Bianca. You're too beautiful to be wasted on a man like McGonagal."

Sir Horace McGonagal was the latest man to offer to marry Bianca. He was considerably older than she, possessed of a competence, and kind. She liked him but knew she would never love him. He was the sort of man Bianca might settle for, but he had three daughters. Bianca had no desire to be a mother to another woman's children.

She still received the occasional offer, especially since she'd come out of mourning. None of them had tempted her. "Beauty is something I was given. I want a man who wants me for myself, for other qualities, ones I worked for."

It was only the truth. It sounded insufferable, but she could think of no other way to put it. She'd love to disguise herself, to become somebody else for a while, just until she could prove she was more than her face and figure. That was unlikely to happen.

"If you were not beautiful, you'd miss it," her mother commented dryly. "You'd want it back in an instant."

Yes, Bianca had to admit that she probably would. But all too often men wanted her for what lay on the outside. And her mother would go on and on until Bianca did something. A week. She'd give it a week.

Bianca met her mother's gaze. "All right then, I'll go."

Chapter Two

A S HER CHAISE rocked its way up the drive of Stonyhurst Park, Bianca became engrossed by her surroundings. The house had the unified exterior of the classical style, but that could be a façade that covered older parts of the house. A double staircase led up to the front entrance. The park was natural at first glance, but of course had been carefully designed a generation or two earlier, so the trees had attained maturity and the whole gave an air of always having been there. That was probably far from the case. The peaks of high hills reared up in the distance.

Bianca had hired a traveling chaise for herself and her maid, which served her purpose, and she'd supplied the company with the plaques that could be hung on the door bearing the ducal coat of arms set in a widow's lozenge. She carried a letter in her luggage in her mother's hand, begging her to return home to Edinburgh, as she had been taken ill. That was her way out, if this visit became insufferable. Which it very well might, if Maria proved unwelcoming.

Hers was not the only carriage outside the imposing doors of the house. Two other chaises, both private, stood there. Footmen in livery were tenderly handing down a lady in vivid red. She must have stopped to refresh herself shortly before arriving here, because there was not a mark on her.

Bianca exchanged a glance with her lady's maid. McMurdo

had come to her in Scotland, and Bianca found herself well satisfied with the older woman. Better than the flighty maid she'd had in London who spent most of her time trying to seduce her husband. Probably succeeding, too, although Bianca had had no idea at the time.

The dip in her stomach reminded her how betrayed she'd felt, but she ignored it and waited her turn.

The other carriage, an older model with no crest on the doors, disgorged a single passenger. He was dressed plainly but well in dark colors, and under his beaver hat his hair gleamed darkly, like a crow's wing. Tall, too, and with an air of confidence. He strode to the double staircase heading up to the main door without looking around, so she could not see his face. But that broad back, and the long legs—yes. A tingle stirred deep inside, in a place that had remained dormant for over a year.

Strange, from just a glimpse of a broad back.

Then it was her turn. She allowed the footman to hand her down, and inside she flicked over to the duchess she had not employed for quite some time. Her dark green carriage dress might be out of date, but she wore it with confidence and flair. Most of her clothes should have arrived, having been sent ahead, but her maid still hauled a bag full of the items she considered too precious to send by mail coach.

Bianca strode up the steps in the wake of the gentleman with the broad back, as if she owned the place. After all, she was a duchess.

Inside, she found her host and the others who had just arrived. The lady in red, who she now recognized as the Marchioness of Broome, was a mature lady with several daughters to settle. Was it three? She was talking to Lord Stonyhurst, who looked even more wizened than when she had last seen him—in a ballroom, leering. Or maybe he looked like that all the time. She couldn't tell, she didn't know him well enough. He had rarely appeared in London, and when he did it was not for long.

The gentleman in front of her glanced around, and Bianca lost her breath. A shot of desire went through her and made her temporarily confused. She hadn't felt that way since her husband's death. Since before his death.

He wasn't exactly handsome. Not like George, whose golden elegance had stunned people, including her. This man had a dark complexion, as if he spent a lot of time outdoors. His clothes were good but not in the first stare of fashion, and they were an indeterminate color somewhere between green and brown. Olive, perhaps. Superb material, though. All the Burrells had an eye for quality. His eyes, dark as night, gazed into hers. His full mouth, uncomfortably sensuous in such a harsh face curved in a smile.

She wanted him. She was honest enough to admit that.

He stared at her as she must be staring at him. Awfully rude. But Lady Broome was still nattering on, her voice echoing around the cavernous hall, so nobody noticed. He bowed slightly. "I suppose we have to wait until we're introduced," he murmured to her. "But my name is Alex."

"Alexander?" Couldn't she think of anything better to say? Apparently not.

"Indeed it is. I've never enjoyed hearing my full name on anyone's lips except my mother's before." He glanced around. "What do you think they're guarding against?"

She smiled. Although she'd never been here before, she'd seen this kind of decoration. The Great Hall bristled with weapons. It felt as if any moment a monster would spring out and the gentlemen present would be forced to grab one of the swords laid in a circular pattern above the huge mantelpiece. And that was not to mention the guns, old, clumsy blunderbusses and a dozen or so flintlocks. Two huge shields bracketed the white marble fireplace. Windows marched around the landing above, but these were free of weaponry, instead holding a collection of portraits that belonged to another age. Probably friends of Queen Elizabeth judging by the ruffs and stiff fabrics.

"It's . . ." she groped for an appropriate word . . . "spectacular." Since she was looking up, the last word echoed around the vast space.

"Why thank you." The marquess heard her remark, and the private moment was over. Still shaken by her reaction to the perfect stranger standing next to her, Bianca moved forward and dropped into an appropriate curtsey.

"So kind of you to come, Duchess," he said, delivering a creaky bow. "I see your mourning is over." Close up, his elegant appearance did not disguise the dry, wrinkled skin, or the yellowish tone of it. He did not look well.

"Not my mourning, my lord, but the outward demonstration of it."

He smiled. "I see. You are planning to reenter society? You arrived like a comet and lasted just as long."

"Indeed, sir." Not very polite of him, or very accurate, come to that.

"My lovely wife is currently resting, but you will see her before long. She will be delighted to see you." He glanced over her head, or rather, past her shoulder, since he stood a couple of inches shorter than she did. By that she knew someone else had arrived. Someone more interesting, no doubt.

The marquess lifted a hand and a maid came forward. "Show Her Grace to her chamber," he said without looking around. "We are delighted you chose our small gathering to reenter society. Dinner will be at the usual time. We do not keep abnormally early hours here." He smiled, then turned his attention to the man standing just behind her. "Can it be that you know Mr. Fraser?"

"Why no, my lord. I'm afraid we have not met before." She would like to, though.

"Allow me to introduce you. This, dear Duchess, is my nephew, Mr. Alexander Fraser. Fraser, this is the Duchess of Whiston."

"Oh! I've not seen you in town, Mr. Fraser." She would have remembered.

"I doan't go to London much," Mr. Fraser said. "Too busy mindin' my business."

That flat tone, the dropped *g*, the way he pronounced "don't" as if it had an *a* in it. When he'd spoken to her a moment ago, there'd been none of that. Why had he adopted a broad Yorkshire accent?

"A duchess, eh?" he said then. "Well, I'm moving with the best of the best now."

He bowed. Although he put his foot forward in the approved mode, his bow was at best stiff, and not as deep as it should have been. Bianca dropped a curtsey and met his gaze as she rose. She read a warning in them. What was he about?

"You'll have to mind your manners," the marquess told him. "You can't molder away in Rotherham anymore."

"Sheffield. I need to get back there quick smart."

The marquess turned to Bianca. "Gracious, is he not? Still, this is a large gathering. I'm sure you'll find some amenable people to associate with."

"I'm still 'ere," Mr. Fraser pointed out. "I'll do me best, though like you say, I'm not used to such fine surroundings." He gazed around, his eyes wide. "Are they for the French in case they get this far?"

"As you may have noticed, the war is over," the marquess said testily. "My ancestors fought hard and well in the Civil War. The Roundheads never gained a place here."

Bianca slipped into her society mask as if she'd never left it off. She was always the peacemaker between her sisters, despite her personal wildness. "That is truly impressive," she said. "Cromwell really was a beast, wasn't he?"

Did the marquess's harsh expression soften a little? She rather thought so. "I would be pleased to tell you more about the family's part in the Civil War. After dinner perhaps?" Her heart sank, but she had asked for it. The abrasiveness between the marquess and his heir had worn at her. She hated bad feeling, especially when she didn't understand it.

The maid stood patiently by, so Bianca dropped a small curt-sey and left the two men to their own devices. She had to find her room, and then she could do the really important things, like discussing her wardrobe with her lady's maid.

ALEX HAD MADE a mistake with the duchess, using his usual accent. His plan was to deter his uncle from making him his heir by appearing too uncouth for society, but she'd made him slip the moment he set eyes on her flawless face. He'd heard about the Burrell sisters, but he'd never seen one of them so close before. The duchess had stunned. Fierce, possessive desire had almost made him dumb. The few words he had managed had been with his normal accent. He'd have to talk to her.

As he followed a footman along a series of corridors, he won-dered how he'd ever find his way back.

His valet was waiting in his room. The chamber itself was surprisingly comfortable, since Alex had expected to be sent to the garret or a cupboard of a room. This was far from a cupboard. Mainly green, with an old-fashioned four-poster bed and with gilt kept to a minimum. The paintings on the walls were mainly Dutch genre works, small intimate scenes that he liked. He owned some himself. "This room used to belong to the heir that died," Fisher said. "The marquess's son. When he came of age, he chose this room as the furthest from his parents' quarters. Wanted a bit of independence, apparently."

"Have you been making friends in the servants' hall?" Alex enquired.

"I got here last night," Fisher answered, "so I put myself about a bit. This house is full, sir. Packed. Agog about the new heir making an appearance. That's you," he added helpfully.

Alex shrugged off his coat. For once, the weather was posi-tively warm. "There are two other heirs, and the marquess has his new wife. He probably wants us here so he can gloat when she makes her announcement. I don't want to stay long, but I would like to know what's going on." He tossed the coat on the bed. "So keep your ears open, if you please."

With a barely heard "tut," Fisher collected the coat and shook it out. He was a middle-aged man, somewhere around forty, and as dapper as anyone Alex had ever met. How he managed to go through the day in the same clothes without a crease, smut, or crumb marring his perfection Alex would never know. Fisher was very good at his job. He turned Alex out with immaculate precision, and he even acceded to his request that his clothes not be skin-tight.

"Do you know anyone here?" Alex paced to the sideboard, where a full tantalus resided, amber liquid glittering in the cut-glass bottles. Paused, and moved on, continuing his circuit around the room. He felt trapped. Something was amiss, and he didn't know what it was. That made him edgy.

"I know a few. I know *of* more that I haven't met," Fisher said, taking the coat to the clothes press. "I am not familiar with this family, sir, but there are a few guests here of some renown. Notorious, one might say."

Fisher turned, his expression bland. "Not that it is my place to say anything—." He broke off when a knock sounded at the door. Alex moved out of sight while he answered it. He returned with a message. "His lordship wonders if you will join him in his study. A footman is waiting outside."

Alex grunted and let Fisher help him back into his coat. He didn't ask if he was presentable, because Fisher knew his work. But a private conversation might move matters along.

He followed the footman, who wore the blue and gray livery of the house. This time the journey was more straightforward. He gathered that the state and family rooms were at the back of the house, and the guest rooms in the wings attached to the main block at right angles.

His lordship's office lay on the other side of the house, beneath the private quarters of the family. At least, he thought so, from the quality of the art on the walls and his knowledge of houses like these. He had not visited many, but enough to know the guests were often housed in a separate part of the building. Or palace, in the case of this establishment.

The study was another spacious room and was filled with modern furniture. Lighter wood and more fluid designs made this as pleasant as the one he'd just left but in a more French style. Except for the man sitting behind the desk. He did not stand when Alex came in, and he waved the footman away. "Come and sit down, boy."

The reference would have made Alex smile if he wasn't on his guard. He took the spindle-legged chair, leaned back, and crossed his ankle over his knee. "I thought you were stuck greetin' people."

"I left my nephew in the hall. He knows what to do. You'll meet the two of them before dinner. Unlike you, they know which side of the bread is buttered for them."

"Aye, 'appens I've more gumption than most." He wouldn't mention that he already knew Adolphus and Benedict. One a clever socialite, the other horse mad.

"And that's how you made your fortune?"

"Aye, some. My father made half of it in India, and I did t'other half in Yorkshire." He'd forgotten to drop the h again. Ah well.

"Your father was a disobedient, foolish man."

"Not the one I knew."

The marquess grunted. "He changed, then."

"Love will do that to a man." And a determination not to allow life to roll over him. He'd known what he was doing when he married. His father had threatened to cast him off, and he did. No doubt he expected Alex's father to crawl back. But he didn't.

"Love." The marquess almost spat the word. "What good has that ever done anybody?"

"My old Dad took what 'e 'ad and doubled it. Then 'e doubled it again."

"Then you doubled it another time." The marquess's thin lips stretched in a smile. "Oh, don't look so alarmed, boy. I'm pretty warm myself. I'm not coming to you cap in hand. No, the matter's more important than that."

Alex said nothing but raised a brow.

"I didn't expect to say this, but you're my heir."

"Mebbe," Alex said, unperturbed. "You found yourself a wife." Who he hadn't met yet.

"I did. But she's not produced, and the way she's going, not likely to."

"So it's her fault?" The marquess must be seventy if he was a day. Alex knew who he would blame. Of course, there were exceptions, but the likelihood remained with the marquess.

"Has to be her. Or . . ." The marquess opened his mouth and then closed it again. "Never mind that. If you're my heir, which you are, for now at least, I need to see more of you." He grimaced. "I never thought I'd say that, either. Never imagined somebody of your father's get would end up with the estate."

Alex ignored the open insult. "Leave it to somebody else, then."

The marquess growled low in his throat. Alex watched, fascinated. Could he give the old man an apoplexy? He didn't want to try. Nothing was more guaranteed to drive him back to his home than this old scroat. For all his fine clothes and grand estate, he was a scrawny, low-minded person. Eager to blame someone else for his own faults. "I can't. Nearly all the inheritance is in the entail, and in any case, dividing a great fortune is a fool's game. Obviously you need educating in the way of great estates."

"I do?" Probably, but he wasn't about to concede that point.

"Yes, you do. I have instructed Villiers to give you an introduction to the estate and how we manage it."

He paused and studied Alex, from the top of his head to his waist, which was all he could see. "You're a good-looking man. Take after your father's side, no doubt. At least you're the only boy, though your mother provided a good litter."

"You're talking about my sisters?" Fury simmered low in Alex's belly. He dampened it down, for now.

"Humph. Yes, them. Glad you didn't bring them."

Stonyhurst thumped his clenched fist down on his desk. For a man of his age, he certainly had some strength of his own, hybrid or otherwise. "Your sisters can marry whoever they choose. I might even help them. But I don't want you marrying."

What business was it of his?

"I've invited a number of young women here, and I expect your cousins to choose brides from them. Has to be quick. You are to keep your hands off them."

He wanted this out in the open. "Because of my mother." He made it a statement.

Stonyhurst nodded. "As you say. Unsuitable blood. Nobody's fault but your father's."

Fault?

His anger burned. But the first person to lose their temper in a dispute tended to lose the battle. He would save his, store it up. Use it against the old man if he had to. "Do you mean you're holding auditions? Or do you want Adolphus and Benedict to test them out one by one?" His mind drifted to that lovely creature he'd met when he first arrived. The beautiful duchess. Though if she was a duchess, she was unlikely to be on the list.

The marquess banged his cane on the floor. "You do not speak of gently bred young ladies in those terms."

Some comment from a man who treated women as chattels and spoke of Alex's family as if they were inferior.

"Straight back on the table."

With an effort, Stonyhurst found his voice. He gulped and sucked in a breath. "It's a house party. Dance with them, walk with them, talk to them. Anything else and I'll have your hide!"

He'd got the old man on the run now. Though outraged by the way the marquess thought he could direct people like puppets and disposed to order Fisher to pack his bags and leave without further ado, Alex gained control over his own temper. It was so tempting to make a scene, to leave and never look back. Nobody riled him like that.

At last he understood why his father walked out. Five minutes in the marquess's company had driven him to this. How much more would years spent with him do? His father had left and gone to India to make his fortune. Which he had. Then he'd met Alex's mother, fell in love with the daughter of a non-commissioned officer, and that was that.

Alex was in a bind here.

"If they like me, there's nowt I can do about that."

"Just don't ask any of them to marry you. Understand?" When Alex did not respond, he continued, "I've invited the other kind of woman to keep you amused. The widows, the wives who are open to dalliance. If you can't keep yourself to yourself, pick one of those. They're all members of society, perfectly acceptable in a gathering like this. They're choice, as well. The season just gone was a poor one. They were all still busy mourning Princess Charlotte."

"Aye, sad business that." The Princess had died the previous November after a terrible birthing. Her son died with her, so the inheritance of the Crown was once more up in the air.

"Indeed. And I won't let the marquessate go the same way. I want this succession settled before I go."

He dispensed with people as if they were toy soldiers on a game board. Alex listened, angry and amused with the man's presumption in equal measure. He said nothing.

"Your cousins are here. We need the next generation," the marquess went on. "The estate needs them. You have no idea of the responsibilities of a man in my position. Even though I expect my wife to produce long before I'm gone, for now you're what I'm left with. And after you, your cousins. None of you are worthy of the position."

How many people would he insult before he was done?

But he hadn't finished. "I want you to spend time with Villiers learning the duties of a marquess and how to run an estate like this."

Alex was forced to see the sense in that. Even if the unfortunate marchioness produced a child, the likelihood was that his father wouldn't live long enough to see the boy come to his majority. He might have to become involved in running the estate. He prayed the marchioness would do her duty by her lord, because otherwise, he'd be well in the soup. But to spend too much time with Villiers would try his temper something fierce. He'd do it, though. It shouldn't take too long to see what needed doing, if anything. Get the lay of the land, so to speak.

"How long is this business going to last?" He would familiarize himself with the estate and the account books, then take his leave from this benighted party.

"I'll probably move them along in a month. But I want you back to carry on your lessons with Villiers. You can use the women in the East Wing to amuse yourself with, and help your cousins choose brides from the young ladies. I'm considering having you live here for a while."

Well, he could whistle for that. Alex had a job to do. The sooner he got out of this place and back to his life, the better.

If Villiers was efficient and honest, Alex could see himself going home by the end of the week.

VILLIERS'S OFFICE WAS in the darkest, oldest part of the house—the central core, the heart. Dark oak dominated, together with stone walls and stairs. If it weren't for the footman who took him there, he wouldn't have arrived this side of dinnertime. As it was, Alex was shown into a narrow office below ground level. It felt cold and damp, despite the cheerful weather outside.

Villiers was as dapper and as on point as Alex remembered him. He stood, as was proper, but Alex only acknowledged that with a nod. "I'm here to learn, your master said." He took care to keep his vowels flat and long.

"Thank you, sir." The last word sounded grudging.

Alex crossed the room and glanced up, to the high, narrow windows that provided the only daylight. "This ain't a good view. Don't your eyes suffer?"

"No. The room is built for security. Do you know the history of the title?"

Alex waved it away. "Later. Let's get to business." Villiers had a large book laid open in front of him on the sizeable, almost black scarred desk. Obviously an account book from the columns and carefully drawn lines.

Alex decided to play this as an innocent, someone who knew nothing about the management of large estates. Let them underestimate him.

Half an hour later, he knew he might have to stay for longer than a week. The accounts were meticulously kept, almost obsessively so, down to the last penny. But something niggled at him. He let Villiers explain how to do double-entry bookkeeping as he studied the figures he was allowed to see. Surely Villiers must know Alex understood that, at least? But he didn't seem to.

"You are thorough," he remarked.

"Somebody has to be," Villiers replied in an unguarded moment. He bit his lip. "That is, I am employed because I know what I'm doing. It is not the place of the marquess to worry about whether the kitchen maid is peeling the potatoes too thickly, or if we can save twenty pounds on a barrel of the best wine."

"Do you watch every detail?"

"The cost is my concern. I do not interfere in the day-to-day business, but I set the budgets and I expect the servants to keep to them. I approve every appointment, and I oversee the inventories. We take a full inventory twice a year."

Inwardly, Alex groaned. How could anyone bear to have such oversight? It was not his way. He found the best people for the job, oversaw them for a month or two to ensure his judgment was correct, then trusted them to get on with it. Nobody worked at their best when they were sure someone was watching their every move.

But this was not his house, he reminded himself. With any luck, it would never be so.

Villiers wouldn't allow him to take any of the books out of the room, but he did furnish Alex with a key. "You may view the books any time you wish, but in this room, or the armaments room," he said. "His lordship prefers it that way."

His lordship probably had no idea. He didn't strike Alex as a person who bothered with details.

Chapter Three

I T SEEMED STRANGE to dress in brighter colors again, but as she stood before the mirror studying herself in the rich red gown, Bianca had to admit that this style suited her better than subdued half-mourning. Black, now, that worked well on her, but when she'd worn unrelieved black she hadn't cared how she'd looked. She remembered to tie a thin black ribbon around her bare upper arm. A symbol of mourning for the Princess. It had been over six months since she'd died, but Bianca didn't want to be castigated for disrespect.

Her simple necklace of tiny rubies sparkled enticingly, matching the tiny drops in her ears. Yes, she could reenter society as a widow out of mourning. This was the start. Red it would be.

She turned with a smile. "Thank you, McMurdo."

The maid handed her a fan, which Bianca looped over her wrist. "Every inch the duchess, ma'am," she said.

"Or the reckless adventurer," Bianca murmured. Either would suit her. With a brief smile at her reflection, she left her room.

Only to collide with a very solid male body. His arms came around her, probably to steady her, but it was the first embrace from a man she wasn't related to that she'd had in over a year.

Her first response was *he smells so good*. Citrus and male mixed. It had been so long since she'd smelled anything like it.

She'd lingered too long. Enough to give the owner of the scent the wrong idea. Since he was taller than Bianca, she suspected she knew the owner of the crisp waistcoat and the alluring aroma. When she looked up, she found she was right.

"I beg your pardon, sir." She straightened and stepped back. She still had to look up to meet his eyes, which was a novelty for her.

"Nothing to beg my pardon for," he said. "I can truly say that it was a pleasure, the best experience I've had since I walked through the doors of this place."

"But you are to be its owner."

He stood by her side and crooked his arm. She laid her hand on the smooth black fabric covering it. Underneath she felt firm muscle. "Perhaps. I still expect the new Lady Stonyhurst to do her duty by her lord."

She tightened her lips. She knew far more about the methods her ladyship would use than she should.

"What is it?" he murmured, glancing at her.

Bianca discovered that his eyes were far too perceptive for her liking. "Oh, nothing. Just that I knew Lady Stonyhurst well at one time. Her mother was kind to us when we first appeared in London."

"Ah yes, the brazen adventurers," he said.

She couldn't deny it, but she was surprised he knew, since he didn't appear in society often. She raised a brow.

"I met your sister once. Lady Langston."

Juliet. "Oh?"

"I'm not entirely ignorant of society. It was at Carlton House."

"You move in exalted circles, sir."

He laughed, a rough sound that reached into her groin. She suppressed a shiver. "I supply the army with uniforms, so the Prince invites me to his gatherings from time to time. Sometimes he insists."

"He must think highly of you." She'd wager few people at

this house party knew of his connections.

"I make what the army requires on time and with the quality the men fighting for us need to have," he said. "Practicality wins over sentiment for me every time."

She liked that. Liked it very much. "So His Highness appreciates what you do."

"And wants it cheaper," he said with a grimace. "But I have shown him what the process costs, and how much it takes to get to that standard. I believe his advisors would prefer to use someone cheaper, but it's a false economy." He stopped abruptly and smiled. "It's their decision."

Oh dear, that smile should be banned.

"You're too easy to talk to," he said. He paused when they reached the end of the corridor and looked up the one they had to turn into. It was devoid of people.

"You're speaking perfect English," she pointed out.

"I'm multilingual," he answered, forcing a laugh from her. He stopped and faced her, meeting her gaze. "Would you keep my secret for a while?"

She was quick on the uptake. "You mean you do not want people here to know you don't speak with a broad accent?"

"Exactly. If someone here has met me before, then I'll have to confess, but I spend as little time in London as possible so it's unlikely."

It could be fun. "All right."

They walked together to the top of the stairs. "This place is a complete warren," he remarked as they descended. "But I learned the knack. There are two great halls, this, and the painted one at the back." His accent was broadening, the vowels longer.

"The South Entrance," she corrected him primly.

"Aha. Of course it has a name. But everything else in the main part of the house leads to one or the other. I can navigate that way."

That was an interesting word. "Were you ever in the Navy?"

"No."

"Nor your brothers?" she ventured.

"Good try." He grinned, a quick flash of that devastating smile. "No brothers. Five sisters, though."

"Goodness!"

"Not all of them are good."

They'd reached the first floor where the state rooms were situated. Easy to locate those, just follow the sound of chattering voices. By the time they'd arrived he was completely Yorkshire. Why did he want his uncle to think he could not speak like a gentleman? What was that for? But she had to admit the deception would be fun, and it seemed so long since she'd had any kind of fun.

The drawing room was full. As it was a substantial size, that took some effort. Was every bedroom occupied? It must be, to have, what, fifteen couples? Together with some single gentlemen such as Mr. Fraser, and a group of young ladies, who would presumably not share a bedroom with their parents. How big was this house, anyway?

Bianca had visited her sisters and their husbands in their country houses. She didn't think the houses were this big. Whiston Hall, the home of her late husband, was huge, a barn of a place, but they hadn't spent much time there. George preferred the excitement of town, and until later in her marriage, so did she.

She showed none of her naïveté in her expression, already practiced at keeping her face calm despite whatever was going on inside. Instead, she smiled as her hostess came forward, both hands extended.

The new polish her maid must have imposed on her made Maria look much older than she was—she had to be five or six years younger than Bianca. But she'd married a man old enough to be her father—her grandfather, even—so looking older would be preferable than appearing as a child bride.

Bianca smiled and said "Maria!" in a soft voice. Maria's fair curls were teased into an elaborate hairstyle, and she wore a delicate tiara threaded through them. She even had a light coating of powder on her face. Bianca had once needed the help of heavy maquillage to cover her tear-stained face, but these days she wore little or none.

"You look well," Maria said. "I am so glad to see you out of mourning at last!"

"It was time," Bianca said softly. "I must continue with my life and not be a burden to my loved ones."

The marquess cut into their conversation. "Ladies and gentlemen, may I introduce you all to my heir?" He indicated the man by Bianca's side. "Mr. Alexander Fraser, of—Sheffield."

The pause told everyone what he thought about Sheffield.

Alex bowed to the company. "I'm glad to be here." The broad Yorkshire accent was firmly back in place. "It's grand to meet you all. I'll get to know your names in no time."

Was that a dig at their host, for not performing more conventional introductions? Of course it was.

Smiles and murmurs rippled over the large room. Even the portraits of ancestors on the walls appeared interested. But if they were present it had to be in ghostly form.

Women surrounded Mr. Fraser. They gently elbowed Bianca out of the way. She was left with Maria, who was still smiling in an eerie way, as if her face was set like that and she didn't know how to change it. "I would love a comfortable coze with you later," she said.

"Or tomorrow, perhaps," Bianca murmured.

Men had kept their distance from her at first, but now they came forward and reintroduced themselves. Bianca curtseyed, but all the time the names were creating horror in her soul.

These men were some of the worst rakes in society, many the husbands of the women who had their sights on Mr. Fraser. What on earth was the marquess thinking, asking them here in the company of so many young girls? It seemed like the worst arranged house party in existence.

Apparently not. Maria spoke with them familiarly and let out that many had been here for some time. "My husband likes men of wit and sophistication around him," she said. "He holds open house for many who are welcome here."

"And artists," one man added. "We cannot forget our artistic community."

"Community?"

"Indeed. His lordship is a great patron of the arts."

Lord Severn laughed. "The house is divided. The younger guests and their families are in the West Wing. You, my dear, are with us in the East. I guarantee you will find much more amusement there."

What did that mean? And since she'd bumped into Mr. Fraser outside her room, did that include him?

At last, someone she knew and liked came forward, and took her hand. Mr. Adolphus Fraser, a renowned wit and man about town, bowed over her hand. His lips brushed the back, but then, he used to tease her like that in the old days. Although he had a fearsome reputation, it was not of the kind most of the gentlemen here shared. "You are in the racy side of the house, with the rest of us," he said. "What is a party without the lovely Duchess of Whiston?"

At least he hadn't called her a dowager. But for the first time Bianca wondered if she should adopt it. It might form some kind of protection. She would be sure to lock her bedroom door tonight. Not against Adolphus, but she didn't trust Severn, or Henry Fotherington-Smythe, a friend and associate of her late husband who stood by a window, smirking at her.

Bianca had made her mistakes, but now she wanted to put that all behind her. Perhaps the red gown had been a mistake. It did not give the impression she wanted. "Stay away," would be a polite way of putting it. She had lived quietly and respectably since George's death. Apparently that was not enough time to shake off a thoroughly earned reputation.

Her instinct was to flee. This was not at all what she wanted.

When dinner was announced, they went in by rank. Bianca

found her seat close to the marquess, with the pompous Lord Waterson between them. "I am glad to see you looking so well."

"Yes, sir. Thank you for your good wishes."

While people chattered around them, Bianca was forced to converse on the weather, the hunting prospects, and other less-than-riveting subjects. She wanted a hole to open up beneath her, especially when she saw Mr. Fraser at the bottom of the table near Maria, laughing and joking with the people around him. He seemed the life and soul of this gathering, but she couldn't hear everything he was saying. Or what was being said to him. So she listened to Lord Salish droning on about his interests, not considering that Bianca might not want to discuss them.

Tedious, but this was the path she'd chosen. She did her best to behave with the propriety and politeness required, but oh, it was hard!

"I'm glad you're here," the marquess said abruptly, interrupting a conversation on the terrible weather of the last two years. "When my wife suggested it, I was doubtful. But obviously you are out of mourning, and you will add a touch of spice to our little gathering."

Spice? Really? All Bianca wanted to do was reestablish herself in society.

After dinner, they convened in the drawing room, the gentlemen not lingering over their port and joining the ladies promptly. The company naturally separated into two groups. East Wing and West Wing, from the look of the participants. Older women in rich colors chattered and laughed, while the pastel-clad debutantes stood around awkwardly. Bianca knew which group she preferred, and it was the one she was supposed to gravitate to. But although she'd made her debut in society later than most, she felt for the poor girls watching wide eyed.

The marquess should never have invited both kinds of guests, and then so obviously housed them in different wings. Someone touched her elbow. She turned to find Adolphus watching her. "Don't," he murmured.

"Don't what?"

"Join the respectables. Oh, we're all nominally respectable, but you know what I mean. You don't belong there."

"They look so uncomfortable."

He smiled gently. "They may have been told why they're here. Don't you think?"

They moved through the crowd, talking softly. "Why are they here?"

"For Benedict and myself. He will have to choose one of the girls."

She tilted her head, gazing at him quizzically. Adolphus Fraser was an inch or so shorter than Bianca, but his lack of height never bothered him. He was delicately built, but according to what her late husband said, he was a force to be reckoned with in the boxing saloon. Wiry, fast, and surprisingly strong. A man of surprises. Not least because he was a chattering man. Also a man of secrets.

"We were always considered acceptable here, you know, but not Alex and his family," he continued.

"Why not?"

A small smile quirked the corner of Adolphus's mouth. "Our grandfather left both his younger sons with a small legacy, but the older sons made it extremely difficult to receive it. Held back the inheritance. My father decided to invest what he had in horse-flesh. Breeding and rearing, and he did very well with it. Alex's father went into trade. That is, he became a successful silk and fabric merchant in India, and when he'd done with that and came home, he built a factory. The war made him rich, but, you see, he was *involved*, and he traded. So after one unpleasant visit he was never welcome here. My family remained cordial with his, but we were invited to Stonyhurst, where Alex and his family were not."

Bianca wrinkled her nose. "Ridiculous."

He nodded. "But not everyone feels that way. I see no difference between my father's attempts to make his way in the world and how Alex's father made his. My father groomed and curried the horses and helped birth foals, and yet a man who oversaw a mill did not qualify for the title of gentleman?" He'd lost his easy smile. For once his mask had slipped and she had a glimpse of the man within. "You don't have to say anything. If society continues in this way, they'll be left behind in the new world that is coming."

"And yet, now that the title is close to dying out, his uncle wants him to marry?"

Adolphus shook his head. "Not him. Benedict. But the marchioness is his first line of defense."

"Are you supposed to choose a bride as well?"

Adolphus laughed, rather harshly for him. "I suppose I am," he said.

He'd taken her to the side of the room where, she supposed, she belonged. Some of the guests here troubled her: roués, men who cared nothing for reputation or for the appearance of respectability. And she was in their sights. Newly out of mourning for a husband who was worse than reckless, and she was available. They would come for her.

Tonight, in front of the debutantes and their parents, they would behave. When the marquess announced that his wife would play for them, they took seats and remained silent. They weren't animals. Bianca sat next to Lady Broome, a widow notorious for her many affairs. Her husband had died young, leaving her with two small sons and a vast inheritance. Now Bianca would be ranked with her. Not that she had the inheritance. Nobody would want to marry her for the pittance she could bring to a new marriage.

That made matters worse, not having that cushion.

Adolphus stuck with her that long evening, while Mr. Fraser fended off a plethora of debutantes and their parents. His accent held firm, what she heard of it, but the room was large and the separation as sure as if someone had erected a silken barrier between them. And yet he was housed on her side of the house.

"I presume he is to make his choice but amuse himself with us," Adolphus murmured to her behind his fan. His was a delicate confection of vellum and ivory, much finer than the one Bianca carried. But he deserved it, he wielded it so expertly. "But I confess, I don't know him particularly well. We are cousins, but not close."

"Your fathers were the two youngest sons of the previous marquess?"

He nodded. "And considerably younger. The old marquess married for duty, had the required two sons, then he and his wife went their separate ways. There was never another child. When the marchioness died, he fell deeply in love with the younger daughter of a country squire. He married her and had two more sons. Alexander's father went to India and returned a married man with a small son. Mine married the woman chosen for him and had four children, two of each sex. My sisters declined to come to this grisly entertainment. They cannot inherit, so they are nothing to the marquess." Behind his fan he yawned.

Maria ploughed through her piece with dogged determination. On her other side, Lady Broome continued a quiet-voiced conversation with the man leaning over the sofa. He must have a magnificent view of her equally magnificent breasts, which she was not shy in showing off. Neither took any notice of poor Maria. She had never enjoyed music, and it sounded like she didn't enjoy it now. She seemed to be on a mission to ensure other people didn't enjoy it, either.

Another guest, Lady Salish, the mother of two of the prospects for the heirs' hand, glared at them over the top of her fan. They took no notice.

"We get to stay in a magnificent mansion, eating, drinking, and living at the expense of my uncle for a while. When things start to get sticky—as they will—I'll slip away."

"I don't think I'll be staying long. I have a home, friends, and family who love me and stood by me at the worst times in my life." A letter from her mother would arrive soon. She'd make sure of it, in fact, as she'd brought it with her.

"But this promises to be very amusing."

Bianca was bored already. Apart from the fascinating man across the room who was currently sitting with Lady Colmondale and her daughter Honoria. Honoria loved horses. Loved them more than anything else in her life, but in order to pursue her passion she needed to make a marriage with a wealthy man who preferably shared her interest. Her mother must be desperate to push her into Mr. Fraser's way. He was an industrialist—it was unlikely he knew much about horses or cared about them a great deal. Had Honoria suffered a horrific season?

Bianca had no idea, but her mother would have known.

She hushed Adolphus with the excuse of wanting to listen to Maria. He shot her a knowing smile but acceded to her request, allowing Bianca to watch the company and listen to the girl fumble her way through a piece of Bach.

After that, Honoria took the seat. To Bianca's surprise, she could play and sing folk songs well. Benedict turned the pages for her. Then they had a respite while supper was brought in.

Ah well, at least she had some convivial company.

The younger women began to drift away with their parents, so Bianca took it as her cue to excuse herself. "Why, is this not early for you, Duchess?" the angelically blond Lord Severn said with a wink. "In town, I don't remember you going to bed earlier than two in the morning. Can it be that we are boring you?"

Yes, you are. "Not at all, my lord. Merely that I only arrived today and I'm tired. Traveling is always so tedious, is it not?" She spread her fan and deployed it. "I keep earlier hours in the country, in any case."

"I see. May I escort you to your room?"

"Pray don't disturb yourself. I am perfectly able to find my way back."

She prayed that was true, but in point of fact, it wasn't too difficult. Upstairs, turn left, and she was almost there. Fortunately, on her own.

Someone must have informed her maid she was on her way to her room, because McMurdo was waiting for her. In half an hour Bianca was in her night rail and wrapper, the one with the lace, and sitting in the comfortable chair by her window with a book in her hand. Her whole body sighed with relief. When McMurdo brought her a pot of tea, her day was made.

This was not the house party for her, but although she knew that, she'd have to be careful about leaving. Unless she assured people she was enjoying herself, they'd know what she was up to when her letter from her mother "arrived." She'd wager several other people had similar letters about their persons. Perhaps she'd stay another day, maybe two. But then she would make her excuses and leave.

Back to what she was before she started out on this mad adventure that had made her into a duchess.

Chapter Four

I F ALEX LISTENED to many more simperings and "Oh, sir, how perceptive of you!" at the least comment he made, he'd go outside, find the nearest brick wall, and beat his fists bloody.

He'd never been the subject of determined pursuit from young society ladies and he heartily wished he'd never discovered it. If that afternoon in Villiers's miserable, damp office had taught him anything, it was just how much he stood to inherit—if he didn't do something about it.

He'd seen rent rolls, inventories, and maps, all designed, it seemed, to impress on him what he might inherit if the woman sitting at the piano destroying Bach did not produce an heir soon. He had to persuade his uncle he was the most unsuitable heir. Then the marquess would leave his wealth to the other two surviving heirs.

He heartily prayed for the eventuality. If the marquess succeeded, he could go home tomorrow and get on with what he really understood. Being a fish out of water didn't suit him in the least.

Meanwhile, he sat next to a girl whose only conversation consisted of her passion for her equine friends. To him, horses were a necessity. They pulled his coaches, let him ride on their backs from time to time, but apart from ensuring they were properly cared for, he had little to do with them. As always, he employed people he could trust, and he paid them well.

It was new to him to be forced to talk to people who didn't interest him.

"Do you know how many 'orses this place 'as to manage?"

That was enough to set her off on another speech. Yes, she knew. Alarmingly, she knew how many horses could be kept comfortably in the stable block, the number that would be needed to work on the Home Farm, and what breeds they should be.

He let her talk. After all, he had all evening. And he was sitting where he could see the beauteous Duchess of Whiston without being too obvious. Her fair curls caressed her shoulders as she spoke with his cousin who was sitting next to her. They seemed to be having a better time than he was, but since he'd gravitated—or been dragged—to the "good" side of the room, that was only to be expected.

The marquess glared at him. This was not going to his plan, and he would have to rely on Alex not taking a fancy to one of the girls and proposing to her. That gave him some kind of power, he supposed.

Pastel pink did not suit Miss—whatever her name was. Neither did sitting in this drawing room entertaining people. She'd be a terrible hostess, unless she were with similarly passionate enthusiasts. He leaned back, smiling, nodding where it seemed appropriate, and watched the other marital prospects on the side of the angels. Their clothing was not their fault. Neither were their duennas, mothers, and fathers. He didn't envy Adolphus or Benedict their part in their uncle's plot. There really was no answer but to study what he needed to, reassure his uncle that he would return, and get out of this benighted place as soon as humanly possible.

Although something still nagged at him. He'd studied the books, and although they looked in order, something bothered him. When he tried to pinpoint it, the thought skittered away like a woodlouse scurrying back to the darkness. He wouldn't rest easy until he'd discovered it, even if it was something innocuous. Which it probably was. Although the steward annoyed him, he knew what he was about. The books were meticulously kept, initialled and signed by the marquess, and in order as far as he could see.

The woman next to him, Honoria Cathcart, daughter of the Colmondales was still droning on about her horses, and thoroughbreds, and God help him, steeplechases. But he would not condemn her or treat her like a disposable object.

So he sat, and he listened to the music, and chatted politely with the woman who bored him until he could decently excuse himself and go to bed.

"I believe we have found soulmates!" her mother said, beaming. "Your knowledge of horses and horsemanship is most impressive, Mr. Fraser."

What, when all he'd done was nod at the right intervals, and ask a few questions? "Thank you, but I'm a mere beginner compared to your daughter, ma'am."

"You should ride out together. My daughter would love a good gallop, but she can hardly do that on her own, and I'm afraid my prowess is not so strong these days." Lady Colmondale wafted her fan. "Indeed, why wait? You do have a horse in the stables, do you not?"

He was forced to admit that he had. More than one, if truth be told.

"Then there is no problem. You could rise early and explore this magnificent park together."

A chill crept up Alex's spine. This was what was meant by a matchmaking mama. If he did not pay enough attention, he would find himself riding out alone with this girl at some ungodly hour of the morning. Someone would see them, her mother would make sure of it, and then his goose would be cooked. He had no doubt he would be hustled into marriage before he'd had time to say no. Compromised into it.

Had the marquess not told this woman of his plan? They

would get nothing making up to him.

His flat Yorkshire accent might have led them to believe untruths, like he was a yokel who had no idea of good manners in society. Or how men were trapped into marriage.

He thought of claiming his horse had cast a shoe, or some such excuse, but then paused. Why should he lie to prevent an encounter he had no wish for? "I'm so sorry, ma'am, that's impossible. I believe it wouldn't be reet for us to ride out alone." Not to prevent him falling on her like a rabid beast, but to bear witness that he had not done such a thing.

"Oh dear." She appeared crestfallen, her mouth drooping at the corners. "I had no idea you were such a prude, sir."

"Not a prude, but I know what's proper. But I look forrard to more conversations like this."

For the next two or three days, at any rate. He'd have to get his manager to call him back. A shame because he wanted to give Acaster that time on his own. Perhaps he could go up to town. He hadn't been to London since his visit to Carlton House last year. His lawyer could use the time to catch him up on his other projects.

"You were talking quite animatedly with the Duchess of Whiston on your way into dinner," the lady pointed out.

"We know some of the same people."

"Who would that be? Perhaps I know the person, too."

"Probably not, ma'am." If he mentioned the Regent, he'd be properly in the soup.

She sniffed. "Somebody northern, I presume. She lives with her mother in Edinburgh these days."

"Does she?"

He looked around. The duchess in question had already gone. Pity.

THIS HOUSE PARTY was nothing but a microcosm of London society, with its mixture of marriageable girls, older, experienced women, and matrons to look down on all of them. Bianca would wager this was not the only house party used for that purpose this year because of the failure of this year's season.

There were a few marriageable men here, but Bianca had done with all that. Only one man attracted her, and unfortunately, continued to do so.

She barely saw the fascinating Mr. Fraser, except when the company got together for dinner. Even then he usually excused himself early. She liked the house very much, although she hadn't expected to. It was spacious, beautifully kept, and full of exquisite treasures. The Stonyhursts were collectors of long standing, and it showed in variety and quality.

She had been given a room decorated in the Chinese style, with black lacquered furniture and rich blue drapery embroidered with small figures engaged in everyday tasks. Elegant. McMurdo approved. Every night Bianca retired as early as she could to read a book or simply to sleep. So far, the visit was achieving its purpose: to reestablish Bianca as a member of society. Even if some of the guests were on the racier side—something that disturbed her when she let it.

The visit passed, as visits did, with the same program repeated every day. Breakfast was served at ten, with food available for early risers who wanted to ride or walk outside. Since this summer was proving fair, much better than the last two, the guests took to the pretty gardens. Bianca sometimes joined them.

After breakfast, several activities were offered, including gentle outside ones.

Maria treated Bianca to big eyes and confidences she did not in the least want, seeking her out to walk with her, if Bianca was not quick enough. She seemed to think their friendship was as strong as ever and made enquiries about "dear Juliet," which Bianca answered as blandly as she could. As the daughter of Lady Rotherham, who'd been kind to the Burrells when they first arrived in society, Maria and Juliet had formed a close friendship. They'd read books together, taking turns to choose. Juliet had given Maria her opinions on various topics, on request, and educated the less-worldly Maria. Unknown to Juliet, Maria and her mother were after prey, a distinguished diplomat recently returned to London. Even though all along Maria loved someone else.

Sadly for Maria, she lost the diplomat, who discovered Juliet and fell in love with her.

Her malleability had come to fruition when she'd agreed to enter into this infamous marriage with a man old enough to be her grandfather, bringing her lover with her in case she got lonely at night.

"I'm so glad everything worked out so well," Maria said, when she'd captured Bianca for a walk around the rose garden. "Except for your loss, dear Bianca!" The day was fine, parasols were out, and people were ambling around.

Bianca couldn't remember giving Maria permission to use her first name. In different company she'd have enjoyed the stroll, but Maria seemed to be under the illusion that they were fast friends. "Thank you for your concern. It has been a year now—time I returned to society."

"Indeed. So brave of you! Especially after the sad passing of your husband's successor."

Not so sad. But Bianca did not say that aloud. "The new duke is a kind man," she ventured, trying for bland and succeeding triumphantly. "And you did well."

"I ended marrying a marquess, so I jumped up a rank." Maria smiled sunnily.

And several decades, Bianca thought, but she did not say that aloud, either, only made a non-committal sound.

Maria patted Bianca's hand. "Now we must find you a husband, must we not? I wanted my husband to invite more gentlemen, but he wants his nephews to marry, so it's mostly women. They must marry young, biddable females."

"Is Mr. Norris part of that plan?"

The name fell between them like a stone. Maria swallowed. "No, not him. He is my husband's secretary, so he's not eligible."

That explained why Bianca had not seen him at dinner or at any of the little entertainments his lordship had arranged. He was Staff, not a guest. And, of course, he acted as stud, substituting for the marquess. Nobody was near enough to hear them, so Bianca broached the subject. If Maria wanted her to leave after she'd had her say, then so be it. She shuffled the gravel with one toe as they walked in the hedged-in garden, the air heady with the rich scent of roses in bloom.

"Is he still your lover?"

Tears sprang to Maria's eyes as if Bianca had called them out. "Yes." She lowered her head, the brim of her bonnet grazing her parasol. "I still love him. But I could not have married him, don't you see? He was poor and he had no status, no rank to speak of."

"He would have gained one in time. Langston said he was very clever, set to go far in politics."

Maria nodded. "But I didn't want that, you see. I'm not made to be the wife of a politician, holding literary salons and that kind of thing. We're much better like this."

So she had scotched her lover's chance of making a name for himself, dragged him here to be at her beck and call instead of letting him stay in London to pursue his ambitions.

"You couldn't marry him without the wealth and status?" If she loved someone neither of those things would have stopped her. The fact that she fell for a duke was coincidental. Except the title had made George—and it had brought him down.

"How could you even ask such a thing?" Maria asked. "When poverty is in the house, love flies out of the window. Someone said that—a poet, I think."

"I saw it on a caricature in a print shop," she said, and re-membered. At the time, she and George were in the news all the time. That was the race around London markets. It had not gone well for George. That was when she'd realized he was flying out of control, and if she did not do something about it, so would she.

Chapter Five

A LEX HEADED TO the office the next day with a sense of foreboding he had no reason for. Perhaps he'd had a bad dream he didn't remember. He rarely remembered his dreams. Vague recollections, strange imaginings, all gone within five minutes of waking up.

He needed to shake this mood and get on. He was nearly there, but the sense of something wrong remained with him, and it irritated him that he could not define what it was. If anything at all.

As usual, Villiers was waiting. He sat behind his desk, his pure white collar so high he could hardly bend his head enough to read the papers before him. Today it was a thick vellum document with a heavy seal contained in a metal holder. Seals became fragile with age.

"What's that?" he asked.

"These," Villiers said with every pompous bone in his body on alert, "these are the letters patent conferring the title on the first Marquess of Stonyhurst by King Charles the Second. I also have the document when the earldom was granted by King Edward the Third." He motioned to another document laid out on a side table. "The title was elevated by the first George, and we have that document, too."

"Aye?" Fascinated by the age of these documents, Alex studied the first one. He recognized a few Latin words, and given time could have parsed it, but he had no intention of betraying his education. "What do it say?"

"Does," Villiers corrected absently. "It is the usual wording. These documents are very precious, you understand, perhaps the most precious of all the objects in this gem of a treasure house. There are, naturally, copies, but these are the originals."

"Aye. Let me see."

Taking a magnifying glass from the table, Alex bent over the document. The wording troubled him. "So this thing is given by the King?"

"Aye—yes." Villiers cleared his throat. "You won't know what it says so I've prepared a translation from you."

Alex read it through. Then he read it again. The formulaic, stately wording conveyed a message he was not ready to hear.

Ten minutes later he was on his way to his uncle's room.

After waiting a further ten minutes, he sent a message that either his uncle saw him, or he would go home this very day. He could do it, just ride away and leave his attendants to pack up and bring his gear along later. He was in enough of a temper to do so.

Lord Stonyhurst sat by a gently glowing fire, staring at the embers. He took his time looking up when Alex came in. "What brings you here in such a mood, boy?"

Being called "boy" didn't help. "I've seen the letters patent."

"Ah yes. I told Villiers to show them to you and explain them. If my wife does not produce a son before my death, you are the next Marquess of Stonyhurst."

Alex gritted his teeth. "I don't want it," he said. "Leave it to somebody else."

"That is not possible." The marquess sighed. "Unfortunately. I should have sent for you earlier, but then, I had three perfectly good heirs before you. Why should I? Now I have no choice."

The documents had come as a profound shock to Alex. Why must there be no choice? Surely a man had a right to leave his possessions to anyone he wished?

"M'father left 'is gold to whoever he wanted to. Are you sayin' that all this don't belong to you?" Anger and a vicious need to rip back drove him now. If that was true, he was in a right mess.

"Oh, it's mine all right." The marquess stared up at him, eyes wide. "But can it be that your father never told you about entails?"

"Why should he? He'd no need. He walked out of this house and washed 'is 'ands of it. Wanted nothing to do with you or the title." He remembered that day so well, especially since he'd returned to the place where it happened. His father in a towering rage, vowing never to return, refusing to tell his son why. Alex could guess, even though he hadn't been in the actual meeting. His father had left him with the housekeeper while he had conducted his business.

They'd knocked the dust of Stonyhurst off their heels and never returned. Only later, when Alex was older, had he told him of the stigma of being in trade. And of the marquess's disapproval of Alex's mother.

For two pins he'd follow his father's example, even though that would leave him in the soup if the marchioness didn't produce.

"She's young enough. You should get to it." And put both of them out of their misery.

"I would prefer Adolphus or Benedict, but you are in the way. Your blood is only partly mine. The other part is not acceptable."

Alex held his temper in check, but only just. "If I go now, I'm not comin' back. Why don't you leave everything except what you need to them? Give them a share."

He strode up and down the Persian carpet, careless of the precious knotted silk.

The marquess snorted. "And impoverish the title? You're mad, boy." He stopped. His eyes went unfocused. "Perhaps that's the answer. I could get you committed."

"Try it." Alex stopped dead and poked a finger at his uncle.

"Go on. Have a go."

"At the very least you can learn to talk properly and familiarize yourself with the basics of civilized living."

The insult to his family mattered more than anything else.

He'd used the accent to deter his uncle from leaving his title and fortune to him. Added to the shame of being in trade and his father marrying a nonentity, that should have been enough. But he saw now that it wasn't going to work.

He could do nothing. He'd never felt so helpless. The shock of realizing there was no way out of this bind short of death shocked him to the core.

Even if the marchioness produced, Alex would be expected to become involved in the baby's minority. The marquess could whistle for that. "Don't mek me a trustee," he said, milder now, his brain working again.

"Too late," his uncle said. "Part of my reason for summoning you here was a desire to see how you managed your business, and how fast you could understand the complexities of the estate. On that score, I'm satisfied. I want you involved in administering the estate in the baby's minority."

At least that was a task Alex could refuse if he wanted to. But seeing all this, he couldn't bear to think of the estate being dissipated or badly managed. Waste made his heart bleed.

"We'll see," he said grimly. With a vague farewell wave, he left the room.

He'd wanted a good row with the marquess, but the man had been strangely subdued. Even strengthening the accent had only earned Alex a mild rebuke. The marquess had everything planned out, and as far as he was concerned, nothing would interfere with that. Not acceptable for the title, was he? He'd show them!

ON THE SEVENTH day, after dinner Bianca settled down in her

room with her book in a comfortable chair.

She was ready to leave. The visit had achieved its objective, to remind people she was out of mourning and still here. Next season she could return to London, perhaps sooner, so she could order a new wardrobe.

Tomorrow she'd regretfully take her leave. No doubt the coaching inn in the village could provide her with a traveling carriage. With so many people coming and going to the Big House, they must have a reasonable stable.

She was reading a new novel, supposed to be a sensation, but she wasn't finding it engaging. Perhaps it would get better as she read on. She'd finished her tea, and wished she'd asked for something else. Her gaze settled on the untouched decanter of what looked like red wine, next to an amber spirit that had to be brandy. After a shrug, she went back to her book.

Someone scratched on her door panels. Since she'd dismissed her maid, Bianca had to answer it herself. Putting the book down, she took a candle and went to the door, opening it a mere crack before widening it enough to let her visitor in.

"What on earth has happened, Maria? You look like you've been dragged through hell," she said frankly, leading the way in. The door closed. Going back to her previous seat, Bianca motioned a chair close to the one she was using. "I take it this visit isn't social?"

Maria seemed not to notice Bianca's abrupt tone. Bianca took her seat and waited. Maria had been crying, her eyes puffy and red, her carefully applied maquillage streaked. Her hair was in a state, as if she'd run her fingers through the light brown curls and pulled out half the pins. She wore a wrapper like Bianca's but clutched it around her body. When she sat she bent over in the chair as if her stomach hurt. This was extreme, even for her. While Bianca had no desire to be as close to Maria as she once was, she did not actively wish the woman any harm. What was done was done.

"What is wrong?" she said, gentling her voice when she realized Maria was genuinely upset. "Maria, are you hurt?"

Sitting up, Maria thumped her clenched fist against her chest. "Only in my heart."

Oh dear. Bianca got up and went to the sideboard. If she'd thought about a drink five minutes ago, she wanted one twice as much now. She poured two glasses and put one on the small table by the side of Maria's chair, together with a clean handkerchief. "Compose yourself. How can I help you if you don't tell me what is wrong?"

Was she expecting a baby at last? Surely that would be good news.

Maria sucked in a breath, then she saw the wine, picked it up like a starving woman and drank half of it in one gulp. Bianca sipped, waiting. When the sniffing and weeping threatened to overcome Maria again, Bianca asked, "Are you expecting a child?"

"Nooo!"

Well, that didn't work. Why not go for the repique? "Is it Walter Norris?"

"Nooo!"

At last Maria mopped her eyes and gazed at Bianca. Her eyes were bloodshot. "He's gone!"

"Gone? Is it your husband?"

"No, no, no!" Maria pulled in a deep breath. Then another. She pushed stray locks of hair back in a vain attempt to tidy it, but it was a sign that she was recovering a little. "Walter has gone away to London."

"At this time of year, when Parliament is not in session?" Walter had been a parliamentary secretary, and still was one, nominally at least, although he'd been notable by his absence recently. "What is he doing there?"

"Stonyhurst sent him away." Maria sniffed. "But before he went, Walter asked me to go with him. To leave this behind us." She waved a hand at the comfortably furnished room, and by implication, the rest of the house. "Of course I can't. Stonyhurst wouldn't let me."

"Since when has a woman asked her husband's permission before she ran off with her lover?" Bianca snapped, struck by the resemblance to her own history. Except she had not been married when she ran off with George. By the time she realized he didn't intend to marry her, Viola's husband had caught up with them, and then George had to tie the knot, especially since Langston had brought a special license with him. Not the best way to start a marriage, as it had turned out. But better than this, apparently.

"We have nothing! Nothing! Who would give Walter a position once they knew what he'd done?"

"He wouldn't be ruined. You would," Bianca pointed out. Men rarely suffered for their impulses. Women always paid.

Maria shook her head. "You don't understand. You've never been that poor. Never suffered like this!"

"Wrong on both counts."

Either Maria hadn't heard her, or she chose not to respond. "I didn't understand why Stonyhurst sent him away, but now I do. Tonight he came to my room and told me to avail myself of the opportunities this party offers. Walter is to stay away until I get with child."

Bianca closed her eyes. The deal with the devil had taken a nasty turn. "You mean your husband is asking you to become a prostitute?"

There was no other way of putting it.

Maria sniffed and dabbed her nose. "He is desperate for a son."

"You might not have a boy first time. What's wrong with your current arrangement?"

"There's been *nothing*!" Maria's tragic expression turned even worse. Bianca hadn't thought that was possible. "Nothing, Bianca!"

"Have you been with your husband recently?"

Maria shook her head. "When we were first married, he tried, but he does not—he cannot . . ."

Bianca had heard of men of eighty who'd succeeded in siring

a child. Lord Stonyhurst had given up somewhat early. But she understood, even if she had not encountered the phenomenon herself.

Another question came to mind. "Why is your husband so set on excluding his heir from the succession? So much that he will turn his back while you put a cuckoo in the nursery?"

Maria's pretty lips curled in a sneer. "Did you see him at dinner? Oh, he's handsome, in a brutish kind of way, but so uncouth! He fumbled with his cutlery, did not know which glass to use, and actually said thank you to the footman! He does not seem to have much conversation, and his accent—he would bring the marquessate to its knees in a year!"

Her words took Bianca aback. She had not known her sister's friend was such a snob. Would she be shocked if she knew the Burrells survived their first season by making their own gowns? That trend they set for elegant simplicity was born of necessity. Bianca barely had a string of coral beads to her name when they'd first arrived in town.

She was tempted to tell the marchioness, but decided against it, instead adding a bland, "I quite like him myself." He was carrying on his masquerade effectively, apparently. Bianca was not sure what he thought he would gain by it, unless it was to be left alone.

"But not as a marquess! He's an industrialist, in trade!"

At least she wasn't crying about it. She was busy drying her eyes and finishing her drink. Bianca exchanged her full glass for the empty one.

"What do you want to do, Maria? If we can help you, we will." None of the Burrells would put themselves in harm's way again for her, but if Bianca could help without risking that, she would.

"Thank you. My mama was good to you, was she not?"

"In her way, yes she was." But only to serve her own ends.

Maria dabbed her eyes again. Bianca fidgeted. She didn't want to go over old ground, especially not with this woman.

On a whim, Bianca got up and went to her dressing table. Her maid had covered it with a soft linen cloth and put Bianca's usual items on it. She found the silver-backed brush and took it back. She just couldn't bear seeing Maria's hair in that state any longer. At the first gentle stroke, Maria whimpered, but she let Bianca straighten her hair a little. Maria had baby-fine fair hair, very different to Bianca's own. While she tackled the mess, Bianca talked to Maria in a soothing tone.

"You agreed to this marriage, Maria. You wanted it. We offered to help you escape with Walter, but you said no, you would do this instead. Once you married Stonyhurst, he became your legal guardian. He has jurisdiction over you. But that doesn't mean he can force you into immoral acts. If you do not want to do this, you don't have to."

"But he arranged this house party for me!"

"And he made you feel you were obliged to him?" Bianca knew how that felt.

"I suppose so," she mumbled. "And I understand why. He is desperate for an heir, especially now that Mr. Fraser has arrived. That made it worse. His accent! Those table manners!"

That rough accent did not conceal his good manners, unless he remembered to keep them uncouth. Bianca had no doubt that if he were not so keen to appear unrefined and unsuitable for the marquessate his manners would be as good as everyone else's. But manners alone did not make a gentleman. There were several in this house party who would not hesitate to take up any offer Maria might make, or even knowingly fall in with her husband's plans. They were not gentlemen, only well-born ruffians with cut-glass accents.

"Ouch!"

She must have pulled too hard. As Bianca walked across the room to replace the brush, Maria got to her feet. "Thank you for listening to me, Bianca. Of course you are right. I must strive obey my husband in all things." Bianca was sure she had never said that, nor would she ever. "I do not know if Walter will return, but I will behave until I hear from him. Then . . ." She lifted her hand and let it drop back to her side with a slap. "I do not know. But perhaps, if I . . ." She bit her lip.

Bianca would have told her husband to take himself to Hades and stay there if he'd made a suggestion like that. In fact, she had told him to do that very thing several times, but not for that reason.

Turning, she shepherded Maria to the door and thankfully closed it behind her. What did the woman expect? Had Norris grown bored or frustrated with the situation? Love dies if it is starved. She knew that only too well.

Alone again, she put her back to the door and leaned against it, breathing out a great sigh of relief. A part of her wanted to stay to watch the drama. This house contained a group of people on the brink of—something. Refreshing that she was not part of it, that she could watch the proceedings like a member of the audience.

Perhaps she'd give it another day or two.

THE MORROW DAWNED bright and sunny, so Bianca decided to stay at least one more day. She went for a long walk before breakfast, pausing by the side of the lake, gazing out at the waterfowl and wildlife. She'd always loved watching nature's creatures. She should do that more.

"Is that a moorhen?"

The deep voice behind her made her jump out of her skin. She clapped a hand to her chest. "Oh, goodness, I didn't hear you come up!"

Mr. Fraser came to stand by her side. "I beg your pardon. The grass is still damp. It must have muffled my footsteps. Should I go away?"

"No, that is, not on my account." Her breathing regained its regular rhythm, and she glanced behind her. "Didn't you use the path?"

"It's quicker to walk straight across." He glanced down at his boots, which were decidedly not fashionable Hessians or even polished top-boots. Thick soles and sturdy manufacture made them practical, but they weren't something any Bond Street dandy would be seen dead in.

She glanced down at her own footwear. She was not exactly a fashion plate herself. She pushed back her old faithful bonnet so she could look up into his face. His smile melted her. She should have prepared herself for the impact. "Yes, it's a moorhen." She couldn't think of anything else to say.

"I should have left you be," he said softly. "I'll go."

"No! I—you just startled me, that's all." She groped for her society face, but it had slipped. "I was thinking."

"What about?"

"Leaving, if you must know."

He laughed harshly. "So was I."

"Really?"

"Really. I came here to see what I was letting myself in for, but it's too much . . ." With a wide gesture he encompassed the park and the house, and by implication, the estate beyond. "I'm not a landowner, not like this." He paused and sighed. "Apparently it will be mine whether I want it or not."

"That's true. The laws of inheritance are complicated, especially when titles are involved. And they can't be changed."

He muttered something low, like "God dammit."

"Did you not realize that?"

He shook his head and bent down, scooping up a handful of stones. "I thought it could be willed away, like property. My father turned his back on all that, so there was no need for us to know anything about entails. Old way of thinking, he told us. I've just been disabused of my illusion. Unless the marchioness produces a child, or I die before the marquess, the title and the bulk of the estate is mine whether I, or the old man, want it or not. And I don't want it."

"Why ever not?"

He threw a stone over the still surface of the lake. It sank without even one skip. "I have my life and I'm happy in it. So are my sisters and my mother. I have my money and my businesses to take care of. It produces more than we need. Maybe as much as the estate, I don't know." He jammed his hands into the pockets of his worsted breeches. "When I came here, I thought I could persuade him to cut me out of the succession, give it to somebody else. Until my uncle's brother and sons died there was little chance of my inheriting, so why should I bother looking into it? I never belonged in this life, never wanted it."

A duck shot out of the undergrowth, squawking and fussing, skimming across the water before it shook its feathers and down. She grinned. "I know how it feels."

He skimmed another stone. This time it took three skips before it sank. He shot a grin at her and dropped the other stones he was holding, dusting his hands together. "You see? I can do it when I'm not in a temper. Your serene presence calmed me down in an instant. Now tell me why you're thinking of leaving."

She'd seen worse tempers than that. She turned away, heading for the narrow path. He fell in by her side. "I don't like the way the marquess is arranging us to his satisfaction. I'm not looking to become a scandalous widow, which seems to be the role he's assigned to me. I'm not looking to remarry, either."

"You're a widow," he said gently. "You can do what you want now. Doesn't your husband's family want to look after you?"

She humphed. How could she tell him about that mess? But perhaps she should tell him what other people knew before somebody else did. "It was hardly a stable marriage. I fell in love, I became a duchess." That was a shock in itself. "We ruled the town for a while. With Byron gone and Brummel fled to the Continent, the wilder part of society was looking for someone to lead it. And for a while, we did it." She paused. "I loved that part.

How could I not? Finally I had a place, and it was so exciting to find myself the center of attention. But we were in debt, and then my husband died."

She couldn't tell him the last part. How to do it? But she tried. "His cousin inherited, but not for long. He was an unpleasant person." And more, but that involved state secrets she had promised not to divulge to anyone. "Before he could eject me from the family home and estate, I left. I asked for nothing but the portion I'd brought to the marriage. He even argued about that. He died last Christmas in a carriage accident, and another cousin inherited. So I'm the sixth Duchess of Whiston, and we're now at the eighth duke." She laughed. "I hardly know the new duke, but he's been very kind, especially considering George and I nearly ran the dukedom into the ground. But he's a good man." Quiet, steady, with a wife and family he loved. Just what the dukedom needed. "I'm happy enough as I am, truly." But sometimes she missed the excitement, the thrill.

And why was she telling him her personal feelings? Giving him a brief account of affairs before somebody else did was one thing, but going into the way she felt? Why should he care, in any case?

"I see." He didn't say more, but she got the feeling that powerful cogs were whirring in his head. What was he thinking? What would he do next?

They reached the path and strolled along it in the direction of the house. Abruptly, he turned. "I don't want to go back just yet. Do you mind? I'll escort you to the door, but I'm in the mood for some fresh air."

Despite the size of the house, they were unlikely to find fresh air there. "Clouds are gathering."

"I know." Pushing back his hat, he scrubbed his hand through his hair. He wore it short but cut carefully into a fashionable style. "Not just in there." He jerked his head toward the house.

"Your valet will hate you," she said with a smile.

"He's used to me. He copes." He set his hat back on his head.

"Yon marquess is determined to make me into a gentleman."

She pushed a stone aside with her foot. "You're not talking like a gentleman in there. Why did you do that?"

They took a few steps before he answered. "I started it to try to put my uncle off the idea of making me his heir. But that's a waste of time now, isn't it? And I did it because they assumed I would be like that. I heard them talking. Frankly, I thought that was all they deserved—that I live up to the person they already believed I was. I'm low-born, in trade, and I work with my hands. So how can I be educated and aware? How can I know others?" Exasperation entered his voice. "Adolphus and Benedict know me, of course. I asked them not to spoil my fun." His mouth twisted. "So much for fun."

They strolled to the edge of a small thicket of beech trees. By unspoken mutual consent they turned and began to walk back. "I don't know my cousins very well," he said. "We're not close."

"Such a pity! But we have only met our grandfather once, our father's father. My brother is heir to his title and estates, though the old man frequently wishes him to the devil. Like the marquess, he married a woman in hopes of siring a new heir, but sadly she died in childbirth."

"That is sad. Losing the child and the mother is such a trage-dy. It happens all too often."

When he crooked his arm, she laid her hand on it. The action seemed natural, somehow. He tucked her close to his body, and she felt his warmth. "It is sad, whoever it is." He patted her hand. Although they were both wearing gloves, the touch was more intimate than any she'd experienced outside her family for over a year.

"I thought I might drop the accent," he said, "but I'm rather fond of it. My father used to threaten to beat me if I did it. I was a headstrong child, ran with the factory children and the ones from the village." He laughed, sharp and short. "He sent me away to school. I hated it, but I worked hard because I knew he was right. I needed to learn how to move in every circle."

"Even this one."

"Indeed." He paused. "I'm reluctant to go back in. That is unlike me. I usually prefer to get unpleasant tasks over with. This time it's as if I'm being trapped, pushed into a corner."

She knew how he felt. "It might help to come up with a strategy of your own. Don't you think?"

He turned and faced her. Her arm dropped to her side. The small loss of his touch went far too deep. Her stomach pitched. But his smile made up for it. "Duchess, you have it right. I came here prepared to learn the situation and go home to think on it. But I can't do that, not straightaway. It's time I adapted my plan. Counter their sword with a shield of my own."

They were nearly at the side door now. He lowered his voice. "I have a request to make. Clearly we are to become firm friends. I'm used to calling my friends by their first name. Naturally that is up to you, but I would take it as a favor if you would call me Alex when we're on our own."

"Are we going to be on our own again?"

"Oh, I think so, don't you?"

He opened the door for her. As she passed, she murmured, "Bianca."

Chapter Six

S HE MET HIM again the next day, and they walked together, always in sight of the house, talking and laughing. And the day after that, and the day after that, until Adolphus Fraser made a remark to her at dinner. "Mr. Fraser must be particularly good company. You seem to enjoy it."

Adolphus had run with Whiston and the rest of his friends for a while, but he had drifted away toward the end, claiming his vices had taken a different bent. Bianca knew him, but not well enough to claim a deep acquaintance. However, certain rumors abounded about his preferences, and without knowing for sure, she gave them credence.

Was he being disingenuous here, or starting rumors?

Bianca did not go out for her morning walk the next day, although she missed her customary exercise. Instead, she went up to the Long Gallery, the place built for the marquess's Tudor ancestors, who were encouraged to walk up and down on rainy days. Not that a spot of rain would have stopped her. Only the thought of meeting Alex again drove her to the sensible route.

She needed to control her reaction to him, to think about him. No man had ever caused such an instant and visceral reaction in her. Well, perhaps one, and that had turned out badly, so she needed to step back and take control of her emotions.

The Long Gallery was deserted at this time of day. Too far

away from the kitchens for the scents and sounds of food preparation to disturb her, Bianca emulated the Tudors and walked up and down. In common with other people who owned such a room, including her sister Viola, Lady Knowsley, the Long Gallery held the official portraits of the family. The ones taken at marriage, death of a loved one, or the set pieces of a family far superior to the thankless observer were mounted here, carefully spaced to show the progression of wealth and power.

Interesting to learn that the family had split in two at the outbreak of civil war, so that Royalist faced Parliamentarian. The portrait of the brothers involved in the conflict taken in the early years of King Charles I showed no foreshadowing. At least she didn't think so, but this artist was a master painter. Was the brother in the elaborate blue satin costume the royalist? She leaned closer.

Firm footsteps on the polished wooden floor made her turn.

There he was. Her attention went from the painting to Alex and back again. Valiantly, she tried to control her beating heart. It pounded like a herd of wild horses. Her breath quickened, and she had to grasp the top of a nearby chair.

"Are you all right?" Closer now, he touched her, grazing her shoulder. She repressed her shiver. "I made sure not to creep up on you."

"I wasn't expecting anyone," she managed. She gulped air. "How did you know I was here?"

"I closed my eyes and imagined you. Then I followed my imagination." She blinked up at him, and he smiled. "I saw your maid coming out of your room and I asked her where you were."

"Ah." She relaxed. For a moment she thought—what did she think? They had not known each other long, so how could she ever imagine a closeness she had no right to assume? She did imagine, though. Last night, as she fell asleep, she didn't think of George, not once. Usually, he drifted into her mind at that time, as if he chose to visit her then. Not last night.

"And you came to find me. How sweet of you."

"Hmm." He wouldn't move away, and she felt no inclination to do so. "Sweet *on* you, perhaps. Maybe." He touched the tip of her nose, so gently that had she had her eyes closed, she wouldn't have noticed. "You are by far the most interesting person here. The one who holds my attention."

"What about all those would-be brides?"

He paused and then turned, staring up at his ancestors painted larger than life. "If I said they were vapid, I would be the most arrogant man alive. It's not that. But the marquess has warned me away from them. Though if I met one who held my interest, I would not let that stop me. But I haven't. I have spoken with all of them, all six. Every one agreed with everything I said, even if I contradicted myself. They do not interest me, although I daresay they would interest someone. They were afraid of me, or they laughed at me because of my accent and uncouth ways. One kindly soul offered to teach me how to use my cutlery."

He huffed a laugh. "If I marry, as I suppose I might someday, I want a woman I can talk to, a friend and partner." He turned back to her. She suspected he had not seen the painted figures at all. "Someone who disagrees with me once in a while, for instance."

"Society has many intelligent, interesting young women," she said, "but your uncle has invited the most sedate and obedient young women he could find. So you won't settle on any of those, not even to spite him?"

"No," he said firmly. He sighed. "He doesn't want me to marry at all, but I don't consider myself bound by his orders. You'll keep my secret, won't you?"

"Of course, if you wish it." She turned back to the painting. "You may find a woman you can respect and love. I'm sure of it."

Why did the thought of that make her unhappy? She should be pleased for him, because this man deserved happiness. She was nothing to him, she told herself, nor he to her, a chance-met acquaintance at an uncomfortable house party.

They could be more than that. The notion crept into her

mind unbidden. She'd been invited as the sinful part of the party. So why not live up to that?

Reason answered her immediately. Because she wanted to be as respected and happy as her sisters, as settled. Seeing their joy reminded her, not of what she had lost, but of what she'd never had. But oh! With this man standing by her side, she was tempted. So very tempted.

"I will," he said with a wry smile, "but to do it to spite my uncle galls me. Even to make him think that." He indicated the painted couple before them. "I have never seen these." They were dressed in the costume of the last century, the lady wearing a wide hooped skirt even in the midst of the countryside. The house, the one they were in now, was depicted in the background, looking much the same. The gentleman stood by the lady's side, a hunting rifle casually tucked in the crook of his arm, pointing downward.

"Quite a set piece," she said. "I see the resemblance."

"In which one?"

"In both of them." She studied his ancestors. "He has the same face shape you do. What I can see of his hair under his hat is as dark as yours, but that might be artistic license. And the lady—elegant, confident. That nose—I'd know it anywhere."

"Would you?"

She turned to see him watching her, not the painting.

"Face shape?" he repeated. Unlike his ancestor, his eyes were gleaming with amusement.

"Long," she suggested helpfully. This connection was too strong. If she stayed here much longer she'd lose her head. All the emotions she'd tried so hard to suppress rose up to trip her. Hastily, she twitched her skirts aside and moved on to look at the next picture. "I wonder how they managed those huge skirts. Do you think the ladies really wore them in the country?"

"When they were having their portraits done they did," he said.

Had he been affected the same way she was, or was he playing with her? After all, only her instinct drew her to him. She knew nothing about his character. Nobody here did. They only assumed they knew.

"They all have a *look*." She stepped back and looked at the portraits lining the gallery. One side was large windows, the other was all paintings.

"Of what? Superiority and privilege?"

"Yes," she admitted. "We both know what it's like to look at that from the outside. Most of the people here would think it strange if they didn't have that look." Another bond they shared. "But not that. The nose, the shape of the face. Although eye color varies. Your eyes are very dark, but your ancestors seem to favor gray eyes."

"I have my mother's eyes," he said, "and her complexion."

"I thought that was from the sun," she said. He was darker than the average fashionable fribble, but she'd assumed that was from the active life he led.

"Not entirely." He moved back a little. "I have her eyes, her complexion, and my hair isn't brown, it's black." He stopped, watching her, evidently waiting for her response. His shoulders tightened.

"She's from the north?" she ventured.

"No, she's from India. Or to be more precise, her mother was Indian. Why do you think my uncle is so opposed to my being the heir?"

Chapter Seven

"BUT THAT'S MONSTROUS!" Bianca spoke without thinking, but she would have said the same thing anyway. If anything, his heritage made him more handsome in her eyes.

His shoulders relaxed, even though his expression did not change. "Thank you for that."

"I thought it was because you are in trade."

He grimaced. "That as well. But he could have taken me out of that circle, brought me here, taught me how to be a gentleman. I know the way he thinks, now." He paused. "But the main objection is my ancestry. Tainted blood, you see."

She felt sick. She'd come across this attitude before, mostly from narrow-minded people. She was sorry to see it in the marquess but not altogether surprised. "And that is why he did not invite your mother?" She'd wondered about that.

"Yes, and my sisters, too, even though they are paler than I am. Apart from Elise." He smiled. "My mother took care to keep them out of the sun and gave them all manner of lotions and potions. But we are not ashamed, nor are we interested in hiding our ancestry."

"I didn't know."

"And now you do, you don't care." His smile broadened. He was truly the most attractive man she'd ever seen. Not the most handsome, not the most polished, but for her, this was it.

"Only that it causes you and your family problems." And, she'd wager, unhappiness. "My experience is mild compared to yours." It was. They had lived frugally, but never starved, never been stared at as "different." The injustice stung her.

"I wouldn't say that. And you faced them all down, did you not?"

They had. The Burrells had entered society with their heads held high, and their secret sewing room well hidden. She smiled at the memory. "It's easier when you have nothing to lose."

His face grew somber. "Unfortunately I never heard of your exploits before I came here. My mother may have done."

"She must have been disappointed not to receive an invitation."

"She was not, or so she says. I offered to bring her anyway, but she refused. And now you're wondering why I came at all. Shall we?" He offered her his arm, and she took it. They strolled up the gallery from the turbulent years of the Civil War, the Restoration, and then the advent of the Georges, with ladies in huge, hooped skirts and men in powdered wigs.

"I came," he said, around the time of George the Second, "because I had little choice. He sent his steward, Villiers, to order me, since I had not responded to his previous correspondence. I realized the old man wouldn't leave me alone until I answered him. So I came." He paused, cleared his throat. "I thought I had better see how things lay. Even then I would not have come if my mother had disliked it. But she told me to open the door, if it could be opened, so that my sisters could visit in the fullness of time, if they wished it."

"They should," she said. "They have that right."

"So they do," he agreed. "Until the marchioness does her duty, I'm the heir. She has produced nothing in a year, and he's desperate enough to call me. But he wants only to assess me as a future trustee for the estate during the young heir's minority. He does not want me to be the heir. He made that quite clear."

They walked up to more recent times in companionable

silence while Bianca recalled Maria's visit to her bedroom. She could hardly tell him what was happening, not without breaking a confidence.

They paused before a collection of portraits. "This must be your grandfather," she said, pausing before a full-length portrait of a tall man dressed in blue satin.

"Yes. And that's his first wife." He indicated another portrait, a lady staring superciliously down on them. Two boys posed stiffly at her side. "That one there, that's the current marquess, my uncle. The other is the next in age. He joined the military, married, and had two sons of his own."

They regarded the portrait in silence for a moment.

"I would not have wished her tragedy on them," he said.

"What was it?"

"A fever took his wife," he said. "Smallpox. The marquess did not believe in inoculation, not even the cowpox method. He ordered the boys taken to a separate part of the house to ensure they did not take the disease."

"My mother had us all inoculated."

"Good," he said. "So did mine."

"But the dangers remain," she pointed out.

He nodded. "People still die. Not as much from the new technique. But they're still dying of smallpox, and the old marquess learned that the hard way."

The next portrait was far less formal. A family, posing in the countryside, with Stonyhurst visible behind them. Alex's grandfather sat next to his second wife on a garden seat, their hands linked. The two boys in this picture wore more practical clothes and were playing with a large dog. "That's him with his second wife. My father is the one holding the dog's lead. The other is my uncle, who died a few years ago—the father of Adolphus and Benedict."

They might not have been like that in real life, but the informality suited them. Recent portraiture preferred to show the sitters in more casual attitudes. Her sister Viola had been painted in fancy dress, as the goddess Diana, a depiction her husband loved. George had wanted to see Bianca painted as Venus, but that commission had never come to pass. Too many debts to settle, too much to do. Like most of George's schemes, it had dissolved into thin air.

"I didn't know my older uncle and cousins' deaths put me in the line of fire. All three of them—father and sons—died at Waterloo."

"That's so sad."

"Yes, it is. Officers above the rank of major are not expected to take the field, but they all ignored that. I salute their bravery." They gave the three men a moment of silence.

"I thought I could ignore all this family duty," he confessed as they moved on. "I wanted to."

"Do you really want no part of all this?" She waved her hand, indicating the estate and by implication, the rest of the marquess-ate.

"I really don't." He turned to her. "I have no interest in old ways and old portraits. I confess, I did want to know if they looked anything like me, but apart from a superficial resem-blance, I favor my mother's side of the family more than my father's. In more than just looks." He smiled. "My curiosity is satisfied in that. But I do want to commemorate the first time I saw my ancestors in an unforgettable way."

"Like what?"

"I want to remember this room as the place where I first kissed you."

Lifting his hand he stroked her lower lip. Not as gently as he'd touched her nose, but he kept his touch light. Sensation radiated through her. She stood still, mesmerized by those dark, liquid eyes. "I want to know how your lips would feel under mine." His voice lowered. "How good you taste."

Lowering his head he kissed her, so gently he made her feel fragile. Untouched, as once she had been. When he slid his arm around her waist she didn't resist, or step back as she should have.

Torn, she waited. He deepened the kiss.

She waited no more. The objections rampaging through her head could just be quiet. One kiss? She would take it.

Bianca flung her arm around Alex's neck, reveling in the fine tremor of his lips on hers as he registered her response. Did he think the desire was all on his side? He was about to discover different.

When he pressed harder, she opened to him, tilting her head so their kiss could deepen, become more passionate.

His tongue entered her mouth, hot and thrusting, desire burgeoning between them. His body hardened, muscles strengthening under her questing fingers. He cinched her close enough for her to feel his erection, as questing as her fingers. She answered him, curling the tip of her tongue around his, teasing, coaxing. Persuading.

He rewarded her with a groan low in his throat, a sound that reverberated through her body.

Then she heard something else. A gasp. Not hers.

Spreading her hand over his chest, ignoring her desire to explore, she pushed him away. "Did you hear that?"

"What?" He shoved his hand through his hair, pushing it into a rough approximation of his style. Hers would take more work. He'd cupped the back of her head while he kissed her.

He lifted his head and gazed at her, smiling. "We shouldn't be doing this, but I'm glad we are."

His words brought her to a sense of reality. Good lord, anyone could come in. Turning, she took a few steps away from him.

At least this place had a mirror, even if it was old and spotted. She crossed the room and examined her tousled appearance. He had not tried to move her clothes. She was still respectable, just about.

He laughed roughly. "Madness," he said. "In this room? Well, if anyone saw us, we'll know soon enough. If you hear, will you tell me?"

"If you tell me. I came here hoping to reenter society quietly, ready for next season."

"Maybe you can still do that."

He hadn't apologized, but why would he? She didn't regret that kiss, only where they'd done it. That, she agreed, was madness. But she did not have to look far for the cause. Passion. That had driven her to a dreadful marriage and forced her into situations she should never have considered. Passion was her downfall, always. Until this visit, she'd put a careful guard on it, determined not to give way, but here she was again.

A widow, a duchess.

In a better position to take a lover.

The thought came into her head as if it had always been there. She turned away from the mirror, setting her jaw determinedly. "We can't," she said.

He arched a dark brow. He knew what she meant. "Can't we?"

"No. Of course not." She shouldn't have said anything. "We are too different, from different worlds with different ambitions. And despite—that—" she glanced toward the door, "—I am not a promiscuous woman."

"No," he said thoughtfully. "You're not. I understand, but that doesn't mean I'll comply. I'm not very good at obeying people when I don't think it's in their best interest. But please don't let this spoil our friendship."

That was the last thing she'd thought he'd say. But she would miss his conversation. He was a complicated man and she'd only just begun to untangle him.

"Will you behave?"

The corner of his mouth quirked up. "I'll try. I can't promise, though." He paused, as if thinking before he added, "But I do promise to do nothing against your will. You may trust me on that."

She lowered her gaze and led the way out of the room.

>>>×<<<

HE WANTED HER to trust him. For some reason that was important to Alex. So he would behave, at least until he'd overcome her resistance. He'd felt it even as he pulled her in, though it had melted soon enough. That kiss had turned incendiary. He'd wanted to kiss her, but not to turn it into what it had swiftly become—the preliminaries to full bed play.

Perhaps he was asking too much, for a gently-bred woman to be an enthusiastic participant, even an initiator. Most were reared to believe the act of love belonged to the man, his to initiate and develop. But he had wished for a woman to be his equal in bed for a long time now. Had he found her at last?

As he walked back up the Long Gallery, he pondered on his life and his desires. Not something he spent much time on ordinarily, but this lazy life drove him to different patterns of thought. It would drive him mad to have to do it every day. Stopping, he gazed out at the park beyond. All carefully constructed and planned to look natural half a century ago, or so Villiers had told him.

All false but, he had to admit, beautiful.

He liked this room. Part of the older section of the house, it had worn oak floorboards and dark paneling, relatively plain, apart from the ceiling which had fanciful patterns embossed on the plaster. But it had mellowed pleasingly over the years to a soft creamy white. The candle chandeliers fitted the style. It had window seats and most of all, he found a still peace up here that was lacking in the rest of the house. The guests tended to stay in the newer parts, the finely decorated rooms with more color and more style. If he had his way he'd stay here all day, preferably with the lady of his choice, but she had gone. Hopefully, without being noticed. Her startlement could well have been imagined. After all, they'd done a bit of gasping themselves.

At the thought, his body tightened. He wanted her, he

couldn't deny that, and he wouldn't. If she was willing, he would share his body with hers in a heartbeat. As long as he could make it last. He closed his eyes, letting the sensations wash over him while they were still fresh. He wanted to remember them as long as he could, in case she chose not to do it again. That would be a great shame. But he'd left the choice with her, and he had to abide by his decision. He would not try to seduce her, not to look at her too much, not want her so badly.

No, that last one was impossible.

A few people strolled along the drive outside the house. Guests, no doubt, from their fine walking outfits, but none he could recognize at this distance. Time to dress for dinner, probably.

As he thought that, the clock on the mantelpiece over the plaster fireplace in the middle of the room struck the hour.

A sudden movement down below caught his eye as he turned away, a woman walking on her own. Not Bianca, unless she had changed in double-quick time. No, he recognized her because she was hatless. The marchioness, his uncle's luckless young wife. She stopped, waited for a moment, glanced around, and went into the maze.

It was a typical maze, easily viewed from above, but not many windows overlooked it at this angle. He watched the woman in the pale blue dress hurry along one line of hedges, then he lost sight of her until she reappeared at the center. She held something, a piece of paper or a handkerchief, something flimsy enough to flutter in the breeze. As he watched, it fluttered out of her hand, caught by the breeze. She spun around, straight into the arms of a man who stepped out from the hedge nearest to Alex. He had not seen him, and apparently, neither had she. She jerked back. Alex stood up, ready to leave the room and race downstairs to save her, but he glanced back.

She was returning the stranger's embrace with all the enthusiasm Bianca had shared with him earlier. Instead of charging downstairs like a knight errant, Alex felt like an interloper.

When he looked back, they were still embracing. Surely other people could see them. What were they thinking, to stand there in full sight of the house?

For that matter, what had he been thinking, to kiss Bianca in the middle of the Long Gallery?

Obviously the marchioness was not in trouble from this man.

He went to the end of the long room and descended the oak flight of stairs. It had a dogleg but no window, so he couldn't see. When he got to the floor below, he went to the window in a small room by the stairs. He could see nothing. A large oak tree spread its branches between the house and the maze. Closer to the maze than the house, he noted, thankful for the foundations of the building. The maze had been carefully situated, because that tree was an ancient one.

The lovers would think they were safe. If he had not been standing by that window at that time, he would have seen nothing. With half the house playing the game of bedroom exchange every night, what was one more? In fact, if this exercise meant a child would stand between him and the title, he'd be truly grateful. He'd thought the marchioness a sweet little thing. His judgment was slipping.

He went down another flight to the floor that held his room. The sooner he was out of this place, the better.

Except for one thing. Or rather, one person.

But no. A flash of temper went through him. Damn the land Stonyhurst was waving before his nose, it was not worth the wasted time. The marquess had kept him kicking his heels here far too long. The rest of the guests and his host could go to the devil. Enough. He would go home. And if the marquess wanted him back, he could damn well invite his sisters too. And his mother.

His sudden decision was nothing to do with Bianca, nothing to do with the kiss that had rocked him to the bottom of his soul.

In his room he dashed off a note to the marquess.

"Unfortunately, sir, I find I cannot stay longer. I have business that requires my presence and unfortunately I must go. I thank you very much for your hospitality."

He sent his valet to find a footman to deliver his missive, then gave orders for his carriage to be prepared to leave early in the morning. Fisher sighed, but he did as he was bid without protest.

Chapter Eight

As Bianca reentered the house after a comfortable stroll with Adolphus Fraser, she found James Villiers standing in her way. The marquess's land steward, a lanky figure, immaculately dressed, appeared to be a gentleman, but had not yet been at dinner, and she had not had occasion to speak with him before. She stood, hands folded, wishing she could go to her room and have some quiet reading time.

"Your Grace." He executed his bow perfectly. She inclined her head in acknowledgment. "If you have a moment, his lordship would appreciate a visit from you."

He was acting as a footman now? Gentleman or not, the marquess was treating Villiers like a servant. "I should change." She gestured to her green walking dress and spencer, which were not the kind of clothes she would wear indoors.

"His lordship will excuse your dirt," he said. "He asked me to make his request straightaway. He feared you would not find enough time otherwise."

She might as well get this over with.

"Very well."

She followed Villiers to the part of the house where the respectable people were housed. It looked much the same as the wing she was housed in, but the porcelain in the glass cases had lighter colors, and the paintings had more people than landscapes.

Subtle differences that probably meant nothing, until they reached the Meissen.

Meissen porcelain was rich and sought-after. So was the Sevres that followed it, particularly the large urns that bracketed the double doors leading to the marquess's private drawing room. As they approached, a footman stepped out of the shadows and threw open both doors. Like entering the presence of royalty. A perverse desire to take a sling and a handful of dried peas to the urns attacked Bianca as she walked through. Those perfectly decorated blue and gold vases, the flowers painted so carefully. Lots of targets.

The marquess sat in a wide, broad-armed chair by the hearth which in this warm weather only contained a flower arrangement in yet another Sevres vase. Everything shone and gleamed. Dust would be banned from this place. It probably never even dared float in through the windows. He put his hands on the arms on the chair and, after a moment's hesitation, stood to bow to her.

And so he should. Her rank deserved it, and she would have that, at least.

Her curtsey was a study in elegance. She made sure of it. She graciously gestured to his seat, and they both sat down. Bianca carefully disposed the skirts of her gown and left her bonnet in place. If she removed it, she would tousle her hair, and she sensed her appearance would be as much a defense against whatever was coming as her title.

"I'm not happy," he said bluntly. Bianca said nothing. "You were invited here for a reason."

"You were not simply desirous of my company?" Hauteur was a new acquisition. She used it now.

His mouth turned in a sneer, but he didn't answer her question. "Let me speak frankly." He shifted in his seat. How frank was he going to get?

She inclined her head.

"Your sister was a particular friend of my wife's and tried to help her elope with someone."

"Your secretary," she reminded him.

"Indeed." He bowed his head in acknowledgment. "You know why I employed him. You may also understand why I dismissed him. He is not suitable for the role I intended for him. A year and no result!" He slashed his hand through the air. "And I cannot accept that—*person* as my heir."

"You mean Alex Fraser?" Her anger flared. "You have a suitable heir. You're lucky to have him."

"Yes, him." The marquess ignored her assessment and picked up a note by his side and flourished it at her. "He says he's leaving. Which brings me to my point—you were supposed to prevent him from doing that. Why do you think I put your bedrooms so close? You were to keep him busy until Maria could find herself a man—someone whose blood is pure, who can give me a true heir. I have reviewed the histories of everyone here, and my nephew is the only guest with tainted blood."

With an effort, Bianca remained in her seat and kept her voice at a normal pitch. "As far as I know Mr. Fraser's blood is not tainted. You would rather accept a bastard as your heir?"

A smirk decorated his thin features. "Not a bastard if I acknowledge the child. Any child my wife bears is mine unless I say otherwise. If I do so, nobody can gainsay me."

Damn him, he was right. He would prostitute Maria to cheat Alex out of his inheritance. The man was far more disgusting than anyone Bianca had met before. This was the dregs of humanity. She was looking at it right now. But she wanted him to say it. "And what do you mean, tainted blood?"

"His mother is only half white."

There it was. The acknowledgment of blind prejudice and an obsession with so-called purity. She had disliked the marquess before. Now she hated him.

"Keep him from leaving and I'll forgive you," the marquess said. "I want him here, where I can keep my eye on him."

"Why do you want him to stay?" It didn't make sense. If he hated Alex so much, why did he want to keep him here?

"Because at the moment he is my heir, and I must at least make an effort to educate him. He seems to have a good head on his shoulders. I would name him guardian or trustee to my child in his minority if he will but apply himself."

Not to inherit, but to educate. To become a servant to the estate. As long as he did not get the title, carry on the name, he was welcome.

"Why should he?"

The marquess's smirk stayed in place. "Because he wants the power and the prestige. How could he not? Everybody does."

"He doesn't need it."

"He says he doesn't. That's merely a negotiation point." He coughed and groped for a handkerchief. Bianca remained still. "But he needs to stay!" He struck the arm of his chair with his clenched fist. "And you will ensure that he does so!"

He expected her to seduce Alex.

Bianca didn't know how to seduce anyone. Not that the man before her would believe her. She turned her head, away, tears clogging her eyes at the audacity and depth of this man's offense. She would not cry, refused to. But if she spoke, she'd reveal her distress.

Duchess, she repeated in her mind. *You're a duchess.*

Anger returned to burn her tears away. "You said you invited me here for a reason. What would that be?"

"I invited you here because of your reputation."

"What reputation?" She felt a bitter satisfaction in making him speak all his basest prejudices.

He shrugged. "A woman of loose morals and low origins." After a pause, he continued. "You cannot deny it. You conducted your marriage in the full glare of the public eye. The reputation you gained then has followed you ever since. You have little idea of the dignity of your position. I did not see it, but my wife did."

She should get up and leave now, but anger kept her fixed to her seat. "Maria told you that?"

"Yes. She was an innocent, whom you attempted to inveigle

into your husband's clutches."

Bianca tried not to gape. "She said *what*?"

He lifted one shoulder in a half shrug. "She's my wife and a woman of impeccable breeding. I have no reason to disbelieve her. And what I have heard from other sources corroborates that."

Numbness spread through her. By her malicious gossip Maria was destroying any chance Bianca had of restoring her good character. She and George had lived wildly, but while he had strayed from their bed, she had never done so.

"You employed your wife's lover to give her the child you could not get on her, and you accuse *me* of immorality?" He would have responded, but she held up her hand and continued. "You were the one who offered to speak frankly. Let me return the favor." She took a deep breath. "Your wife has been spreading malicious and untrue gossip about me, impugning my character and my behavior." She took a chance, but then, when had a Burrell ever done anything else? "If I hear her promulgating that kind of nonsense to anyone, I will employ a lawyer and take her, and you, to court. Do you hear me?"

"Can you prove you did not take lovers? Or that you inveigled my wife into eloping with an unsuitable man?"

"Yes," she said without hesitation. "She cannot name one lover, because there were none. As for the second matter, does not the fact of your own behavior tell the story? I will bring all this to an open court, the facts laid bare for all to see. Win or lose, your machinations will be in the open."

The supercilious smirk remained on his face, but his cheeks whitened. He'd heard her all right. "I'll speak to my wife," he said.

"See that you do."

She left the room with all the dignity of her rank, but inside she was raging.

This farce was done. Over. If she returned to society she'd do it on her own terms, not at the whim of this awful man. It only went to prove what her mother had always said. Rank did not make a scoundrel into a gentleman.

BIANCA SENT AN excuse down to dinner, and spent a miserable evening in her room, brooding. Allaying her maid's advice that she should take a paregoric and lie down, she managed what food they sent up, although she could not have said what she ate if someone had asked her afterwards. The food here was truly uninspiring. Perhaps Maria did not take proper control of the kitchens.

She would not listen to Maria anymore, and if she came knocking at the door again, Bianca would resolutely ignore it. The woman was poison. After pushing her plate aside and going to the window seat to find her book, Bianca wondered if Maria had ever been Juliet's friend, if indeed the various schemes to use the Burrell sisters had come from the daughter and not, as they'd assumed, the mother.

Sighing, she found her place. An hour later she woke up with a start and gave up, taking off her robe and climbing into bed. She would only miss one person when she left this place. Since he was leaving, too, there was no reason for her to stay. She'd given her maid instructions to pack and tell the coachman to find a chaise to take her home. If necessary, she'd travel on the stage. It wouldn't be the first time.

Her maid woke Bianca at seven with hot chocolate and the inevitable slices of bread and butter. "I've packed, ma'am. The coachman has not found a chaise. Apparently the inn could not provide one."

Bianca sat up. "Perhaps we can get seats on the mail," she said.

Her maid recoiled, her hands held in front of her as if warding off evil. "Madam!" Bianca let her maid put pillows behind her back, but her hands were trembling. "We cannot possibly take the common mail coach," McMurdo said.

"Then we must stay in rooms at the inn until we can hire a vehicle. Or travel to the nearest large town where we can obtain a private chaise, because I vow I will not spend another night under this roof!"

"But Your Grace!"

Bianca picked up a slice of bread and butter, and rolled it into a neat coil. She was pleased to note that her hands were totally steady. "We don't have to use my title on the road. Not until we must. I have no desire to draw attention to myself. Most of the luggage can be sent on."

If she confided in her lady's maid and hinted that the information was not in absolute confidence, the story that the marquess had insulted her beyond bearing would be all around the servant's hall before dinnertime. And serve him right. But no, she would leave with her dignity intact. What was left of it. "What are they talking about in the servants' hall?"

"All kinds of things, ma'am." The maid went to the dressing table where Bianca's substantial monogrammed vanity case stood, ready to accept its final contents. "The Midas of the North, for one thing. How handsome he is, and how generous to the servants." The man must give good tips. "They like him. Some of the other guests, now, they've had run-ins!" She clicked her tongue. "Least said, ma'am."

"What about me?"

"Nothing in my hearing, ma'am."

Yes, that was the hallmark of a loyal maid. That they did not trust the gossip to be repeated to the source. But she did learn one thing; that they were talking about her. Why wouldn't they? A duchess with a scandalous past?

"They call this the Wicked Wing, ma'am," McMurdo said, busy with brushes and crystal pots.

Bianca burst out laughing, even as she realized she shouldn't be. But who wouldn't laugh?

"Am I the Wicked Widow or the Desperate Duchess?"

"I'm sure I couldn't say, ma'am." Bianca heard laughter in her maid's voice. The Wicked Widow, then.

"So unoriginal!" She yawned, feigning boredom.

Would the reputation Maria had assigned to her ruin her forever? That went far beyond being a wicked widow. It pushed her into evil country. She would not bring this home to the new holder of the title of Whiston.

The new Duke of Whiston was a quiet family man, totally uninterested in public affairs and society matters. Truthfully, he had a lot to cope with. He didn't need a scandalous widow adding to his problems. She'd have to retrench, as her soldier brother would have it. *Nil desperandum*, something he also said. A good motto. Never despair.

First she'd go back to Edinburgh, to her mother, before going to Viola's. She could consolidate her reputation there, instead of trying to do it here.

The thought made her heart sink, though. So many condemning dowagers, so many traps to avoid! Deep down, she was the same Bianca as ever, the fun-loving, adventurous Burrell. Being forced to spend months, perhaps years, in decorous disguise would just about kill her.

But not quite. Imagining Maria's chagrin when she heard Bianca had restored her reputation would help no end.

As Bianca was finishing her breakfast, her maid came in with the duchess's clothes for the day. A simple gown of spotted muslin and a deep red redingote. Comfortable enough. Instead of the cheap canvas of yesteryear, her footwear was sturdy brown leather half-boots. These little touches and differences made her life so much easier.

She let her maid dress her. It did not take long since Bianca declined face paint and an elaborate hairstyle. After, she sent McMurdo down to the back hall, firmly assuring her that she meant her word, and they would take the mail coach to the nearest large town, where they'd find a chaise to hire. She left a letter on the small desk before the window, informing her hosts that she had been called away unexpectedly, two full weeks before the assumed end of the house party.

Other guests, sensing the lack of scandal, would drift away, no doubt moving on to other great houses, with more guests. Bianca firmed her chin. She would not give them any reason to gossip about her.

They had a carpet bag each. Bianca would send for the rest. Although McMurdo grumbled, she followed Bianca down to the side entrance. Not the one leading to the stables, because guests would already be using that, but the one on the other side of the house.

When Bianca led the way out of the gardens, McMurdo groaned. "You cannot mean to walk, ma'am!"

"Can't I?" Bianca turned to confront her maid. "I told you I would not spend another night in that house, and I meant it. You may go back if you wish, but I will make my way to the village and bespeak a room at the inn. I will take the mail to the nearest town. If you leave me now, I will not take it kindly."

McMurdo sighed and shifted her bag from one hand to another. "You are set on this, ma'am, I see. I cannot leave you alone, but if I may speak freely, I think you are being too forward. We could arrange a better departure if you would consent to stay another day."

"No," Bianca said firmly. After what the marquess had said to her, how could she even consider it?

She turned and continued to walk. If McMurdo wanted to follow her, she would. Bianca had found herself in far worse positions than this.

The sound of booted feet trudging behind her told Bianca she still had a maid. They continued in silence until they reached the wall that separated the estate from the main road. Following it for half a mile gave them access to a small gate. Once through it, Bianca sighed in relief. The village couldn't be more than five miles from the house. Less, if she was lucky. She'd marked it when she arrived, but not really taken note. Her mother would probably have measured the distance. Very thorough, her mother.

They followed the road and within two miles found the village. Just as well, because McMurdo had stopped her remarks and suggestions, which had flowed over Bianca all the way. Now to face the inn. It was a coaching inn, so it would be large enough to cater to a couple of unexpected guests. She turned to McMurdo. "I'm Mrs. Cavendish here," she said.

"If you'll excuse me, ma'am, you won't be easy to forget," her maid said. "They'll most likely recognize you."

"We did not stop here on the way, did we? Then let us see how this plays out. If they recognize me, so be it."

That was when it started to rain. They still had half a mile to go, since the inn stood on the other side of the village. Bianca didn't care. She'd found the walk exhilarating, a proper walk instead of a ladylike stroll. She could stretch her legs and breathe good, clean air.

The village was a large one, cottages straggling away from the church and the inn. By the time they reached their destination their hats were completely ruined, and they were both soaked.

Bianca still felt relief that they'd escaped the confines of Stonyhurst.

Now she had to brazen it out. She had her story ready, but would the landlord believe her? The man in question came to greet them, wiping his hands on his apron. "Ladies?"

"I would like to bespeak a room for myself and my maid," Bianca said calmly.

The landlord paused, frankly studying them. Bianca put up her chin, not meeting his gaze directly, just like a proper aristocrat. "Your horses, your coach?"

"Just the two of us," she said.

"Hussies!" The hiss came from behind them. The landlady had arrived. Bianca wasn't sure they were supposed to have heard this. When she came around the solid bulk of her husband to stand beside him, she was regarding them with a skeptical eye. "We can offer shelter for a few hours, but no more. Sorry," she begrudgingly added.

Bianca was used to that kind of treatment, but not so much since she'd become a duchess. Her maid, evidently, was not. McMurdo stepped forward. "Woman, I'll have you know—"

Whatever the landlady was about to find out was lost as a male voice boomed out from behind them. "Landlord, is there a problem?"

"N-no, sir," the man stammered. Startled, the landlady glared over Bianca's head. That as much of the voice told her who had entered.

"Mr. Fraser!" The landlady gasped.

Alex had not passed by, then. What was he doing here? When she ventured to glance at him, she found him gazing at her with absolutely no expression whatsoever. She swallowed.

He pushed up the brim of her bonnet, which had lost its stiffening in the rain.

"This woman . . ."

Alex came forward to stand beside her. Firmly he took her arm and slid under his. "I will not have you catching cold." He turned to the landlady. "This woman, as you called her, is a friend of mine. She is the Duchess of Whiston." He ignored the gasps and continued. "That you did not recognize the quality of her clothes, much less her person says much about your lack of perspicacity. Please show her to the room I have engaged for myself, and find something suitable for her to wear."

"I have clothes—"

Sharply, he cut her off. "Ensure she has transport back to Stonyhurst when she is ready."

"But Mr. Fraser, your room . . . ?"

"Yes, my room. Or are you objecting to having a duchess in your establishment?" He stared down his nose at the landlord.

That did the trick. The landlord changed from a stern over-lord to a cringing servant. She hated to see both, but the cringing was worst. After all, this was his establishment, and he was entitled to admit who he wished.

Even worse, the man bowed low. "Your Grace, I beg your forgiveness."

She glanced at Alex, and then at the landlord. "Very well," she said with all the dignity she could muster.

"I will desire tea to be sent up," Alex said.

"Your Grace?" the landlord said.

Alex turned his attention to the landlady, as if the landlord had not spoken. "You have prepared a room."

The landlady dropped a curtsey. "Of course, sir. As soon as we heard. I did not know you would be bringing anyone."

Alex patted her hand. "I am not. I am merely offering Her Grace the use of my room. I will spend the night elsewhere."

Perversely, Bianca wanted to shove his hand away, but she had just enough presence of mind to stop herself. Her escape had ended before it began, because this man had her now. While she had no fear of him, she felt trapped again. The walk to the inn, despite the inconvenience and the rain, had been exhilarating. Being on her own, except for McMurdo, striding along the open country, had brought her joy like she'd hadn't known for years.

Instead, behaving as the duchess she was, she lifted her soaked skirts and followed the landlady upstairs to a pleasant room, fairly spacious for an inn.

An old-fashioned four-poster bed dominated the space. A table was set by the window, and there was room for a couple of chairs by the fire, which, she was disappointed to see, was not lit.

The landlady dropped a curtsey. "Begging your pardon, Your Grace, we didn't recognize you. My husband is a dolt, and so I'll tell him."

They took Alex's word where they would not take hers? Incensed, Bianca sucked in a breath, and let it out slowly. By the time she'd done that, the landlady had gone. Probably assumed she was too proud to speak to a mere landlady. If only she knew!

McMurdo hurried in. She carried both bags, which she

promptly dumped on the floor. "We must haste to get you changed, ma'am. We don't want you catching cold." She kicked the door closed with her foot.

Bianca was amused to see the maid wedged a chair under the door latch before she helped Bianca off with the drenched redingote. "You must undress too, McMurdo," Bianca said as the maid handed her a towel. "I can't have you catching cold, either." When the maid hesitated, Bianca moved out of reach, removing her stays and shift herself.

Within twenty minutes both were dry and dressed in clean garments. Bianca had unearthed an old blue gown, comfortable but far from the fashionable garb she used these days. Ladies did not travel in their best clothes, although they might stop at a nearby inn to change before they reached their destination.

Bianca handed the wet towel to her maid, piling it on top of the other garments to be laundered by the landlady. "I'll get tea sent up, ma'am," the maid told her. She moved the chair and left.

She glanced outside. It was still raining. At least the fire was laid.

Taking the tinderbox from the mantelpiece, she struck a light and dropped the flaming scrap of rag onto the coals before taking a taper to light the fire from beneath.

"Very skillful."

His entrance made her drop the taper with a little scream. She had to scramble to rescue it before it set fire to the room or her clothes. The reminder made her shake even more, but she managed to get the taper into the fire. She straightened. "Thank you for the use of your room, sir."

"It was the least I could do." His mouth ticced up in that half-smile. "Especially for you."

She lifted her head to meet his gaze, and his amusement changed to concern. Quickly he hastened across the room and took her in his arms. "Oh, my dear! Was it the fire?"

She shook her head, dislodging the tears. "You know?"

He nodded.

Knowing was one thing. She'd gone over that day so many times, and still it always turned out the same way. "It happened in an instant, Juliet said. H-he just c-caught." She gestured to the fire. "I wasn't there. I should have been. I dream of it."

The tears came as never before, as if this, finally, was her time. He let her cry, just held her, making soothing sounds occasionally. He moved, and sank down, probably onto the bed, still holding her safe and tight.

She didn't know how long she cried. She heard a door open and close but took little notice of it, lost in the moment, in the horrible reminder. "I just kept thinking that he could have escaped. It was so sudden, so final."

"Yes, I know."

"How?" Lifting her chin, she gazed up into his face. He gazed down at her, and produced a handkerchief, which he used to dab at her wet cheeks.

"Have I seen it, you mean? No, but I've seen other things. Other deaths."

"You have?"

"I own several manufactories. I go into work every day—I'm not a distant master. They're dangerous places, my—dear."

His—what? He hadn't been about to say that.

He mopped up her tears, making soothing noises, tsking when she tried to apologize. "You've been holding this back for a long time, haven't you?"

"I—I suppose so. I wasn't even there."

"And that's part of the problem, isn't it?"

She rested her hot cheek on the comfort of his strong shoulder. "Yes, I suppose so."

By now she'd stopped crying. "I feel better," she said wonderingly.

"You will feel better still." He still held her and showed no sign of releasing her. He was marvelously comforting. "You needed to let it all go."

"I thought I had. I've cried before."

"Not like this."

"No, not like this."

Bending his head he gave her a kiss, so tender, soft, and warm it made her yearn for more. But he drew away. "Do you want to tell me?"

Surprisingly, because she'd never talked about it before, she did. "We had a love match. That was what society understood. But he took a mistress, Lady Owen, and he flaunted her in front of me. So I left him. That and the constant criticisms drove me away." She let herself go back to that time, safe in the circle of his arms. "I went with Lady Langston, Juliet's mother-in-law, to a villa they owned just outside London. Juliet wrote to me. He'd visited her, assured her he would never do anything like that again, begged me to return. Juliet believed him, but I found it hard, so I lingered. If I had not—it might have been different."

Telling someone who'd never known the Duke of Whiston was both difficult and simple. From the outside it seemed so straightforward. But there were nuances few people knew about. Lady Langston had understood. She'd gone through a similar experience herself.

"That wasn't all," she confessed, reaching for the right words. "He was a duke, spoiled and indulged. I was an Irish brat, dragged up in poverty, forced into situations George could never have dreamed of. I think that was where it started. He assumed I was inferior to him, in status, intelligence, and everything else. And he resented that he had to give up a lucrative potential bride for someone like me."

He sucked in a sharp breath. "He never meant to marry you."

"No," she said.

"He did not respect you."

She'd never heard her situation described in that way before. But it fitted. "No, he didn't," she said. "He constantly corrected me, said he was helping me, so much that I became afraid to do anything without seeking his approval or anything that might not please him. It was not all his fault. I do not think he even knew he was doing it."

He growled, low in his throat. "He had no right. You are perfect as you are because you are you."

She nodded. "I know that now, but sometimes I feel so helpless, and all my confidence falls away from me. Visiting new places, for instance, even coming here." She paused. "That's why my mother wanted me to come on my own, and it has helped, I think. I stood up to Stonyhurst when he spoke to me as if I were nothing."

"What did he say?"

"Oh, the usual things," she said. She didn't want to tell anyone, not yet, how badly the marquess had humiliated her. Almost as if it was her fault. She knew the guilt and shame she felt was underserved, but she still experienced it. "I told him to go to the devil." Not in those words, but her threat to take him to court should hold him for a while.

"Good," he murmured, pressing a kiss to her forehead. "You are worth ten of him. Titles mean nothing, only that a person was fortunate enough to be born into wealth and privilege."

She recalled a sound. "Did someone come in while I was crying?"

"Your maid," he told her.

"Oh God, no!" Bianca closed her eyes. How could she have forgotten that? It must have been when the door opened and closed.

"I believe she is bespeaking dinner for us both."

It seemed so long since she'd set out that morning. "It's too early for dinner, isn't it?"

"Probably, but I'm hungry, and I'll wager you are, too."

As he spoke, the clock on the mantelpiece bonged out the hour. It sounded rusty, and so loud.

Alex stood and seemingly effortlessly, settled her lightly on her feet. "We should go once you're ready."

Bianca went to the stained mirror over the chest that served as a dressing table, and took the pins from her hair, before reaching for the brush. She only noticed him watching when she'd smoothed out the curls. "Oh!"

"One day," he said, his voice harsher than she was used to, "one day I would like to do that for you."

Since she started and ended every day with her hair up, Bianca recognized the intimacy. No man had seen her with her hair down for over a year.

Quickly, she twisted it into a knot, and secured it with the pins. The only bonnet she'd brought with her was on a side table, carefully spread out to dry. She felt bare, as if she'd removed more than hairpins. Especially the way he was looking at her. Raw desire etched his features into her memory.

And the way he'd appeared when he had cradled her in his lap. She knew what desire looked like, but tenderness in the object of her desire was new to her. Combine them and she was in trouble.

"Thank you for being with me during my storm." She turned and faced him, a little more herself once more.

"You're welcome," he replied in the same polite tone. "I'll go downstairs. The rumors will have started by now. We're too close to Stonyhurst for people not to hear."

"Rumors?"

"I've been up here with you for at least half an hour."

As he spoke, the rusty clock chimed the quarter-hour, followed by the church bell.

"Enough time to . . ." He spread his hands in an eloquent gesture.

"Let them," she snapped. "I don't care. I'm going home."

He raised a brow. "Home?"

"Edinburgh." She turned her back as if primping at the mirror, but she could still see his reflection. "I've had enough of that place, and of the company, too."

To her shock, he burst into laughter. "Well that will make them talk," he said eventually. "Because I'm leaving too."

"I heard," she said dryly. "Why?"

"Because my uncle sickens me with his plans and his attitude. He expects me to dance attendance on him because of his rank. I have work to do." He paused. "Plus, his refusal to invite my mother and sisters grates badly. He had to ask me because of my position as his heir, but he wanted to bend me to his will. And ignore my family. That will not happen, and he needs to know that."

He ran his hand through his hair, raising the dark locks into spikes. "There's no help for it. But I can be the heir at a distance and pray that the marchioness finally bears fruit."

"It won't be his." Why had she said that? But why shouldn't she? Maria had not exactly behaved as a friend should. Bianca carried on. "She was not spending her nights with her husband. She was spending them with her lover, the marquess's secretary."

He went completely still. "What?"

"It's true. She loved Walter in London. We tried to help her to elope, but she refused to do it, and accepted the marquess's proposal instead—as long as he employed Walter Norris too. He is her lover, and he shares her bed, not her husband. But the marquess has sent him away because they weren't producing 'the desired result.'" She paused. "This house party is for her to find a new lover, in part. The other part concerns you and your cousins. The old man wanted me to seduce you to keep you at Stonyhurst so he could teach you to become the baby's guardian and trustee."

He closed his eyes. "What in God's name does he think he's doing? Who does he think he is?"

"God, I think."

He touched his thumb to his mouth. "Probably." He grinned reluctantly.

Her simmering fury abated in the face of his amusement. There was a funny side, to be sure. She had not lost much, after all. Only her disappointment that this house party was not the return to society she'd wanted, but a seething mass of intrigue and unhappiness.

"Aren't you concerned that you will lose the marquessate?"

"I don't want the title. It will take me away from my work, from what I do best. Despite his riches, I'm probably as rich as he is or getting there. I don't want to have to live here or learn how to manage a great estate. My sisters don't want to be members of society. They have turned down the offer to be presented at court."

"You don't want it at all?"

He shook his head. "Not one bit." He paused. "But I take his efforts to replace me as a deep insult. The extremes he is taking are appalling. I might be relieved if Maria bore him a son, but to do this . . ." He bit his lip. "Not like this."

"It's not fair. Or right."

He nodded and glanced at the door. "I've stayed in here too long. Is your maid likely to spread gossip?"

She bit her lip. "I don't think so, but she is quite new to me. She came to me in Scotland, and so far she has been excellent."

He nodded. "I will, if you don't mind, drop a couple of yellow boys her way."

"A good idea." Guineas were always useful encouragers.

He went to the door. "I'll order dinner served in a private parlor downstairs, then we'll decide what to do."

Chapter Nine

THIS WOULD NOT be the first time Bianca had brazened her way through a situation. Although only mid-afternoon, she was sharp-set and followed her maid downstairs with eager anticipation.

He was waiting for her and stood when she entered the cozy parlor fragrant with the scent of baked meat. When he held her chair back for her, she could have sworn he grazed the back of her neck before he went to his side of the table and sat. "This was a good idea," she said as she shook out her napkin. "But what do we do now?"

"We eat."

They suited actions to words and exchanged little more than requests to pass the salt or for another refill of the excellent robust red wine the landlady had provided. A beef pie was followed by apple fool, the first tender and hot, the second cold and creamy. Better than the elaborate, two course meals with twelve removes each offered by the marquess, because this was hot.

At last, with a sigh, she leaned back and tossed her napkin next to her plate. "I feel much better," she said. "But I still want to go home."

"And then what?" he asked as he topped off their wine, finishing the bottle. The windows on this floor were small and cloudy, the glass old and closely mullioned. Branches tapped the glass and a sprinkle of rain hit it.

She shrugged. "I thought I'd go to Edinburgh, back to my mother and Scottish society. And the gossip." She sighed. "I swear it's worse than London. Probably because it's smaller than London. But we are staying with my sister in a few weeks' time, so it won't be for long. Having the scandalous duchess in their midst is an invitation to gossip."

"About you."

"Yes. But I did bring the scandal on myself."

His face, so grave, gave nothing away. "Did you? My uncle's library holds a mass of old newspapers and journals, so I undertook some research." He glanced at her, then looked away. "If you will allow me to give my opinion?"

She nodded.

"I think your duke was on the road to perdition before he met you. You were impressionable, beautiful, and if you'll forgive me, a trophy."

Except that George was not going to marry her at first. She only thought he was. She still felt like an utter fool for going along with George's plan to elope. "I was an adventuress, that's all, and I was lucky."

"Lucky?" he echoed. "He was the lucky one. Any man would be lucky to—." He broke off abruptly, took a deep breath, and started again. "You know that I admire you."

She liked that word. "I admire you, too." She did. He'd taken what he had and made the most of it. Added to that, she had never reacted so instantly, so viscerally to any man. Not even her late husband, not to this extent.

The landlady came in to clear the table. She brought a maid with her, and they took their time, or so it seemed.

Alex held the door open for them and closed it gently behind them. Eating together like this was mildly scandalous, but eating in the public rooms would have been worse.

He turned to her. "What were you doing walking with your

maid—with your luggage?"

She clicked her tongue. "Only a couple of small bags, enough for a few days, that's all. I arrived in a hired chaise. I could not hire one from this inn for my return—there wasn't one available—so I thought to catch the mail to the nearest town where I could hire one. I had no intention of going all the way to Edinburgh on the mail." The thought made her shudder.

"I should think not!" He folded his arms. "You will forgive me for saying that your move was reckless."

"I've traveled on the mail before. I am not entirely new to the experience." She lifted a shoulder.

"As a duchess?"

"I would hardly use my title," she scoffed. "I don't have my jewelry or my better gowns with me today. I would have sent someone to collect those. The marquess could hardly expect me to stay after the insults on my character he offered me."

"I see." His chest moved in a sigh. "It is unforgivable, but he has offered insults to most of us in this visit. Myself most of all."

"Is that why you decided to leave?"

He shook his head. "Not entirely." He paused. "I think he intends to have me tutor or become a guardian to any heir his wife may give him."

"That's terrible!"

"So he called you a trollop, and tried to make me an unpaid servant to his changeling." His mouth turned up in a wry smile.

She fixed her gaze on that mouth, hastily looking away when she realized what she was doing.

"We can either return to the house in my carriage, or we can part for a time. I have unfinished business with my uncle. While I was willing to accept a child of his as his heir, I will not accept a random child begotten on his wife by someone else."

"And yet you didn't care before you came here."

"Well, now I do. My uncle's deception does not only reflect on me, it reflects on my cousins, too. They would be cut out of the succession, pushed out by a stranger." He paused. "What he's doing is deeply wrong."

"What if she falls pregnant?"

He glanced away. "I will ask questions. If the child is his, then I will accept it, with a great deal of relief. But I need to know more. You may take my traveling carriage if you want to return to Edinburgh."

"I can't do that!"

He straightened and returned to his place at the other side of the table. "You can't catch a mail coach to a random town in the expectation of hiring a chaise. Good God, woman, what were you thinking?"

She swallowed. "That I did not want to spend another day in that house."

He sighed again. "I see. I admit that was my sentiment also, even as you told me about his plans. But on reflection, it will not do. Perhaps I should pay a visit to Edinburgh when I've sorted out the situation here."

Her laugh rang around the room. "You have no business there, do you?"

"I can find some." Deliberately, he walked around the table to face her, with nothing between them. He put his hands lightly on her shoulders. "Bianca, I want you. Surely you know that? Do you feel nothing at all for me?"

Meeting his eyes, staring into those liquid depths, she couldn't lie. "Of course I do."

"You're so desirable." He pressed a quick kiss to her lips. "We could go back to the house. Say that you went for a walk and got caught in the rain. I came upon you and rescued you."

"Yes, I suppose that is possible."

He continued. "I warn you that I won't let our friendship die. If you wish to go back to Edinburgh, I will follow you as soon as I can, but in the city we will have to behave like the duchess and the gentleman. No trysts, no private time. Not with the gossips watching us. So choose, Bianca. Will you come back to the house, or will you go back to Edinburgh?"

He was right. The gossips watched Bianca and her mother all the time. If he came at all, their acquaintance would have to be carefully decorous. And they only had a few weeks. She could ask her sister to invite him to her house party, and unlike the marquess, she would have his mother and sisters invited.

On the other hand, at Stonyhurst, here, now, today . . .

She made her decision. "Let's go back to the house."

THE WHOLE HOUSEHOLD saw them arrive in a country gig. Once the rain had passed, Alex drove, leaving his grooms to take his traveling chaise back to the house. Open carriages were respectable. Closed chaises were not.

They discussed their strategy on the way back. Sharing a meal with a man in a private room at an inn was not too scandalous. Spending half an hour together in a bedroom was slightly more so, but they could deny that part.

They made no secret of where they had been, only changed the story a little as they'd discussed. To reinforce their story, Bianca handed the butler her bedraggled bonnet. "This is unrecoverable. Dispose of it, if you please." While the footman was busy, she went to the small table where mail was left, and retrieved the letter she'd dropped there earlier. She wouldn't need it now.

Back in her room, Bianca felt helpless, as if all she'd done had achieved nothing. McMurdo busied herself with unpacking the trunks in the middle of the room. Here she was again. Perhaps she should have borrowed Alex's chaise, after all.

But no. She wanted Alex, and this was the only way she could have him with any chance of coming out of the affair cleanly. The marquess had arranged this house party carefully to allow those who wanted to indulge a way to do it without condemnation and without being observed.

Although she would still receive opprobrium from the strictest society matrons. But there was no pleasing those.

Once her hair had dried, McMurdo brushed and curled it, then put it up into a loose knot, while Bianca stared into the mirror and thought. Hard. But she couldn't get past the simple admission that she wanted Alex. So much that she had abandoned her escape and come back to Stonyhurst. Declared herself willing to obey the marquess, who had told her to seduce Alex. Did she have no pride left?

Perhaps she'd never had any to start with.

McMurdo arrayed her mistress in a green silk gown, exquisitely embroidered with spring flowers, but with only a single deep ruffle at the hem. A simple string of excellent pearls around her throat and matching drops in her ears was all the jewelry she used. As McMurdo spread a silk scarf around Bianca's shoulders, she hummed. "The perfect duchess," she murmured.

"Not exactly," Bianca said, but she thanked the maid and left the room. She left a couple of guineas on the dressing table which would be gone when she returned. McMurdo deserved that at least, and the tip, added to the one Alex gave her, might help to remind the maid where her loyalties lay.

The murmur from the drawing room sounded louder. When she entered, immediately Lady Broome came over to join her. Alex had not yet arrived, Bianca noted after a quick sweep of the room. "You created quite a stir today," her ladyship commented, evidently inviting her response.

"I truly cannot think why. It was inordinately kind of Mr. Fraser to pause his journey for me."

"A damsel in distress," Lady Broome mused. "Truly a story to rival Elizabeth Woodville's."

Bianca frowned. "I don't see the similarity." She'd never heard of the woman.

Rescue came from an unexpected source. "Really?" Adolphus Fraser said, lifting his quizzing-glass to Lady Broome. "I was not aware that the duchess was a mother."

A pang went through Bianca, but this was not the place to reveal personal vulnerabilities. "I am not," she said.

"Elizabeth Woodville was. I'm not sure it was raining, either." Adolphus turned his attention to her. "Do you recall the story?"

If she admitted she didn't know, she could be holding herself up to ridicule. While she counted herself a friend to Adolphus, he could never resist a good story, and perhaps her being ignorant of this Woodville woman would become one of them.

Fortunately, before she could answer, Benedict came to her rescue. "Not everyone is an aficionado of history. It happened four hundred years ago. Why would Her Grace be interested in that?"

Relieved, Bianca smiled her thanks. "I'm afraid I've only ever had a passing interest in history."

"Indeed," Benedict said, his soft low voice almost soothing. "Elizabeth Woodville stood in the rain with her two young children to waylay King Edward the Fourth and beg for the pension she believed her late husband had left her. She made quite the picture. The king was so taken by her pleas that he married her."

Ah. Fairly mild, considering what the reference could have meant. She could cope with that. "If I had known Mr. Fraser was driving out, I might have walked the other way." A laugh rippled around the room. So everyone was listening to her. "I would not have delayed his journey for the world. But he kindly took me up and conveyed me to the inn, where I could dry off and change my dress."

"A gentleman at heart, then," Lady Colmondale remarked.

She laughed. "Indeed he is. I so missed the long rambles I used to share with my sisters that I took my maid and set out for a walk. There was no sign that it was going to rain, but half a mile from the village the skies opened up and we were drenched. Mr. Fraser took us up and lent me the use of his room at the inn. When my clothes had dried, we all returned in a hired gig. He kindly deferred his journey to rescue me, that is all."

She had the maid, the open carriage, and the chance meeting all set out. With any luck, the listeners would take notice of those points.

"I never thought of him as a knight in shining armor before," Adolphus said in tones of great amusement.

She caught sight of Alex, who stood in the doorway of the room, surveying the company. "Neither did I," he said, as he bowed to her and walked past her to bow to the marchioness.

A few guests exclaimed at his chivalry, and others made ribald comments about medieval armor.

Maria seemed more cheerful tonight, smiling and conversing with the guests. Perhaps she'd become reconciled to her lot, although Bianca suspected that was not the answer. Maybe she was employing her gift for acting, as she had with Bianca's sister. She appeared adept at that particular skill.

Bianca gave her a cool nod. Maria unfurled her fan and smiled as she offered Alex her hand to kiss. So sweet, such an obedient wife. Murmurs around her attested to that, so they must be right. Mustn't they?

While talking politely to other people, explaining her morning's predicament more than once, Bianca kept calm and refused to let anyone break her duchess façade. She'd learned how to do that during her brief marriage, both in public and in private. Now, she could listen to people telling her that she must miss her husband very much, and that he was a hero for pushing her sister out of danger as he burned to death.

Yes, in that moment he'd been a hero. He was not such a hero at other times. But nobody knew that. And because of his terrible death, George was forever a hero. She concentrated on that rather than going anywhere near Alex or looking at him. If she did, she might reveal her agitation. Or should that be excitement?

She'd never been so nervous.

Should she look at him? And if she did, how much? She felt

like she was starting all over again. All through dinner she tried to behave normally, discovering that actually doing that was far more difficult than ever before. At least she wasn't sitting close to him. That would have been agony.

"You seem a little tense, Duchess," Lord Severn remarked. He was watching her a little too much for her liking. He was a collector of women, or so he'd told her once, which implied a man who was more interested in ticking their names off a list than in giving pleasure.

She forced a smile. "Not at all, sir. My ducking earlier merely gave me an hour or so's discomfort. I do thank Mr. Fraser for his timely rescue, so the adventure had no serious consequences. I am quite well, I assure you."

"Nevertheless, I have a warming brandy in my room. I'd be honored if you'd accept some of it before you retire." He'd be in his dressing gown, no doubt.

"Truly, sir, I am perfectly well. Your concern is touching but unnecessary."

What a nuisance. Now she'd have to wait for his inevitable visit before continuing her plans. She knew his type. He wouldn't give up easily. The last thing she wanted was to become an on-dit at this blasted gathering. If she were to meet Alex later, it would be with the discretion of everyone involved.

The man was showing signs of his dissipation on his face. A cynical expression without the interest and amusement that made the same trait acceptable in Adolphus, or even his brother, whom she knew less well. That leer, which Severn probably considered an interested smile, and the way his gaze lingered on her bosom irked her. The evening was the only time she went without covering her breasts completely, so he had only a few hours to admire her cleavage. Much too long, but to wear a tucker or partlet would be to admit defeat.

And Lord Severn was not the only known roué in this company. That was what made this house party so unbearable. That and the marquess.

Bianca turned her attention to the buttered peas, even though her appetite had completely gone. She managed a few bites, even though the vegetables were overcooked and nearly cold. The kitchens must be some distance from the dining room.

When she dared to glance down the table, Alex was in deep conversation with Honoria Colmondale. A pang of jealousy unexpectedly ran through Bianca, though she had no cause to be jealous, no claim on him. At the head of the table, the marquess was smiling at his wife.

AT THE DOOR to the music room, Lady Broome stopped Alex, her gloved hand barely resting on his arm. "I have something special to tell you," the countess murmured.

They were standing close to the door he'd just held open for Bianca, but her ladyship had not given him time to leave.

"You seem happy tonight," Alex said, wondering when he could leave her side and go somewhere else—anywhere else.

"Indeed I am. I have much to be happy about."

"I'm glad to hear it, my lady."

"Oh, call me Amelia, please! It would be quite foolish for you to use the formal address all the time, and that is something I do not at all wish for you to do. You could use my first name when we are alone." She beamed at him as if she'd conferred a favor. Her thin pink lips gleamed in the candlelight.

Alex controlled his shudder. She was a beautiful woman wearing rich colors, lavish decoration, and diamonds, but beneath it all, a woman Alex was not disposed to like. One who insisted on having her own way. A widow, he recalled, with two young sons who were not here for this visit. And wealthy.

"It's not reet." He lapsed into deepest Yorkshire, but that did not stop her.

She laughed as if he'd made a joke. If there was one, the joke was on him. "You are funny, sir! Or may I call you Alexander?"

"If you want." He would dislike it excessively, but what could he do?

"Well then, Alexander, some of us have made a little arrangement for tonight." She leaned closer. She'd been eating the onion-laden pork in white sauce concoction that he had assiduously avoided at dinner. "There is a little game people in town are playing. Obviously not something for the young ladies, so don't get ideas in that direction! But in the wicked wing only."

His stomach twisted. He didn't like this. He'd suspected something was afoot, but not what it was. "Not her then?" he said, gesturing to the company. A young lady, he couldn't remember which one it was, sat at the piano and settled her music on the stand. After smiling at her mother—ah yes, it was one of Lady Bewes's daughters—she began to play.

"No, of course not!" The marchioness struck his arm lightly with her furled fan. "Don't be so foolish."

Behind her someone hissed, and they were forced to remain quiet while the Bewes girl finished her piece. After the patter of applause, another young lady took her place and glanced at Alex before she, too, opened a leather folder and got out her music. More tedium. Alex liked music, which was why he disliked the mangling of it by people who should never have learned a note. At least nobody was singing. Yet.

During the pause, conversation resumed. Lady Broome leaned closer. "At the end of your corridor, there is a pair of potpourri containers. Chinese ones. You know them?"

He did. Large porcelain dishes covered with perforated lids. Dragons twined around each other on the wooden base to the piece. Hideous, he'd thought them, but his mother always insisted he had no taste.

"The potpourri has been removed. The dishes are empty apart from a number of items. Keys, to be precise. Now if you remove a key from the container with the blue dragons, you will find it opens a lady's door. You are to select a key and discover which room it opens. Inside you will find your prize. We are sure you will find your heart's desire in one of them. At least for tonight."

Alex was horrified. He was sure Bianca did not know. And of course that made their proposed meeting later totally impossible. People would be running around all night.

How could he warn her? Severn leaned over where she was sitting on the other side of the room with an infuriating leer. The man could win any leering competition he went into.

"Amusing, yes?" the countess said, laughing low in her throat. Alex was tempted to ask her if she had a cold. "My room," she said, "is the third on the right. Do not worry that we might be caught at our frolics. This scheme was of the marquess's devising. He wants us to enjoy ourselves, he said. His only caveat was that we were to remain in the wicked wing, and not venture into his side of the house."

Infamous. He should have left after all.

ANOTHER DEEPLY TEDIOUS musical evening. Bianca even contributed an Irish folk song. Although she had an indifferent voice, she was applauded warmly. Perhaps because she followed Maria stumbling through a piece of Mozart. Some guests urged Bianca to take her place at the piano, and Lord Severn offered to turn the pages for her. No doubt that would give him a better view of her cleavage. She demurely refused. In truth, her piano lessons had been rudimentary to say the least. The Burrells had spent much of their early years traveling, avoiding debt collectors for the most part, so any continuity of education had been marked only by its absence.

"I find your teasing charming, Duchess," Severn said, a smile playing about his mouth.

"If you detect teasing, it is purely in your imagination, my lord."

The murmuring from the occupants of her wing in particular seemed almost feverish. She did not care. They could do what they wanted.

Again, she took care to keep away from Alex, although she didn't ignore him—a difficult balance when all she wanted was to go to him. She had never taken a lover before, despite the rumors circulating around London when she'd lived there. People here seemed to prefer the rumors to truth, but then the rumors fitted their opinions of her.

The music room held a charming arrangement of sofas and well-cushioned chairs rather than the serried rows of uncomfortable wooden seats some hosts preferred. By now the company separated naturally into the groupings they preferred, although Alex continued to keep the marchioness company. Bianca wondered what he was about but had no desire to join them.

Eventually, when Severn had finally stopped in his efforts to persuade her to play again, Adolphus took the empty seat beside her. "Was that all you did today?" he asked. "Or did you try to escape?"

As usual, he'd gone to the nub of her dilemma. While she liked him, she didn't entirely trust him. "Just a walk," she assured him, "but I will confess that I got hopelessly lost. I had no idea I was close to the village. I wanted to visit the pretty temple on the hill that I can see from my bedroom window. Not visit a country inn."

"Ah, the folly," he said, and from his tone it was not clear if he meant the temple or her foolishness. "Didn't you notice the rain clouds?"

"Unless they are actually black, I find difficulty discerning rain clouds from an overcast day. I needed the walk."

"Restless?"

"A little," she admitted. Yes, he was right. She was more than restless, if only he'd known.

He sighed. "I fear the rain might set in for a few days. Which will turn the roads into quagmires, and mean none of us can leave the house, even for a moment."

"Oh, I doubt that," the marquess said, with a hearty expression Bianca didn't believe for a moment. "It is summer, after all."

A few people laughed. "The season of rain and clouds," Adolphus pointed out. "As if God was displeased over Waterloo. We haven't had a decent summer since."

"Waterloo was fought in the mud," Lord Severn pointed out.

If it did rain as hard as it had last year, when the party broke up nobody would be able to get away.

At last, the clock struck ten, and as if they'd all breathed a collective sigh of relief, they set out for their various rooms. As Bianca went to the door, miraculously Alex was there, the closest he'd been all evening. "Not tonight," she heard in a breath, so low she doubted he'd said anything. He did not accompany her. Adolphus did that. Outside her door, he kissed her fingers. "Sweet dreams, dear lady," he said. "Keep your door locked."

"I always do," she said.

Adolphus hesitated, then shrugged as two people entered the corridor. "It is very wise of you," was all he said before he moved on.

What was Alex doing? Had he fallen under Maria's spell? What was going on? And what did Adolphus mean, or was this a general warning? As the well-dressed men and women passed by before she entered her room, they bade her a polite good evening, and she did the same. Everything seemed normal.

Still wondering, she found McMurdo inside, and they went through the usual night-time routine of undressing, washing, and hair brushing. *Not tonight?*

Sighing, she climbed into bed and found her book. Although she'd meant to wait, just in case he changed his mind, she was asleep before she'd finished a chapter.

She woke suddenly. It was still dark, so still night. And she was no longer alone.

Although she'd expected her first affair since her marriage to have a more emphatic start, she wouldn't complain. She rolled over, into his arms.

"Good evening, dear lady," he murmured.

Bianca screamed.

Chapter Ten

THAT SCREAM HAD come from Bianca's room. Before he had time to think properly, Alex was across his room and through the door that led to the little sitting room that separated his room from Bianca's. He'd run toward the noise, rather than using the more indirect route. He saw the door at the other side of the room and fastened his blue banyan on his way, not hesitating as he shoved through into her bedroom. If the connecting door had been locked, he'd have broken it down.

The light of the single candle in the sconce above the bed showed him the scene. Bianca was out of bed, clutching a sheet to her bosom, facing a naked Lord Severn. He had his hands out in front of him in a gesture of placation, but it wasn't very convincing, due to the state of his lower body.

Alex didn't bother to examine him. Grabbing a garment from a chair, he tossed it at Severn and went straight to Bianca, folding her in his arms, shielding her from Severn.

Now she shrieked at him. "Let me go, damn you!"

Startled, he released her. She stepped out and faced her aggressor. "What gave you the right to think I would welcome this . . ." she swept her arm around in an encompassing gesture, ". . . insult?"

Not terror, but anger. Bianca was furious. Alex didn't blame her. So was he.

Severn moved to the door and picked up a robe that lay just inside. A gentleman's banyan. With his back to them, he quickly shrugged into it, so that when he turned back to them, he was at least half decent. "In answer to your question, ma'am, I was told of the evening's entertainment by Stonyhurst himself. I thought you knew."

"I was *asleep!*"

"I thought that charming." He seemed to be recovering. Instead of the shocked expression, he wore his usual cynical half-sneer again. "And it was."

Alex moved closer to Bianca again. "Stonyhurst said you could do this?"

"He encouraged me," Severn said. "You know about the games planned for tonight?" Alex nodded. Bianca shook her head.

Had nobody told her? What had Adolphus been thinking?

Severn sighed, and fastened the toggles that held the robe together, rather than holding the crimson banyan around him like a towel. "I see. Perhaps Stonyhurst thought it a fine joke. It would have been, if you'd been expecting me."

He went to the mantelpiece and collected a taper before crossing the room to take a light from the single candle. He walked around the room, lighting the half-dozen candles set in the wall sconces while Bianca turned to Alex.

"What is this? What is going on?"

Alex explained. "The female guests in this wing were told to leave the keys to their chambers in one of the Chinese pots at the end of the corridor. Then everyone would take a key and see which door it fitted."

"But I didn't put my key there . . ."

"They used the housekeeper's keys for the pots," Severn said. "Otherwise how would people leave their keys and also lock their doors?" His banyan safely fastened, he spread his hands again, this time in a gesture of surrender. "I cannot apologize enough, ma'am. I may enjoy little games like this, but not with an unwilling woman. I prefer my pleasures to be mutual. If you wish, I'll leave in the morning. In fact, I think I will leave anyway. I have no desire to stay in a house where I am used for our host's amusement." He stepped to the door but turned back before he left. "Once again, madam, I humbly beg your forgiveness."

"Stop!"

Alex's sharp command made Severn turn around to face him, one brow lifted in query.

"If he arranged this, he probably also arranged for someone to be outside, someone who can bear witness to who paired up with whom."

Severn shook his head, grimacing. "You're right. Do you have a servant's door, ma'am?"

"Go through the door I used," Alex said. "Then through the one on the other side. You'll find yourself in my room. The servant's door is on the other side of the room, near the large clothes press. If you do that we can say that you came to my room for a drink and conversation."

Severn nodded and crossed to the open door. "I'm definitely leaving in the morning. And anything I saw or did not see here tonight remains with me. A roué is not a successful one if he doesn't know when to keep his counsel."

He didn't look back.

They didn't move until they heard the door open and close on the other side.

"Did you know about this?" Bianca turned to face him, arms akimbo.

Alex turned away. "For God's sake, put something on."

A gasp was followed by the fumbling and rustle of silk. Before this moment he had not realized how close to naked Bianca was, and the glimpse he'd had nearly undid him. She wore a night-rail of white lawn, so fine that when she put her hands on her hips, the fabric drew taut over her magnificent breasts and deliciously curved hips. He could not even think of her in those terms. Not tonight, not after the shock she'd received.

"All right, you can turn back now," she said.

She wore a robe of pink silk, which covered her nakedness, but not her shape. He couldn't prevent his body reacting in the inevitable way. But he was a gentleman, and he would behave like one if it killed him.

"Are you recovered? Should I leave now?"

Bianca laughed. Shakily. "Do you think this is the first time a man has tried to compromise me?"

Going to the bed, she drew something from under the pillow. The blade of the wicked hunting knife gleamed in the moonlight filtering between a crack in the curtains. "I always have this with me."

He blinked. That was a knife that meant business. "Always?"

"Well, when I'm in a house I don't know well. One never knows." She placed the knife on the bedside table. "Except one often does. I wasn't always a duchess, you know."

Her calm statement spoke volumes. His heart ached for her.

She went to the lacquered chest of drawers. "Brandy?" She lifted a tumbler.

"Absolutely, thank you," he said. So she did not want him to leave immediately. From the fine tremor of her fingers when she removed the decanter's stopper, she was not as recovered as she claimed. Severn had given her a severe shock.

"I knew nothing about the marquess's vicious games," she murmured.

"Clearly. He must have told the others to keep you in the dark. I thought Adolphus would tell you when I saw you with him in the drawing room."

"He tried. He told me to keep my door locked and was about to say something else when we were interrupted."

He took the brandy with a smile. As his fingers grazed hers, her gaze flew up to his face. If not for that telltale tremble, he'd have acted on their attraction, but he would not take advantage of her while she was still upset. Like Severn. "Who'd have thought that the notorious Lord Severn would have had a conscience?" she said. She didn't move away.

"A roué who prefers his women willing. There are a few of them around, and we were fortunate to meet one."

She sipped her drink. "Why would Stonyhurst condone such a thing, much less promote it?" Indicating the daybed, she went and sat. He waited until she'd settled before joining her.

"My guess?" She nodded as she took another sip. Alex put his drink aside. He didn't really want it, but he suspected she wouldn't have had one if he'd refused, and she needed something to steady her. "I think it was simple revenge on you. You did not do as he wished, so this was your punishment."

"Is he that petty?"

"Not just that." What he'd learned today had rocked him. That his uncle was willing to allow such behaviour was deeply disturbing. "We know he is so against me inheriting that he wants his wife to take a lover and conceive a child. The last one did not work, so he provided a confusing situation that would allow her to take another."

"In what way?"

"With all the running about, a lover could easily slip into her wing, and claim he was lost in the confusion. It makes the presence of people in their nightwear in the corridors more understandable."

"Oh yes, yes I see."

He leaned back, careful not to move closer. The last thing she needed was for him to make an advance. The arrangement they'd made earlier in the day had died when she found a strange man in her bed. He was lucky that she allowed him to stay. "He wants everyone under his thumb."

"Including you."

He nodded. "Including me." He paused, waited for the atmosphere in here to settle. "I think we should both leave this house as soon as we can." He would deal with the marquess's vicious games on his own ground and in his own way. After he'd informed his cousins, who were equally involved in this.

"You do?"

Only there was one problem. "At the inn, I made enquiries about a chaise for you. The marquess bespoke the two the inn usually holds. That meant you were never going to get them. I wouldn't have put it past him to buy all the available tickets on the mail coach, too."

She frowned. "Is he that bad? Why would anyone do that?"

"Control. Over me, his wife, and everyone here. As long as they do as he wishes, they are welcome. We did not."

She shuddered. "How terrible. Do you think he would read the letters that go out? I left one in the hall when I went to the inn, but I retrieved it when we came back. I daresay he could have read it and put it back."

"Thus knowing you planned to leave. And knowing you couldn't." His lip curled, but he kept the curse hovering on his lips to himself.

"And he planned to take his revenge when he ensured I would not know about tonight's little game." She bit her lip. "I have coped with worse."

"Worse than this?" He found that hard to believe. She'd almost been raped tonight. But for Severn's conscience—who could have guessed?—she could well have been.

She shrugged. "My mother, my sisters, and I have faced the world alone since my brother joined the army, which he did, by the way, to earn enough to help us." Her expression lightened. "I could send a letter to Viola. We're staying with her next month, so I will just arrive a little early. She'll send a chaise for me."

"It would still take days for this to come about. If the marquess deigns to send your letter at all."

"You can still leave, as you were trying to do today."

He smiled. "Yesterday, to be precise." She had not noticed the clock chiming the hour. He sighed. "My uncle commands people like an emperor. If that does not work, he takes other paths to get what he wants. Take his wife, for example. He tried to get an heir on her by fair means or foul to cut me out of the succession. Then he compounded the insult by wanting to use me as a guardian—

an unpaid one." He paused a moment to control his anger. It was none of her doing. "By forcing us together, as he thought, he could also keep me under his thumb. I would stay here for you, if not for him."

"So you decided to leave."

He nodded. "I'd have returned, sometime, to discuss the matter with him. At my convenience, not his. But I cannot leave you here alone, can I?"

"Why not? I can manage well enough until I can leave. Either to Viola's or back to Edinburgh."

He admired her spirit. She had clearly come about after her distress this afternoon and then again this evening. "You know I assumed you had your own vehicle that you could use whenever you wished. But I have no doubt he would have subjugated you to his will, one way or another."

Bianca snorted. "Not likely."

He smiled at the charming inelegancy, appreciating how much she relaxed in his company. "Probably blackmail. He knows you want respectability after your—turbulent marriage, so he threatened to destroy it."

"Yes," she said softly. "But he wouldn't have succeeded. If it came to a choice between my reputation and my freedom, I would never choose the former."

"You're sure?"

"I've coped with worse." She said again and smiled.

"I have another choice for you. I can lend you my chaise to take you wherever you wish. It can take you home and return to my house. My home is a mere thirty miles away, so I can easily ride there. I arrived in state for a reason."

"Yes, you did, didn't you?"

"I brought trusted servants, outriders, and my traveling chaise. I wanted a show of strength. And now they can take good care of you, if you want to use my carriage to take you home."

She bit her lip, as if thinking about his offer. "Thank you. I may well take you up on your offer."

He should leave now, but he didn't want to. He got to his feet anyway, determined to give her some peace.

"No!" she cried as he turned.

Immediately he faced her again. "What is it, sweetheart?"

He had no idea how the endearment escaped him.

Bianca stood up. "Don't go. Please." They stood apart, gazing at each other, drinking the other in. "If we only have this night, so be it. I want you, Alex. Very much."

How could he resist her? He didn't even try. Cupping her shoulders, he drew her closer, watching her all the time to ensure she had no doubts.

When his lips settled on hers, he felt as if he was coming home. When she opened her mouth and returned his kiss, he felt like a giant.

She'd stopped trembling.

THIS TIME THEY would not stop at a kiss. The knowledge made Bianca's knees weak and her heart throb against her ribs. Desire heated her veins, ran through them like living fire. When he touched her, sliding his hand up from her waist to her breast, she shuddered, letting him feel her response, touching him in her turn.

Banyans fastened with large, elaborately braided toggles. She found the first one at his throat, felt the fabric tighten as he gulped. He didn't stop, didn't pull away but kissed her again, cupping her cheek in a gesture so tender she melted, sighing into his mouth.

Finally she got the last toggle undone. Wasting no time, she slid her hand under the heavy silk, the softer silk of the lining grazing the back of her hand as she came into contact with his bare skin. A shock like a streak of lightning coursed through her. She'd expected a shirt or night rail, but she found only him.

Spreading her hand over his chest, she savored the strong muscles, smoothly flexing under her hand, broken only by the coarser sensation of a light smattering of hair.

His lips left hers as he gazed into her eyes, his own hooded and sultry. "I had no time to make myself decent," he said, his voice low and intimate. "Do you mind?"

A laugh shook her. "No."

She wanted him to touch her as she was touching him, greedily exploring. When her hand grazed his nipple, he gasped and spread his larger hand over hers, the robe pushed aside. More than his hand pressed into her. Moving against him, she explored his erection through the clothes she still wore. Large, insistent, altogether the object of her desire. Her body softened for him, the sensation moving up through her body until she wasn't sure if she could stand on her own anymore.

"Shall we?" she managed to say, pulling away to move to the bed. He followed as if glued to her, smiling down at her.

"We shall."

He busied himself with her robe, easier to remove than his, but then he had her gown to tackle. He made short work of it. She'd wondered if he might tear it off, and thrilled at the prospect, but he didn't do that. Instead, he unfastened the buttons on her sleeves, then the ties at her neck with excruciating slowness until part of her wanted to pull away and drag it off as fast as possible. But she'd fallen under his spell, and gazed into those dark, long-lashed eyes as he lifted her last garment to her waist, and then over her head.

Her nighttime braids had already come partly undone, and as she shook them free of her night-rail, they unraveled the rest of the way. She never wore them tightly braided, as that left unwanted waves, so it was a matter of seconds to pull them free.

Alex watched her, smiling, and when she had done, he reached out and threaded a strand around his fingers. "So silken. Like a maiden locked away in a tower, waiting for adventure."

"In case you haven't paid attention, I'm no maiden," she

reminded him. "Though I don't have as much experience as some would have it."

He raised a brow. "I don't care. I only care that our first time will be glorious. No pain, only pleasure."

That sounded like a promise. He scanned her as she stood there, and she felt nothing but pride that she could arouse this man to such intensity of desire. Candlelight flowed over them both, and she was glad Severn had lit more.

Stepping back, he followed her example, letting his robe fall away completely. Alex's skin glowed golden in the light. Greedily she examined him, letting her gaze encompass all of him now, from the strongly formed feet to the top of his head. He was magnificent. He stood as she had, proudly, without shame.

With a groan, he came back to her and picked her up, laying her on the bed. Lifting her arms, she welcomed him as he joined her, holding his body over her, resting on his elbows. "You," he said, touching his lips to the tip of her nose, "are glorious."

"Are you going to ask me if I'm sure?"

He chuckled. "No. I trust you to know your own mind. If you're not sure by now, you're not demonstrating that very well."

"I want you."

"If I told you how many nights I've lain awake, thinking of you, wanting you, you would not believe me."

"I have never wanted anyone so much." She would not mention her first husband, but he was the only person she had to compare to this man. She would not do it.

Bending, he kissed her. Their bodies touched, from their mouths to their toes, sealing together, discovering. She spread her hands over his back, exploring, touching every part she could reach, claiming all that skin for herself. He moved softly against her, and when the kiss ended, continued down, touching his lips to her throat, and the pulse that throbbed frantically against him. Down and down, kissing her tight nipples, licking them, learning them, making her tingle all over. He murmured something, words she didn't catch but felt, vibrating against her skin.

He touched whisper-soft kisses down to her navel, where he played. Then he touched her, parting her lower lips gently and stroking.

Bianca nearly came off the bed.

Her reaction didn't stop him. Holding her more firmly, he continued to play while he came back to her, opening her, exploring. Now he was within her reach, too, and she circled the hard base of his erection, enjoying his deep groan and the way his eyes fluttered closed before he kissed her again.

Both exploring, discovering, but all too soon that wasn't enough.

Lifting his hand away, he finished the kiss and came to her, his knees between her thighs. As if they'd done this before, she lifted her knees high up, hugging his hips, spreading her hands over his back as he finally—finally!—joined their bodies together.

Alex's mouth dropped open and a stifled gasp escaped, as if he'd caught it in his throat. Bianca forced her breath out. The moment he'd entered her, a thrill had gone through her, right along her spine, delivering something akin to an orgasm.

It couldn't be. But—it was.

By the time she'd caught up with herself, he was moving, in and out, in a rhythm she felt in her soul. She responded naturally, let her body guide her into the dance.

"Did you come?" he murmured.

"What? Yes, I mean, yes, I think so." If he felt it, she must have done.

A sensuous smile curved his lips. "Let's make sure of it, shall we?"

He soon had her gasping again. Pressing the soles of her feet against the bed, she responded to him, bracing her body. The strokes increased in pace and depth. Oh, how she'd missed this! But she had not understood how much, fooling herself into believing it didn't matter. It mattered.

Especially with someone like him, a man who took care to

ensure she was as satisfied as he was.

They lost themselves, time losing its meaning as they watched each other. This time the feeling built gradually, thrills chasing the warmth. When he kissed her, she hooked one arm around his neck, his back muscles rippling as he settled.

Abruptly, he dragged his head up, and gasped, then cried out as he moved swifter than she could process, out of her body. Wet warmth pulsed onto her belly.

ALEX LEANED HIS forehead against her shoulder as he panted out his orgasm. He couldn't believe he'd nearly stayed inside her. Too close for comfort.

Hard on the heels of that thought came the wondering response—did he care if he impregnated her?

Only if she objected. Otherwise, no. Tonight had merely strengthened the feeling that in the Duchess of Whiston he'd met his match. In every meaning of the word.

Practicalities first. Swinging out of bed he headed for the washbasin where he found a cloth. The water was cold, but it would serve. He soaked it and strode back to the bed, where Bianca lay on her back, one arm curved over her tousled golden curls. "You look like Sleeping Beauty," he said as he cleaned her stomach.

She flinched at the application of the cloth but opened her eyes and gazed up at him. "You read Perrault?"

"I have five sisters," he reminded her. "All younger than me."

"Didn't they have a nanny to read them stories?"

"Did you?"

Smiling, she shook her head. He returned the cloth to the basin and then himself to the bed via the sideboard. She was watching him, and he rather enjoyed it. He waited until she'd sat up before handing her the glass of wine. She'd left enough space for him to join her.

His heart had nearly regained its usual rhythm. If he concentrated on telling Bianca about his sisters, he had a chance of not jumping on her like a rabid beast. Because once was most definitely not enough.

"Caroline is my youngest sister. The others fit between us in age. In answer to your question, a nanny is not a substitute for a relation. I used to read to her, and she started to insist if I could not." He chuckled. "A little madam was Caroline."

"Why were your sisters not presented at court?"

He leaned on to one elbow, gazing at her. "We had no reason, and when I suggested it, they turned the offer down." After all, he'd been a guest of the Prince of Wales, so they could have been presented. He should really insist, but although he had no problem insisting on things outside the house, he was no match for six determined women. Especially women he loved. "I'd like you to meet my family."

"Would you? I'm flattered."

A thought began to filter through his mind, but he would keep quiet about it for now. He was not sure how his mother would take to the idea, for one thing. "I don't want this to end. One taste of you isn't enough." He took their empty glasses and put them on the nightstand.

"I'm still here." Laughing, she levered herself over him, and all conversation stopped.

Chapter Eleven

TIME TO CALL his uncle to account. Having quelled the vicious anger he felt over his uncle's attempts to supplant him, Alex strode to the marquess's apartment with a list of complaints.

He would start at the top.

The marquess only admitted him reluctantly, complaining that he would not be at the bidding of his nephew.

Alex heard the tail end of the complaint as he entered the elegant apartment.

"You treat me like one of your employees much more, my boy, and out you go!"

"With pleasure," Alex said. He left the door open, uncaring of who might hear their conversation. After all, everyone except him seemed to know about the marchioness and her lover. "Once I've spoken my mind, I won't be staying long."

The marquess waved to a nearby chair. Alex ignored the gesture, choosing to loom over the man. "You'll stay. If you want your share of the inheritance, that is."

"I don't. Your influence and your poisonous plans are anathema to me. I don't need your money. Or your influence."

"Yes you do." Stonyhurst folded his hands over his flat stomach. He wore a waistcoat and coat in the height of fashion, but he still looked like a wizened old man. He was barely sixty. Alex had known men of seventy with more vigour than him. He flicked a glance up at Alex. "And what happened to your accent?"

"That? It won't help me anymore."

"So you used it to try to deter me?"

"Yes." He didn't want to talk about that. It was irrelevant. "I came here to inform you that you will not foist a changeling onto the title."

"An interesting word. Did your mother teach you that?"

Alex steeled himself not to fling the insults at his uncle that the man deserved. He had not come here to lose his temper. What was the point?

"Your meaning?"

"She is a mongrel, neither one thing nor the other. Therefore, so are you. I will not introduce impure blood into the line."

Idiot. Deluded idiot. "I will not deign to defend my family, because we need no defense. If that is all you have to say, then our association is close to an end."

"Then go," he said roughly. "I will use everything in my power to assure you will not inherit my title."

"Try." Alex felt the very air was tainted. "But if you acknowledge a child not of your get, I'll ruin you. That is a promise. And I can do it."

"And how do you propose to do that?"

"I will take you to court. I will appeal to the Regent, who claims that he owes me a favor." For providing the material and design for a particularly fancy military outfit, but the marquess didn't need to know that. "I will declare to everyone I know, and you may ask my cousins how many men in power I can claim acquaintance with, that the baby is not yours. I will drag you through the mud, as you have consistently tried to drag my family."

Finally that smirk left his face. "Empty threats." His voice lowered, rough-edged, revealing a temper at last.

"It's up to you to discover how empty those threats are." Alex had the upper hand. He felt it, knew it. He'd learned how to hold his temper in check. The marquess had not.

"So much for not wanting the title. I can drag you through the mire, too, boy. Your line isn't pure, your ancestry forever tainted."

"I still don't want the title. But I will not see the estate, its employees and servants, brought down by a man foisting a changeling onto it. You will not do this, not only for my family's sake, but for my cousins', too. You will be displacing them, too, breaking the natural order. I will not see that happen."

"I am the marquess!" He sprang to his feet and roared.

With an effort, Alex kept the pitch of his voice steady. "You are, and when you die, if a son of your blood does not inherit, I will. Despite my dislike of the whole business, I will accept it." And all it meant, God help him. He lifted his hand, pointed a finger at the man. "Don't try me. Don't fight me on this, because I will win."

"You didn't care before. How dare you come in here and try to lay down the law!"

"Not only will I try, I will succeed. Don't push me, old man. Or on second thought, do. I can't wait to unleash my legal team, to let your sordid secrets out in public. If you're thinking of retaliating with my mother's ancestry, you need not bother. We have already made it known. We feel no shame."

Now he'd started, he let it all out. "You treat people as if they are all subservient to you. That you have only to snap your fingers and it is all as you wish. But only here, not in the wider world. You've allowed your wife to take whoever she chooses into your bed. Last night you promoted it, acted as her pander. You are nothing more than a desperate man, old before your time, wearing yourself out with efforts that will not succeed."

"How do you plan to stop it? You can't, can you? Any child my wife bears is legally mine unless I say otherwise."

Alex delivered his last shot. He had others in reserve, but he didn't need them. "I can ruin the marquessate. You gave me the ammunition to do that. I know where your investments lay, how much you owe, and who owes you. I know your lands, and I know which bank holds your treasures."

Someone tapped at the open door. Alex did not look around. "If you insist on this ruinous course, everyone will know why the title and estate sank into oblivion. You hear me?"

Without waiting for an answer, he whirled around and left the room, pushing past an open-mouthed Villiers as he went.

Chapter Twelve

REPORTS OF THE argument between the marquess and his heir were all around the house within hours of it happening. Naturally, everyone behaved as if they had no idea of it, but small groups talking in low voices became normal, and as the weather improved people took to walking outside, discussing the rift.

Alex remained at Stonyhurst for now. He had more to learn, he said, but he would leave soon. The marchioness barely acknowledged him, and the marquess mainly kept to his room, loftily ignoring his heir when forced to be in the same room with him.

Bianca had decided she would stay until he left. She wanted to be with him as long as possible. She hadn't had enough.

And people approached Bianca about his change of accent, as he had totally dropped the Yorkshire accent now. "Did you know?" Lady Broome asked her as they promenaded in the rose garden one fine afternoon.

"I did," she admitted. "He spoke to me just before we were introduced. Enough for me to know the accent was assumed. He asked me to keep his secret, and I promised to do so. His cousins knew, too."

When Alex had appeared at dinner the evening of the argument, he'd spoken to everyone in the same tone of voice, making light of his Yorkshire accent, assuring people it was "nobbut a joke."

Some took offense, but not seriously. Some were stiffer when they spoke to him. Others were warmer, mainly the ones with eligible daughters. He behaved the same to all of them, with distant politeness.

BIANCA WAS IN danger of becoming too involved with Alex. Over the next week, she spent every night with him. Because of the sitting room between their chambers, they could conduct their affair in relative privacy, unlike the other guests in this wing, who changed bedrooms with monotonous regularity. They would hear a giggle, or the thump of bare feet running past the bedroom.

He was always gone by morning. Bianca should feel relieved at that, but instead, a sense of melancholy filled her when she turned over and she saw he'd left. He always covered up any trace of his presence. No dent in the pillow, no rumpled sheets on his side.

They occasionally met on their morning walks, but they were careful not to make a habit of gravitating to one another in public. By now Bianca did not want to give the marquess the satisfaction of knowing his ruse had succeeded. It had owed nothing to the old man, after all. If anything, his ordering her to seduce Alex had deterred her.

The lovemaking was better. Just, better. Perhaps because she was more relaxed than with George, having learned how delightful lovemaking could be. Or not being with a reckless scoundrel with a temper that flashed and whose moods were so changeable.

One evening, after their passion had temporarily abated and Alex fetched their wine, memories shot vividly back into her mind. It seemed wrong to lie here with her lover, thinking of her dead husband, but she had not done it deliberately.

She gasped, and he caught her glass as it tipped crazily to one side when her attention slipped. He put them aside.

"What is it?" Alex leaned over her, cupping her cheek. "You left me. Where were you?"

"Oh, it's nothing. Truly."

"It's something. If you don't want to tell me, I won't press you. But I'd like to know what disturbed you so much."

"It was George," she began.

He stilled. "Your husband?"

"Yes."

"Do you miss him?"

She bit her lip. "No." She'd never confessed that to anyone before, but the impulse was too strong to resist. "That's the first time I said it aloud."

He nodded. "Sometimes things are hard to say. Your husband died a hero, did he not?"

She nodded. "I wasn't there. I think I told you that I'd already left him by then." Her attention flew to his face. "I couldn't take it anymore."

"Did he hurt you?" He stroked her stomach in a soothing gesture, but he did not pull her closer. He gave her the room she needed, but she felt the tension in his hands, heard it in his voice.

"He never laid a finger on me in anger. It was not like that. He told me I was useless, kept telling me. At first it was little corrections, like telling me the colors that did not suit me or that I was using words not popular in society—the occasional Irish dialect."

He huffed a laugh. "Sithee, we're nairn fancy, like, in York-shire."

That made her smile, despite her distress. "Then it became worse, as if it was a habit in him. He blamed me for forcing me into marriage, said I had seduced him into it, planned it all."

"Did you?"

Appalled horror filled her. Grabbing the sheet, she pulled it up to her neck. "Out," she said stiffly. "Just go. How dare you even suggest that? How could you think that of me?"

He pulled in a breath. "Bianca—"

"No." If he didn't leave, she'd end up crying in front of him. The tears welled up in a great lump in her throat. "Go, just go."

Silently, he left the bed and picked up his banyan, throwing it over his shoulders before he left.

When she heard the door to his bedroom close, she let go.

She'd never cried like this, not even before, even when she'd wept for the waste of George's death, even when she'd cried in Alex's arms at the inn. The secrets she divulged, the way she'd felt so free and open in his arms was all an illusion. People assumed she'd seduced George, and since she couldn't disabuse them, she let them. But for her lover to think it . . . no, that was too much.

She'd been his victim, not the other way around. The injustice hit her, and she buried her face in the pillow, sobbing her heart out.

Arms went around her, holding her close. She knew from the touch who it was, but she had no strength of will to push him away again.

"I'm sorry," he said, urging her into his arms, holding her while she wept. "I'm so sorry. Such a stupid thing to say. I was so wrong. I should have thought more, thought better of you, and of myself. I have no excuses. But I can't bear to hear you cry alone. Just let it go, sweetheart, let it out."

What he'd said, those two words had broken something inside her. Burst the barrier she'd put in place when George had died. She'd been so determined that nobody would see the grief churning inside her, the confusion of missing him and the relief that she wouldn't have to listen to his tirades anymore.

Bianca had no more resistance, so she did as he suggested and sobbed.

Alex demanded nothing, only murmured words of comfort. Eventually the storm passed, though she'd no idea how much time had. Her eyes hurt, and she felt as if she had run a hundred miles, exhausted and wrung out.

She couldn't remember when she at last cried like that. If she ever had. Even back at the inn she had not released all the tension that lay inside her.

From somewhere Alex produced a large linen handkerchief, which he used to dab her cheeks. Then another.

He stopped. "This is no use," he said, and laid her gently down on the sheets. He went over to the wash basin and soaked a clean cloth before wringing it out and bringing it to her. He paused and looked at her before he scooped her up again. "I think you'll be all right now." When he applied the cold, damp, cloth she sighed in relief as the coolness transmitted to her overheated skin.

"This is so much better." As her senses returned, she grew increasingly aware of her vulnerability. "I'm sorry," she mumbled into the soft heat of his silk banyan. "I never do this."

"Never?" he said, amusement tinging his voice. "Not even now?"

She shook her head, the tangled locks of her hair tickling her cheeks. "Never before. Not like this." She took the cloth from him and applied it herself, folding it into a strip before pressing it over her sore eyes. Whether she did that for comfort or to avoid looking at him she wasn't sure. A bit of both, probably. "I don't know what got into me."

"You've been holding that in for too long," he said.

Recognition hit her in a jolt. Yes, that was it. Confused reactions to her husband, relief mingling with her grief, and then having him die in that gruesome way. "Perhaps he wouldn't have had the accident if I'd been there."

"Who can say?" He touched his lips to her head. "Nothing you did was wrong. You are not responsible in any way for his death."

"Really?" After removing the cloth, she looked up and met his gaze. "How can you know that?" A touch of irritation crossed her thoughts, that he claimed to know something he was not there to witness.

"Because I know you."

"After such a short time?"

"Sometimes that's all it takes."

Cradled in his arms she felt ridiculously safe. While she knew that was an illusion, for now it was enough. She would survive, as she always had, but for now she could rest and take a hiatus from reality. Only now did she understand how much she needed it. "I thought living quietly with my mother in Edinburgh would give me the rest I needed. I forgot how critical Edinburgh society could be. They welcomed the duchess but disliked the holder of the title."

"Then they're idiots."

She loved his uncritical support. She'd so rarely received that from anyone, even her mother and sisters. "I tried so hard to be part of Edinburgh society."

"It's their loss, not yours."

He could put her down now, but she didn't want him to. She snuggled closer.

"Was it all bad, your marriage?"

"Oh no. I had a riotous two years. My husband was terribly handsome, the most charming man I've ever met, and I fell head over heels for him."

She paused. What should she tell him? Everything? No. Yet again she was thinking too much. She needed to stop. So instead, she just talked. "I never paused to think that we did not need to elope. Oh, I was so foolish! He was of age, and so was I. I didn't know that he planned to set me up as his mistress, not his wife— not until we received a visit from my brother-in-law, the Earl of Knowsley. He compelled George to marry me. In fact, he had the special license in his pocket."

"Good man, Lord Knowsley."

"Yes, yes he is." She smiled when she thought of Gerald. A childhood friend of George's, he could say things to him that no other would dare. "Although George married me, and I think loved me in his way, he always resented the fact that I balked him of the heiress who would have paid his debts."

"He did that, not you."

"We were extravagant, went deep into hock. What shocked me was the level of debt that was tolerated because of his rank. I thought of all the people he was cheating out of their money, and I remonstrated with him."

"That was when it started?"

She knew what he meant by "it."

"No, it had started earlier, just after our marriage. He would joke about it and called me a provincial, a bourgeois, because I didn't know the people he did. I'd never moved in circles like that. Most people were accepting of what I was, but George wanted me to be perfect, and I could not be. He criticized my clothes, the way I spoke, even that I thanked servants when they performed a task for me."

"That's just good manners, to thank the servants."

"He preferred to pretend that they were not there. You don't thank air, he told me once. Since he'd been brought up in those circles, been a duke almost since he reached double figures, I believed him and tried to do as he said. But then he found someone else." She paused. "Lady Owen. He flaunted her at balls and meetings, rode with her in the Park. She was everything I was not, and I felt superfluous, stupid. He wanted me to feel like that." Truths came to her as she spoke, details of her marriage that had never occurred to her before. "He wanted me to feel inadequate, didn't he? He never wanted me to behave like a proper duchess. It made him feel superior, I suppose."

He crooned to her, rocked her as she poured out her story.

"So I left him. Juliet's mother-in-law, Lady Langston, took me away to a house by the river where I could rest and think. She was the first person I'd ever met who understood. I was recovering, and I decided to go back to London and tell George to mend his ways or I would leave him for good."

Events poured through her mind, coming clearly to her, with

details that had evaded her before. George had played her so cleverly, perhaps not even aware he was doing it. At the end, she'd been so uncertain of herself that she could not make even the simplest decision without consulting him.

"Where was your mother?"

"My mother was visiting an old friend. Everything happened so fast. She returned to London and accompanied my sister to Whiston House—they had been living there as well. And that's when George died. I felt nothing, Alex! Not for weeks!"

"That's normal in some people when someone close dies. They are numb, frozen."

"Has that happened to you?" Finally it seemed she could think and speak about George without guilt and grief overwhelming her.

"Yes. My father. It was sudden, an apoplexy. He collapsed in his office, and he was gone. Just gone. I took charge, ensured everything was done, and it was a week before I realized he would never be coming back." He gave a harsh laugh, no humor in it. "I said I was going away to see our man of business in London, but I stopped at an inn on the way, somewhere nobody knew me."

"You were alone?"

A pause before he said, "Yes. I wanted it that way." He kissed her forehead. "I wept for two days straight off."

Now she could offer sympathy, return some of the comfort he'd given her. She held him tight, felt when he drew in a deep, shuddering breath. But he did not weep. Only rested his chin on the top of her head and melted into her.

Five minutes later, he unwound, and drew her up into his arms to share a deep kiss of reconciliation which slowly turned into arousal.

This time their loving was deeper, gentler than they'd experienced before. A long, shudder of deliciousness. They moved slowly against each other, knowledge of their bodies adding extra dimension to their actions. They said nothing, only sighs, groans and cries punctuating the still air around them. The bed became their everything.

They came together, becoming equals in love.

BIANCA FELT REFRESHED when she awoke to the clock chiming three. She lay in Alex's arms, and it was as if she'd awoken to a new life. Beside her, he stirred. "I should go," he said, his voice thickened with sleep. "I should never have fallen asleep."

But he'd remembered to "keep her safe" as he put it. She'd been disappointed in that. But not in anything else. "It's only three," she said.

"But if I sleep again, I probably won't wake until your maid comes in."

That was true. But she wasn't ready for him to leave.

"Sometimes I wake up wondering if I have to dress in a hurry."

"Why?"

She chuckled, her breath returning to her from his shoulder. Looking back, the incident seemed funny. At the time it was far from that. "We had to leave Ireland in a hurry, because we hadn't paid the rent for three months. The landlord said we should pay when we could, but then he expected us to earn the rent on our backs." Ignoring his sharp gasp, she went on. "Needless to say, we did not do that. But we had to leave quickly in the middle of the night with only what we could carry."

The memory that halted her was her sister's problem. She had sustained a slight wound to her toe, which festered on their erratic journey to Scotland, and eventually had to be amputated. Such a small injury to cause so many problems! Viola had been lucky to keep her foot. The rest of the journey, desperate though it was, brought out the best in the sisters and their mother. By the time they reached sanctuary in Edinburgh, they were a strongly bonded family unit.

He sat up. "I wish I'd been there."

"But you weren't. We managed."

When he sat up, she went up with him. She put her hands on his shoulders, gazing into those dark, dark eyes. "Don't tell my brother about that, if you ever meet him. He doesn't know. He'd be furious and probably try to seek out the Irish landlord."

"I'm tempted to do that myself." His eyes were hard. He meant what he was saying.

"Then I shan't tell you his name." Cupping his cheek, savoring the rasp of his incipient beard, she said, "It was years ago. Long gone. Ancient history."

He smiled wryly. "Perhaps I'll find out. Is what your landlord did any different to what my uncle tried to do to you?"

"What he did or did not do means nothing. I shall go to Viola's soon, and I will go in the knowledge that what I did was my choice."

Alex put his hands either side of her waist. "I have an idea."

"Oh?"

He laughed. "You look so adorable when you tilt your head like that. Like a robin waiting for a crumb."

"A robin?" Nobody had called her that before. She'd heard all the extravagant compliments known to man, so why did this one strike her to the heart?

"Exactly like." Leaning forward, he kissed the tip of her nose. He leaned back against the pillows, still holding her. "I would love you to meet my mother."

"What?" Had she heard him right?

After regarding her closely, he finally spoke. "We have something, do we not? A connection, more than a physical attraction, although that, for sure, would be enough."

"We're friends," she ventured. What did he mean?

"Yes, we are. But perhaps there's more." Yes, perhaps there was. "I know I have no right talking to a duchess like this . . ." He smiled. "But I dare, because if I don't ask, I'll never know, will I?"

"Know what?"

"Let me make myself clear. If I offer anything, it will be what I have now, with no expectations of anything else."

He was proposing? Her heart beat faster.

"The old man will cut me out any way he can. I'm a mongrel, he tells me, not fit to hold the title." When she would have protested, he shrugged. "I don't care. Truly I do not. I'll take the title of Midas of the North over Marquess any day. But you—you're different. You're a duchess, a member of the highest of high societies."

"I was a penniless girl from Ireland, the child of a squire's daughter and a man who'd been cast out by his uncle, an impoverished viscount."

"You're much more than that. I will fight for justice, and if that includes inheriting the title, then I will do it. But it may not come to that."

"No," she said faintly.

"You know how I feel about you."

"You're not . . ." Confused, she didn't know what to ask.

"It's too early to jump to conclusions, is it not? We like each other, perhaps more. What I feel for you . . ." He paused. She waited. "I've never felt like this before, but a month ago we hadn't even met. I don't want to let you go away. Everything in me tells me not to let you go. But you need more time, don't you?"

She bit her lower lip. He understood. She'd married George in haste and lived to regret it. If she were to marry again, she wanted more time.

"I would like to invite you on behalf of my mother to stay with us for a while."

"Does she know?"

His gaze slid away and then back to her. "She will. And I promise you, she won't object. I have a house in the countryside, where my mother and sisters live. I also have a much smaller house in town, which I use when I'm working there. Usually, I stay there during the week, unless my mother is holding a dinner or a musicale or something that she wants me to attend. I can travel to the country house instead. I will, if you're there."

"Oh!"

"I want to know you better. If you feel the same, come for a visit. Find out more about my life, my real life. Meet my mother and sisters. See what I do."

Yes, she did feel that way toward him. Nobody since George had affected her in this way. Alex's lovemaking was glorious, unselfish, and passionate, but he was right: she needed to get to know him better before taking a step like marriage. "I could," she said. "Yes, yes, I will."

He kissed her then. But not with the desire earlier. Tenderness marked this caress. They lingered over the sweet embrace.

When she pressed her body against his, he gently laid her down on the bed. "Rest, sweetheart. Sleep. You need it. I'll see you tomorrow, and we must try not to show too much fondness for each other, though it will be difficult. For me, at any rate." He kissed her again, touching his lips gently to hers before lifting the sheets and blankets to tuck around her. "But we can show a little now. We'll leave soon. The end of the week? That will give me time to write to my mother and get her response."

"We would travel together?"

"I'll ride. It's about thirty miles to the country house. Sheffield is a little farther, but we won't be going there, at least not at first. My house is not as large or grand as this, but I do think it's elegant. Will elegance suit you, rather than magnificence?"

"Oh yes," she breathed, and as he left her room, she sank into a dreamless sleep and didn't wake until her maid came in at eight the next morning.

Chapter Thirteen

"I'M AFRAID I must leave soon, too," Bianca said at breakfast. Alex had just announced that he was leaving and then left the room to see Villiers, or so he said.

"Oh dear!" Lady Salish, the mother of two aspirants to Alex's hand exclaimed. A tall, ascetic woman, not quite as tall as Bianca, but getting there, she tended to dress in delicate fabrics in light pastel colors. "And I was wishing for a quiet word with you. Unfortunately, we must leave soon, too, delightful though this visit has been." She glanced at her husband and shrugged. "We have enjoyed your hospitality, Lady Stonyhurst."

Maria was present, though her husband was not. She appeared considerably brighter these days. Perhaps she'd found a new lover. As long as her husband acknowledged any child she bore as his, the child, whoever his father, would become the marquess. Though if the marquess didn't take heed of Alex's warning, all hell would break loose. With the marquess's three heirs in the house, the respectable wing had better sort itself out and decide who was marrying whom.

"We've hardly exchanged a word since you arrived," Lady Salish said with a pout. "Would you walk with us after breakfast? The day is so lovely, it would be a shame to spend it indoors."

Since she could not excuse herself without appearing rude, she agreed to the stroll. Lady Salish had treated her coldly during this visit, but perhaps Bianca had redeemed herself without realizing it.

At any rate, she found herself in the company of not only her ladyship, but two of her daughters. They had to walk a little apart, to avoid the clash of parasols. Bianca soon put hers down, since the day was overcast, and her bonnet would shelter her face from the sun, but Lady Salish's daughters spun and flirted with theirs, despite there being no gentleman present.

"This house is astonishing," her ladyship began. "Do you not think so?"

"It certainly holds its share of treasures," Bianca answered cautiously. "And everything is displayed in the greatest taste. But . . ."

"Yes?"

Well, why not explain her misgivings? "A treasure house doesn't make a home. Every room is carefully arranged. Some of the sofas have legs so thin I dare not sit on them."

"Oh, the ones his lordship obtained from the Versailles auction?" Her ladyship twirled her parasol and glanced up at the sky before following Bianca's example and putting it down. She moved a trifle closer. "Though one does not like to ask how he obtained them, it has to be admitted that they are of the very best. Perhaps the poor late queen sat on those sofas or used that charming bonheur du jour in the music room."

"It's possible." Bianca didn't really care for the over-gilded, over-designed pieces, but she wouldn't say so, since her ladyship obviously admired them.

"And if her ladyship doesn't make haste to begin her nursery, it will all go to the mongrel."

Bianca closed her eyes, forcing the reply back when her ladyship used that hateful word.

"That is how his lordship refers to him, did you know? I consider him a handsome gentleman," she continued.

Not so bad. But even to repeat such a disgusting allegation was to perpetuate it. Bianca wouldn't dream of using it. "He is handsome," she said. Though his looks came from his personality. He wasn't a golden god like George, and she was heartily glad of that.

"And most taken with you. Mind you, one cannot be surprised at that. You have always been an accredited beauty. Your sorrows do not seem to have dimmed that. I was so pleased to see you here, recovered and out of mourning."

"Thank you," she said. This woman did not lack for words, as long as they were her own.

"Indeed. And as women of the world, you and I know that men need what they need. We can overlook that, can we not?"

"I didn't," she said, wondering where this conversation was going. "Of course, it's a matter of choice. His, usually."

Lady Salish tittered, covering her mouth with delicately white-gloved fingers. "We must strive to excuse them their little foibles."

Bianca held her tongue. It was either that or give her considered opinion, which did not include excuses.

Fortunately, her ladyship did not need more than the occasional prompt. With her daughters trailing behind, she continued her speech. "Mr. Fraser appears to be a gentleman. You would know better than me."

"We are staying in the same wing of the house," she admitted. And the same bed, but she wouldn't mention that. "He has kindly escorted me down to dinner once or twice."

Lady Salish gave Bianca a roguish glance. At least, she probably meant it to be that, but it came out as more of a leer. "Of course. And the cruel trick he played on us all—the accent he did very well. But I can forgive him for that. A man with prospects like Mr. Fraser's needs to fill his nursery, at the very least. And the sooner the better. I wondered if you would do me the greatest of favors by telling me a few of Mr. Fraser's preferences. Does he like horses, for instance?"

"He rides them, but I don't think he is particularly interested in them." A wicked notion crossed her mind. She let it brew a little.

"The theater? Does he prefer women who are modestly silent, and accede to his wishes, or does he like a spirited girl who can discuss political issues and other thorny matters?"

Oh yes. She would do it. Serve her ladyship right. Nobody would insult Alex like that in her hearing. "In our conversations, I have discovered Mr. Fraser enjoys the theater very much. He has sisters, you know, and they encouraged him. He also enjoys modern novels when he is not working. Something to relax with, I think he said." He probably read technical manuals for relaxation. Let them underestimate him. "He has visited London of course, but only as part of his business. He does not move in society. I daresay he would appreciate a few helpful hints."

Lady Salish would be eager to comply. "As the marquess's heir, he will naturally have to attend events in the City more often. One does not like to comment, but I heard he had the epithet of Midas of the North. That would imply considerable—substance."

"Oh yes," she said happily. "In provincial terms he is most well-to-do. And the marquess has two heirs after Mr. Fraser," she added. "Mr. Adolphus Fraser and Mr. Benedict Fraser."

"Oh, those two!" her ladyship exclaimed. "We have known them this age! But they are useful to know. Adolphus knows all the on-dits, and Benedict, although a man of few words, can always be relied upon to successfully predict the winner of a sporting contest. Besides, Adolphus is not the marrying kind."

"No, he is not. However, the marquess would be severely disappointed, should the young ladies focus their attention only on his current heir."

"Oh pooh!" Her ladyship waved away her concerns. "I am of a different opinion. Even without the marquessate, Mr. Fraser is an attractive prospect. My husband has made a few discreet enquiries. He is a wealthy man. True, he needs a little Town polish, but I'm sure that can be achieved with application and a good example set before him."

Bianca suppressed her instinct to laugh. Instead, she continued with her story. "Mr. Fraser appreciates a woman who knows her place. His sisters are meek individuals. He rules the roost at home, or so I understand."

"So he is not for you?"

"Certainly not!" She did her best to appear shocked, fanning her face with her hand. "My dear, late husband never required that of me. What civilized man would? Mr. Fraser is undoubtedly a powerful-looking man, but he is not strictly good-looking. You knew my late husband." Lady Salish nodded. "He was most handsome."

"You were noted as the most beautiful couple in society."

"Yes." Lowering her chin, she lowered her lids and looked up. While she could not use that coy expression as effectively as her sister Juliet, who was a few inches shorter, she could still use it to feign bashful innocence. "I'm afraid we were. Misleading, however. I saw many who could overtake us on those stakes." She had not, but it didn't hurt to be modest.

"And now you are on your own," her ladyship said in a sympathetic tone.

Yes, she was. But hope had bloomed in her breast. Alex was a completely different prospect to most of the men she knew. He was not dependent on getting a legitimate heir on some vacuous young woman, or on making the social rounds, tediously trailing from country house to country house all summer, and then London in the spring. His life would be completely different. She still expected to live the rest of her life on her own, but . . .

And she would fight for her dream. Even if it meant putting other women on to the wrong track. She would also support him. Serve the wicked gossips right.

ALEX ENTERED THE armaments room, prepared for another brain-numbing session of accounts.

Villiers had a set of accounts and inventories concerning the estate open today. Used to studying the account books of his own business, he was accustomed to seeing patterns on a page, so that when something was amiss, he could stop and pay deeper attention. But once Alex had begun that sort of closer inspection in another set of books, they'd never come out again, but perhaps it was only his unfamiliarity with property details that kept him uncertain.

And most likely the man resented Alex invading the space he'd carved out for himself. Added to that, they had a lot of ground to cover before Alex left the house. Villiers seemed to be as eager as Alex to get this business done.

Today, Villiers discussed the extent of the estate, how rents were collected, and the kind of repairs tenants demanded. "Frequently," he said, "they will ask for the thatch to be renewed on their properties a mere ten years after the last time it was done. They believe I do not have a memory, or that I do not know how to look at the records. It is tedious but necessary to keep those lists precisely."

"I have a few tenants of my own." Alex gave the list of repairs a good, hard look. At first glance, they were in order. The names of the tenants, the repairs recorded. "Some of these names are repeated often. The houses seem to be in poor repair. Perhaps it would be better to tear the old place down and replace it completely."

"In some cases, it would be more appropriate," Villiers admitted. He came over to study the same book. "The Walker cottage, for instance. That is a local one—on this estate—close to the village. The cottage was built by a Walker a century and a half ago and not very well. He built it near the river on uncertain ground. The place is regularly flooded. I have suggested to his lordship that we replace the cottage with a sturdier construction half a mile away on firmer ground, but he will not have it. He likes the half-dilapidated place. He says it adds character to that part of the estate. He told me he did not have to hire a hermit while the Walker cottage remained." Villiers heaved a sigh. "In their case, the repairs are usually required and not fabricated."

"You travel to the estates," Alex said, continuing to study the records.

"Yes indeed."

Someone rapped at the door and Villiers went to open it. He did not let anyone in, but closed the door gently, the old latch barely rattling in its gate. "His lordship wishes to see you," he said.

"Now?"

"Now."

Alex could guess what it was about. He'd made his announcement that he would soon be leaving at breakfast, in the full hearing of the guests and servants. His lordship would undoubtedly have heard. Alex prepared himself for battle.

When he entered the stifling heat of the marquess's chambers, he was surprised to see his cousins there, also. They sat on a sofa before the fire which, unlike the one in his room, was lit. The brothers sat at either end of the sofa, as if they couldn't bear to touch.

The marquess waved to him to sit in the only vacant chair left, and in the same gesture waved away the servants hovering by the door. "And no listening at the keyhole, either!" he said.

They bowed and left.

His lordship banged his cane on the floor, evidence that he was in the habit of doing so left by the thin patch on the Persian rug. "Now then." He addressed Alex, his pale blue eyes remarkably sharp. "You had the effrontery to announce you are leaving without informing me first. You will not leave, hear me?"

Alex took his time replying, tamping down the spark of irritation that inevitably struck him at those words. "I've a business to run. I told you before that I'd leave when I'm ready, not at your convenience."

"You have duties here!" He banged the cane again. "How

could you even suggest it? Were you expecting more leniency? Perhaps an allowance, even?"

"I have no need of any allowance. If you give me one, I'll donate it to the local foundling hospital." Of which he was already a patron.

"Effrontery! Are you used to frittering money away on useless orphans?"

Alex didn't dignify that remark with a reply. Instead, he tried to make a conciliatory gesture. "I don't live so very far away."

"Humph! But I have need of your presence here. You will obey your elders and betters, sir!"

"I will." He paused. "But I'll still leave on Friday."

Unexpectedly, the marquess turned to his other nephews. "You hear that, boys? That is how a man conducts himself, even a mongrel like Fraser here!"

Anywhere else, at any other time, Alex would have got to his feet and left after that kind of insult. If the marquess had been younger, he'd have struck the man.

He contented himself with a brief, "If you continue to call me by that name, I will find something equally derogatory to call you. I thought I'd made myself clear on that score."

"You will not be inheriting anything, you two, if you don't start fending for yourselves! Your father left you well provisioned, did he not? Live within your means! When you do so, I will be generous. And while you have been idling the day away, Fraser here has been spending time with Villiers, learning the ways of the estate. I plan to send him on the rounds in the autumn, so he may see the land for himself."

He spoke as if Alex's arguments meant nothing. "You want to make Villiers lead me on a dance around the country looking at old houses? I will not."

Adolphus got out his snuff box. Benedict did not show any change of expression. Perhaps they were used to such attacks. Alex was not and did not intend to make it a part of his everyday life.

"But I have some good news," the marquess said. His mood changed abruptly. He was almost smiling. "My wife informs me, in fact she is certain, that she is in the family way."

Alex drew a deep breath, but all he said was, "Congratulations."

So the marchioness had finally done her duty and would present a baby to her husband in due course. If this were a child of her husband's, and if it were a boy, that would remove a great burden from his shoulders.

The marquess watched him closely. "Are you not disappointed?"

"No. I will require written assurances of the child's origin, of course."

Lord Stonyhurst put both hands on the end of his cane and leaned into it, regarding the three men carefully.

Before he could challenge Alex, Adolphus spoke. "Indeed, many congratulations." Benedict glanced at Alex before adding his felicitations.

"Now she's not very far along, so we don't want the others knowing yet," the marquess said. "But we are sure. Which means," he added, turning his attention to Alex, "that I will need my nephews around me so we can make arrangements for the boy."

"Boy?" Adolphus said with a lift of his slender brows.

"Aye. If she has one she can have another. So even if this one is the wrong sex, she'll have proved her worth and we'll get another. I had to pay a King's ransom to get her parents to agree to the marriage. But she's a well brought up girl and she knows her duty. Unlike some." He shot a fulminating glare at Alex.

"I know my duty, uncle." Was that the first time he'd called the marquess uncle? Yes, it was. But his relief had made him lightheaded. After what he'd said the other day, surely the marquess would not dare to foist a changeling on the estate.

The marchioness must have fallen pregnant before Alex had thrown down his ultimatum. If it was after the marquess had sent her lover away, Alex might be brought to accept the situation. Certainly he would prefer it.

He could get on with his own affairs, perhaps make a few calls on Stonyhurst, and that would be that. He would not be dancing attendance on the old man.

"Well, I can't deny I was worried for a time, but she's a good girl. Of you three," he continued, passing the glare on to Adolphus and Benedict, "Alexander is the best prepared to provide adequate guardianship. Matters being as they are, I may not survive to the boy's majority. You'll be well rewarded."

"Count me out."

Lord Stonyhurst went on as if Alex hadn't spoken. "And your sisters can be presented at court, Alexander. They'd like that, hey?"

They'd already refused the honor, but Alex wouldn't mention that now.

"We'll see," Alex said. "You want us to keep mum about this?"

"For another week or so. I've sent to London for her ladyship's personal physician. She refuses to be examined by anyone else. He'll confirm her pregnancy."

"And it's yours?" He wouldn't make any excuse for being blunt.

The marquess beamed. "Yes, it is. Wholly mine, and I will sign anything you wish to that effect."

Alex still didn't trust him, but he would bide his time and do his best to ensure that the marquess told the truth. The marchioness was a weak vessel, a pretty little thing with a deceptive way about her and a habit of bending to the wind. A little gentle questioning wouldn't go amiss.

The marquess laid his chin on his folded hands. "Good news. A shame I won't see the boy to adulthood."

"There's a man of ninety in our village," Adolphus said.

Benedict remained stoically silent. Would the news be a blow to them? Or would their uncle provide them with a better income if he expected them to take a hand in their baby cousin's upbringing?

The marquess got up. The other three followed suit, ready to take their leave, but his lordship turned and stared into the glowing embers of the fire. His shoulders hunched. "Peter should never have died," the marquess said.

Shock rippled through the room. Since Alex had arrived, nobody had mentioned Lord Youngman, the marquess's only son who had died of smallpox. Alex had never known him, but from the portrait in the picture gallery, he knew Peter had the long face and strong nose that characterized most of the family. Until he got here, Alex assumed his nose had been from his mother's heritage, but now he was not so sure.

Alex said softly, "No man should see his son die."

The marquess was still staring into the fire. "He was a good boy."

Since he said no more, the three men glanced at each other and quietly left.

When they were half a corridor away, Adolphus let out a long breath. "Well. So there we have it. He's cut you out of the succession, coz."

"So he has." Alex paused. "He wouldn't have told us if he wasn't sure, for all he's asked us to keep silent about it."

Benedict leaned forward. "Can the child truly be his?" He spoke barely above a whisper.

"Perhaps," Alex said. "We should do everything we can to prove that it is."

As Benedict strode away, Alex touched Adolphus's elbow, causing him to hold back for a moment. "You're not likely to produce a child, are you?"

Adolphus sighed. "No."

"I think we're all sorry that Lord Youngman died."

He was, truly, and not just for himself. Especially considering the marquess's last words. He missed his son. It was the first time Alex had been aware of true humanity in his uncle.

Chapter Fourteen

Before dinner that evening Alex was besieged. Young women who wanted to know his opinion about some Shakespeare play or another. When he answered, "How would I know?" when asked if Feste was the best clown in all Shakespeare, the girl laughed, and said he was the wittiest man she knew. What devil had told her he cared for Shakespeare? He enjoyed a rollicking farce as well as the next man, but to sit through the tedious wordsmithing that went before was more than he could bear. If he went to the theater, he tried to arrive at the second interval.

But as he opened his mouth to inform this young woman, her sister—or another so like her that she could have been her sister—tapped him on his arm with her fan. "For shame, sir, we know perfectly well how much you enjoy the Bard!"

Did they?

Miss Garvey, a toothy young woman with a real gift for coy looks and fan deployment, continued. "But sir, perhaps that is not your favorite Shakespeare play. Which one do you prefer above all others? *Hamlet*, perhaps?" She was one of Lady Salish's brood, he recalled. Hadn't he seen Bianca with them earlier?

He was on the point of answering strongly in the negative. "My sisters saw that play. Over four hours long, one of them told me. I don't have time for that."

"So you have not seen it?"

"No. I've seen *A Midsummer Night's Dream*," he added. His parents took him when he was a child, but he had not been impressed and his mother had declared herself shocked at the goings-on.

"Ah yes, so charming!" She fluttered her fan. Alex, no slow top, realized what his lover had done. Torn between laughter and irritation, he listened to Miss Garvey extolling the play. He nodded at intervals, knowing his ordeal wouldn't last for long because they would be going in to dinner soon, and Miss Garvey's seat was nowhere near his.

However, once seated at dinner, he discovered that both young ladies who had heretofore gazed at him in awe or showed no interest in him at all now seemed desperate for his opinion on topics he knew little about.

Alex eyed his plate, deciding the ragout was not only cold but close to inedible. But eating that was preferable to talking about Shakespeare. While he dug in, her ladyship loudly pronounced her opinion. "The actors of today do not understand that audiences require entertaining, not being made unhappy by killing the hero at the end of the play. It is most unfortunate that they have decided to restore the original, tediously miserable endings to his tragedies."

Alex chewed and swallowed, and decided that maybe the conversation was better after all. "Doesn't somebody need to die in a tragedy?"

"But does it have to be the character you've learned to love during the course of the play?" Miss Garvey said. Her sisters murmured agreement.

Alex gratefully put his knife and fork down and beckoned the footman to remove his plate. They would be serving the second course soon. "I don't take much interest in old plays. It's not in my line at all."

The second course brought a fresh selection of dishes, one of which was apple pie. Alex didn't mind apple pie cold. He refused the rest in favor of the dish he knew best. Even spiced it tasted fine. Only fine, though. His cook did better, and she didn't call herself a chef.

Alex let the conversation run around him until Miss Rosamund Garvey, the younger sister of the other one, determinedly dragged him back in. "Sir, have you visited London?"

"Once or twice," he admitted with reluctance.

"But not to society. Not to the season."

"No."

She lifted her fan and tittered behind it. Were her teeth bad, so she had to cover them up? "I suppose not, but a man of your substance would be most welcome there, I am sure."

"Perhaps," he admitted reluctantly.

Another Garvey, this one sitting opposite her, broke in. "Oh Rosamund, for all we know Mr. Fraser runs tame in White's. After all, they welcome all kinds of gentlemen there."

After placing his silverware carefully on his plate, Alex leaned back. "All kinds?"

"Yes indeed," she hurried to explain. "From all walks of society."

He waited, watching the slow blush rise in her cheeks. It didn't improve her, unfortunately. This Garvey was a strawberry blonde, and if allowed in the sun, would freckle charmingly. Alex had no objection to a freckle or two. But the fiery blush did not become her. "Yes of course," she continued, seemingly determined to dig the whole even deeper. "That is . . ."

Alex took pity on her. "I'm not grand enough for White's."

"You will be now," Miss Rosamund Garvey said. "I'm sure they'll welcome you."

"Perhaps," he repeated. "But I'm not in London often enough to make it worth my while."

"Oh!" The girls looked at each other, confusion reigning in their expressions.

They'd probably never come across a man who didn't belong to a prestigious London club. As it happened, they still didn't know one. Alex had joined White's, at the urging of the Regent, although he'd never bothered to go more than once. He preferred Watier's.

He should try to persuade his sisters to go to London, though. When he went home, he'd ask them if they wanted to try again. Perhaps some good would come of this ridiculous situation, after all.

Apart from meeting Bianca, that was.

"So you do go to London occasionally," Miss Rosamund Garvey said. "That must be useful for your business."

"Aye, it is. We provide uniforms to the army, you see. The Regent takes a personal interest."

Silence fell for what felt like eternity.

From the other end of the table, Lady Salish leveled her lorgnette at him. "Am I to understand that you claim acquaintance with His Highness the Prince Regent?"

Realizing his error, Alex tried to underplay his acquaintance. "I've met him a time or two." Made him a uniform, in fact, working with his tailor to ensure the details were correct. And obtained the gold bullion for the tassels at a knock-down price, which pleased the Regent no end. "But I don't move in society, as such."

"Well, that's about to change," his uncle boomed from the other end of the table. "I'll put Villiers onto it. I'm sure he can find you a tailor and whatnot."

Remembering the high points of Villiers's shirt collars, Alex doubted that. He would not be taking sartorial advice from that man-milliner. Neither would he be parading around in town.

"Mr. Fraser looks every inch the gentleman," the oldest Garvey girl said. "He is, I'm sure, perfect as he is."

Alex felt vaguely sick, and it wasn't because of the food.

AFTER DINNER IN the drawing room, the women gathered around him, asking his opinion on this and that as if he were the arbiter of everything in the world. He couldn't decently excuse himself and discovered a desire to listen to insipid pieces played on the piano rather than any more of this nonsense. All the time Bianca sat next to Lady Bewes watching him indulgently and exchanging gossip, their heads close together, dark and fair. They made a lovely vignette, but Alex was not sure if Bianca realized it.

He was certain Bianca had started this hare. The Garvey girls were especially persistent. Shakespeare came up again, but that was cast aside in favor of a discussion about the merits of an ideal bride, which Alex listened to, appalled.

"She should be kind and never speak too loudly. Her husband should always have the last word in any discussion, of course. A lady should be modest and gentle," Miss Rosamund said firmly. A giggle from the sofa made him glance at Bianca suspiciously, but she refused to meet his eyes. Seemingly she was in animated discussion with Lady Bewes. Alex narrowed his eyes, but there was little he could do about it.

He waited for half an hour after she had excused herself to go to bed before he went up to join her.

Twenty minutes later, he strode into her room after a perfunctory knock. "What was all that about?"

She sat up in bed, drawing the covers up around her shoulders. Tilting her head on one side, she regarded him with raised brows. "Why, sir, I have no idea what you mean. Lady Salish expressed her desire to recommend her daughters to you. She has discovered the extent of your wealth and suddenly finds you the most attractive man in the world. I told her you had a secret passion for Shakespeare and preferred a wife to be obedient and passive."

Her eyes danced with mischief as he strode over to the bed and pulled the covers away. And groaned.

Beneath the sheets she was naked.

"You know how to deploy your weapons, do you not?"

She rolled on to her side to lean on her elbow. "Were you not amused?"

"Amused?" Tilting his head back, he stared at the ceiling as if he could find answers there. "What have I done to deserve this?"

A rustle of sheets heralded her movement. She was kneeling on the bed, busy at the single toggle he'd fastened before coming here to confront her. She pulled his banyan aside and spread her hands over his chest, making a "Mmm" sound of approval. "I love a man with a little hair on his chest."

"Hmm." But he couldn't deny he appreciated her attention. The body of a courtesan in the person of a great lady. As far as he was concerned, she was both. He had never met anyone remotely like her before. He doubted anyone existed who could come close.

Her unbound hair tumbled over her shoulder as she explored, smoothing her hands agonizingly slowly over his body. Every nerve, every one of those damned hairs responded to her, rising at her touch, sending prickles of sensitivity through his whole body.

Then she touched his erection, so gently he could hardly bear it. "Don't stop," he said, rough and hoarse.

"Oh, I have no intention of stopping."

She followed her caresses with kisses, at first gentle, then firmer, leaving a damp trail down his belly. She licked him, as if savoring a favorite dessert. Alex didn't dare move, but he couldn't help his shudder. He stood while she knelt, going on all fours to pleasure him.

Alex dug his fingers into her silky curls, responding with moans of pleasure. His agitation when he'd entered the room melted in the power of her onslaught. He would do anything for her, anything in the world, if only she'd continue.

When she pulled away he cried out, "No!" but there she was, kneeling on the other side of the bed, beckoning to him. Her lips were damp. She'd brought him to the brink and pulled away, the rush of cooler air when she left him almost forcing his culmination.

But not quite.

He was bigger, taller, and stronger than Bianca, but right now she had him in her thrall. He lunged across the bed, catching her around her waist and pushing her down against the mattress. She fought him, catching him off-balance, rolling them so she ended on top.

With a wicked gleam in her eyes, she took him in hand, guiding him into her wet warmth. Now it was her turn to moan. Throwing her head back, her hair tumbling almost to her waist, golden strands gleaming in the candlelight. A goddess. A wicked one, to be sure, but his, all his. He watched their joining, helped her as she moved, pleasuring herself on him. Using him. Alex loved every second.

He cried out and bucked, pushing inside as deeply as he could go, the motion instinctive and inevitable. For the first time since they'd become lovers, he pulsed helplessly inside her silken depths.

Bianca fell over him and to one side, as he panted, wordless sounds of ecstasy escaping their lips. Then he kissed her. A sloppy, careless kiss, the best he could manage. He had lost control. Alex barely had the strength to tug the sheets over them both before he fell into a deep sleep.

WHEN ALEX WOKE, the candles were still alight. He blinked, letting his mind come back to life. Bianca lay in his arms where she belonged, with one leg curled around his. They lay entwined, as if they'd always slept that way. When he woke, she stirred, but then settled with a little sigh that stirred the hairs on his chest that she said she loved.

What he'd done shook him profoundly. He could have stopped, but he didn't want to. That was the part that shook him the most.

He had to face what he'd been hiding from for a while now. He wanted her badly. He'd already made his mind up, and he would not give in unless she told him to stop. Inviting her to stay with his mother was a much more important decision than Bianca would assume. He'd never done that before. The young women she'd introduced to him in the past were acceptable, but no more. He liked them, but he felt no passion. Only friendship. He wanted more, and now, finally, in the least expected place, he'd found her.

From the first time he'd seen Bianca, the first time he'd touched her, the first time he'd talked with her, he'd known. Only it had taken him this long to accept it. Now all he had to do was to persuade her. Her turn about this evening had only strengthened his desire to have her for his own. And showed him that she did not want anybody else to have him. When she entered a room, he felt her presence even if he could not see her.

If her reputation was even half true, she'd had more lovers than he, but he had strong suspicions about those particular rumors. Alex himself had never found much time for love affairs. Now he wanted to spend all day and all night making love to her. He didn't care who she'd had before, only that she was his from now on. He smiled. She was certainly skilled. He'd come in here annoyed, but she dissipated that in a matter of minutes. Seconds.

She stirred again, and this time her lashes fluttered against his shoulder as she awoke. He kissed her the rest of the way awake.

"What time is it?"

"From the light, I'd say about two. I've not been awake long, and the clock hasn't chimed yet. We have plenty of time." He went up on one elbow so he could meet her eyes. "I'm sorry I lost control."

"I'm not." She snuggled closer, smiling. "I like it when you lose control."

"But it has implications."

"Hmm. Yes, I suppose so."

This was difficult. "If there is a—result, we must marry."

"I don't see why."

Mustering his arguments, he started to list them off. "Because I will not willingly condemn a child to the life of a bastard. Because I take responsibility for my actions, always. Because—"

She touched a finger to his lips. "I'm glad you accept responsibility, but it's unlikely there will be any result. So don't worry."

"What do you mean?"

Her lips flattened. "I mean that all the time I was married to George there was never any hint of a child. It was one of the things he resented in me. He wanted an heir." She met his eyes fearlessly. "He said his mistress had given him a bastard. I checked, and yes, he had a child by her."

Alex touched her chin, making her look up when she tried to look away. "This affair was before your marriage?"

"And during." A tear leaked out of the corner of her left eye. She dashed it away with an angry gesture. "I thought I'd cried enough about that. In my innocence I thought I was the only one right up until he flaunted Lady Owen at me. I was not. He said I must learn that a man had more needs than one woman could fulfill, and that I must put up with it, as all wives had to."

Fury simmered deep inside Alex's chest, but he suppressed it. She did not need that now. "He was wrong. Very wrong."

She nodded. "From my sisters' experiences, it seems he was." The ghost of a smile flickered over her lips. "After he died, I tried to find the woman. After all, the baby was his and should receive something. But she'd gone. I couldn't find her."

"That was good of you."

"George was careless with money, so it was likely he had not provided for her. I couldn't bear the thought of any child of his going without. I don't have much to offer, but more than I'd had before."

He swallowed. "How many people have you told about this?"

"Just you. I did tell my mother and sisters that he had a mistress, though."

"Good." A docile woman she was not. He touched his lips to hers. "After George . . . ?"

Bianca stared at him until the moment of realization hit her. "After? Nobody. Not until you. To be clear, there have only ever been two men in my bed."

"But I heard . . ." Good Lord. She should be sleeping in the family wing, not here with the reprobates.

"People assume things. Because George did, they assumed I did, too." Reaching up one slender arm, she palmed the back of his neck. "So you see, there will probably be no result from what we did tonight."

He wanted to hit something. The wall or the door. How could she allow people to assume these things? "But there still could be a result."

"I—I wanted you. I still do, to be honest. I thought I'd remain a widow for the rest of my life if I could not find a man who did not need an heir. It wouldn't be fair to let a man believe that I can give him offspring when I cannot."

"You don't know that!" What on earth made her believe she would be childless? Two frantic years? Nowhere near enough. "Sometimes people are married for years before they produce a child."

She shook her head, strands of her hair clinging to the pillow. "I don't think so. I would not consider it. It isn't fair to deprive a man of his nursery."

"It is if the man thinks it's well worth the sacrifice."

"And an heir? Doesn't he need an heir?"

Ah. His uncle's news took on a fresh significance. Alex's life didn't depend on children. This frantic getting of heirs seemed ridiculous to him. "I choose my own heirs. There is no entail or condition imposed on my property. I will choose someone capable of running the business. Ownership will be divided between my sisters and my mother." And his wife, though he sensed she would not accept becoming that. Yet.

But she would.

"Soon you will meet my family. Whatever comes of the visit, they will enjoy your company."

She closed her eyes. "I won't be going. I'm sorry, I really am, but I can't give you false hope. I can't let you believe something that is improbable to say the least." She opened her eyes and stared up at him, her own stark and vulnerable. "Please believe me. I'll stay here a few extra days." She was panicking.

"No. You accepted, and I will hold you to it. Whatever else happens is up to you. Except of course for this." He rubbed his bare skin against hers. "We cannot do this in my mother's house. She'd have my hide." He smoothed his hand down her body, trying to remember every part of her. He would have to forego that pleasure at home, and he would miss it terribly. "Sweetheart, children are not essential to my happiness or my property. I don't need a male heir to inherit everything I own." He snorted. "Such nonsense. Surely everyone should have the power to leave their property to whomever they wish. I'll leave my property where I choose. To you, if you like."

At least he made her laugh. "Very well. I'll come."

He paused, gathering his thoughts. If he didn't tell her, she might shy away again. "You must not tell anyone else, but the marchioness is pregnant."

"What?" She stared at him, eyes wide and shocked. "She is?"

"She has told my uncle so. He wants us—my cousins and I— to keep our counsel for a time, until her physician gets here from London. He will confirm it, and presumably make arrangements for the birth. He swears it is his, and it could be, if it happened after he sent her lover away."

"Goodness!" she said faintly. "Maria came good. Her mother will be thrilled. Lady Rotherham, that is."

"I neither know her ladyship nor do I want to know her. You, on the other hand . . ." He kissed her. When the kiss ended, they remained close, a bare inch separating their lips. "Which means, in case you had not worked it out, that this changes nothing between us. Not that I cared to start with, but it should ease your mind."

He watched belief dawn in her eyes. "I suppose it does," she said slowly. "How very radical of you." Humor had returned to her voice. He guessed she coped with many of her troubles with humor.

He had to calm her, and assure her that childless or not, she was the only woman he wanted in his life. She would take some persuasion, but he was up to the task. That quick retreat, the attempt to back away, which he'd only just headed off, showed her mood. He loved that.

He touched the tip of her nose. "You'll enjoy the visit. Although I'm having second thoughts about letting my sisters meet you. I'm concerned they'll lead you astray. They're perfectly capable of it." That should pique her interest. "They refused to be presented at court because they said they had no interest in having a bunch of people they did not know staring down their noses at them."

"They're as radical as you."

She was coming around. But he would have to step carefully until he could persuade her that she herself was essential to him, not just any child she might or might not bear.

The clock struck four. Later than he'd thought. He grimaced and rolled over to swing out of bed. "Damn. I must go. The servants will be up soon."

"Yes." She sighed, but she smiled when he leaned over her and tucked the covers around her. "Thank you."

Bending down, he gave her a sweet kiss. "I will see you very soon. If I don't go now, we'll be caught out. My valet already suspects."

"So does my maid." She gazed up at him, wide eyed, forcing him to kiss her again. "You don't seem in the least concerned."

"I want this subterfuge over."

"Goodness!"

"Not goodness at all," he said, standing up and reaching for his robe. "Merely practical commonsense. My stock in trade."

And an intense dislike of anything to do with this family, and the way they treated his mother and sisters. That would never be acceptable to him.

He left, blowing her a kiss as he reached the inner door.

Chapter Fifteen

McMurdo stepped back and regarded Bianca critically. "There, ma'am. That will do fine."

Bianca barely nodded. She was deep in thought.

She cared for Alex far too much for her comfort. The visit to his family was to get to know each other better, and Lord, she needed that. The revelation that she could have a young man, one without an heir, had stunned her. She had a chance of happiness. Alex could name his own heir; he did not have an entail to his name. But the pressure on an aristocrat to produce a full nursery was little short of insane. The war had taken so many, perhaps they thought they were in danger of dying out.

She would write to her mother and her sister later today, let them know what was happening. Neither of them would rush over to see her unless she asked for their help, but there was no harm appraising them of the situation. Besides, her mother had every gossip sheet and journal known to woman, and if there was any information Bianca should be aware of, she'd let her know.

Bianca glanced in the mirror. "Thank you, McMurdo." She needed only a glance. The pink muslin had served her well for a year now, and it would work for today. In line with current fashion, McMurdo had added a ruffle at the hem, and a tiny, frilled collar at the top of her partlet. She wore the pearl brooch George had given her the day after their wedding. McMurdo had packed for a siege, and for all seasons. That reminded her. As her maid draped a scarf becomingly over her mistress's elbows, Bianca said, "We will be leaving this house early tomorrow morning. I am going to stay with Mr. Fraser's mother, since she was kind enough to invite me. The journey won't be long, so you may remain behind tomorrow to finish the packing. I will send the carriage back to collect you and the bulk of the luggage." She sighed. "I knew I was optimistic, hiring a chaise. I should have brought my own." But it was the one with the Whiston crest contained within a widow's lozenge on the door, the one that announced her presence to everyone on the road. She had not wanted that.

"If you're going somewhere else, ma'am, you could ask your lady mother to bring more clothes for you."

"I will."

"But ma'am—"

Before she could speak, Bianca interrupted her. "The journey is a mere thirty miles. We'll be there long before nightfall. Mr. Fraser will ride, I will travel in the carriage. The proprieties will be observed, and so you may tell anyone who asks you."

Alarm flashed in McMurdo's eyes for a second before she murmured acceptance and moved away to tidy the dressing table. Yes, Bianca was taking a risk, but only a small one. After all, she was a respectable widow—a semi-respectable one, at any rate— not a sheltered virgin.

The future was looking decidedly rosy. With a new and brighter outlook, Bianca left her room and made her way to the main landing, and the stairs leading down to the breakfast room.

That was when she heard the scream. High pitched, desperate, but not a feminine scream. A man hurtled toward her, his hair disheveled, eyes wild. He ran past Bianca, then turned back, facing her for a bare minute. "He's dead!"

Shock rippled through Bianca. She grabbed his arm. "Who, who is dead?"

"My master!"

Well that didn't help much. He was clearly a servant, perhaps a valet to one of the gentleman guests? The madman had run from the family wing, so Bianca let him go and headed there herself. She would get no sense out of that man. At least she knew what Alex's valet looked like, otherwise she might have panicked as well. As it was, her senses were alert, the fine hairs on the back of her neck still bristling.

The house was still full of guests. Whose valet was that? Who was dead?

Alex stood outside the marquess's room, his face pale. The door to the chamber lay wide open. When she ran up, he put his hand on her arm. "Don't go in there."

She did not have to go in. She could see inside without that.

Her first thought was for privacy. This should not be open for every passerby to see, and spectators would be arriving soon enough. Stepping inside, she reached for the door.

Alex got there before her. As if he understood her intention, he closed the door behind them.

The place reeked of blood and human waste and shock. It reverberated off the walls, sent those little hairs on her neck and arms crazy again. The bed's elaborate draperies and coats-of arms mocked the man who lay in it. The covers were thrown back, revealing the gouts of blood that had spurted from the marquess's throat when his throat had been cut. Bianca planted her feet firmly on the floor, apart enough so she did not keel over.

"I told you not to come in here."

She waved him away like a fly. "I'm here now. Good God, who did this?" She kept her second question to herself for now. Why?

"You shouldn't see it. I think it's driven his valet mad."

"He certainly appeared that way when I saw him." Why were they talking in hushed voices? It was hardly likely they'd wake the man up.

The door behind her opened. Alex left her but was too late to stop the marchioness seeing the gory sight of her husband sprawled on the white sheets in a pool of his own blood.

Nobody screamed like Maria. Her piercing, high-pitched shriek was enough to give anyone in the same room with her a headache, but Bianca would forgive her now. This time she had reason. This was not a mouse or a bird trapped in a chimney.

She turned to see a man enter the room and scoop Maria up. "I'll take her to her room." He glanced at her. "Good morning, Your Grace."

Walter Norris had always been polite.

"What are you doing here?"

Alex watched them as Norris, his arms full of a marchioness in her night clothes said, "She called me back. Excuse me, ma'am." Just as if he were in her sister's drawing room.

Alex turned to her as Norris left the room with his lady. "Who was that?"

"Walter Norris. Maria's lover." No time for polite euphemisms now. "The marquess said he was not doing his job and sent him away."

The facts sounded even more disgusting when she said them aloud.

He remained silent while the clock chimed the hour that the marquess would never hear. "This could make you the marquess," she said, knowing, as nobody else did, that he wouldn't welcome the news. And knowing that this changed everything.

"We must pray that the marchioness keeps the baby and does not startle it out of her body with her hysterics. And that the baby is a boy. And her husband's, rather than her lover's."

She nodded. A movement behind them told her they were no longer alone.

Benedict Fraser swore, using several words that ladies were not supposed to know, although most of them did. He turned to murmur to someone just outside, then came into the room. "What in God's name went on here?"

"As you see," Alex said smoothly.

"My brother will stop anyone else coming in."

Alex nodded. As if to disprove Benedict's words, the valet entered through the servants' door. His hair was roughly smoothed back instead of standing on end and he was no longer shouting. "I will see to his lordship."

"No." Alex spoke in such a commanding tone that the valet stopped in his tracks. "Leave him be until the magistrate has seen him."

"You want someone else to see my lord in such a terrible state?" Tears started in the man's eyes. "How could you be so cruel?"

Alex walked toward the bed and walked slowly around it, staring at the occupant. "How many people have seen this?"

The valet sniffed and discovered a linen handkerchief in his pocket. "I found him. A maid came in and screamed, and the housekeeper took her away. So they saw him. And you, of course, and the duchess, and Mr. Adolphus and Mr. Benedict Fraser."

"Send for the butler and Mr. Villiers. They should see this. After that, you may attend to his needs. You do not have to perform the office yourself. If you wish, I can send my valet to help. He served in the military."

He was thinking fast. Bianca's mind had only just begun to work again. Yes, the heads of the household staff should witness this. And "witness" was the right word. It was highly unlikely that the marquess had done this to himself.

The valet left the room, sniffing into his handkerchief. Adolphus Fraser came in, staring at the bed, but after a moment he turned his attention to Alex. "Has anyone found the weapon?"

A pertinent remark. "No," Alex said. "It may be in that mess . . ." He waved a hand to the gory body. Because that was all the late marquess was now. A dead body.

Just like George, just like her father, whom she barely remembered.

But seeing the mess on the bed, breathing in the stink of death, Bianca sensed burning. It filled her nostrils, the stinging sensation of burning paper. She had dreamed the scene so many times. Nothing was on fire, it was all in her mind, but knowing that did not help.

The vision swam before her eyes. She reached out.

Alex caught her hand, drew her close, steadying her. "You should go," he said. "If you can bear it, go down to breakfast, tell them the news, but don't go into details. I'll arrange everything here." He leaned closer. "I'll come to you when I can."

Gently, he turned her. Alex and the Fraser brothers gazed at her as, on shaky legs, she left the room.

"SHE WENT AS white as that sheet," Benedict said. He held up his hand. "No, I mean as white as that sheet once was. Oh God, who could have done this?" His eyes glossy with unshed tears, he glanced at the bed once more.

Alex shook his head. Adolphus checked off on his fingers. "The valet, a maid, his wife, his wife's lover, anyone who was passing in the night, you . . ." He let his voice trail away as he looked at Alex.

"Why me?" Alex demanded.

"You are the heir if the marchioness's baby is a girl, or if she does not carry the child to a healthy birth. If the child is a boy, we will be the baby's guardians. You win either way." Adolphus walked to stand before Alex, meeting his gaze steadily. "It has to be said now because others will say it."

"And you," Alex said. "You win too."

Adolphus shrugged. "Of course. We are guilty in our innocence."

After puzzling over the remark, Alex gave up. Why anyone would want to make a witty remark, or attempt one in this situation, passed his understanding.

He took a moment to order his thoughts.

Instead of going to the door, he called out. "I want a footman!" After all, he wasn't going to wake anyone up. Exasperation, a totally inappropriate reaction, hit him hard. How could he cope with all this? Why should he?

A footman in full livery entered. He was wearing a black armband, which was all Alex needed to see to know that the household knew and was reacting to the news. "Has the magistrate been sent for?"

"Yes, my lord—sir," the footman replied. That slip was obvious. Alex pretended not to notice. He'd deal with that later. "The local officials have been notified, including the vicar and the constable. Mr. Villiers is on his way, and a rider has been sent to fetch the magistrate."

No sooner said than arrived. The steward burst into the room. "Is this true?" Villiers clapped a hand to his mouth when he saw the mess on the bed. "Oh, my lord, oh sir!" He shook his head as if to remove the vision and turned his back on the bed to face Alex. "Who did this?"

Alex nodded to the footman, who obediently left the room, closing the door quietly behind him.

"We need to find out," Alex told Villiers. "I expect you to make the arrangements for the announcements and the funeral. I want you to deal with that side of the business. My cousins and I will talk to the guests."

"And the marchioness," Villiers said.

Alex had never seen the man so disordered. He'd only knotted his neckcloth, instead of the elaborate folds he usually employed, and he had not shaved. "Did we wake you?" Alex asked him.

"N-no, sir. I planned to visit some tenants today. I had to change into something more suitable before I came here." He swallowed. "I had no idea I'd find . . . this." He gestured to the bed.

"Well, you cannot do that now. Please prepare the necessary documents."

Villiers spared a glance at the bed, and then looked away, shuddering. "Yes, sir. This event . . . means you are now the marquess."

"No." Alex was firm on that. "The marchioness informed her husband that she was expecting. We will send for a physician to confirm the pregnancy."

Villiers blinked. "She is?"

"She says so." No point hiding it now. The marchioness would have to declare her pregnancy to the officials in order to stake her claim in the will. Alex wanted everything made clear. No secrets now. He'd had enough of those.

"The funeral." Villiers seemed to have regained some of his usual hauteur. "His lordship must be interred in the family chapel."

"Here?"

Stonyhurst had a small but exquisite chapel. Were people buried there? He'd seen the memorial plaque dedicated to previous marquesses and their families, but these days the chapel was only used for family and servants' prayers.

"In St. Cuthbert's, in the village," Villiers said. "Naturally."

That explained why the church in Stonyhurst village was a fine one. Alex breathed a sigh of relief. Call him squeamish, but having a recently dead marquess on the premises was one dead body too many for him. He couldn't understand the aristocratic penchant for keeping one's ancestors close.

His cousins watched him dispense his orders. Once the steward had left the room, Adolphus plucked the inevitable snuffbox out of his pocket. This one glittered with tiny diamonds. He opened it and took a leisurely pinch, but he did not offer it to Alex and his brother, as he usually did. And his hand trembled when he lifted the snuff to his nose.

Alex felt strangely detached, as if none of this mattered to him. Intellectually he knew the events here tonight would have an effect on his life, one way or another, but he couldn't seem to care.

He'd seen dead bodies before. He'd even seen bloody dead bodies, and he'd cared about every one. Felt for the families, sympathized with them. But this? This death that would mean so much more to him? Nothing.

Yet.

"You're handling this well," Benedict said when Villiers had gone.

"I'm used to thinking about three things at once," Alex told him.

Adolphus walked to the bed and gazed down at their uncle. "No more criticisms about the way I dress or the money I drop on the gaming table. No more summonses to come here, never mind what I'm doing or who I'm with."

"He didn't know about you, did he?" Alex said.

Adolphus turned away, back to his brother and Alex. "He did. A couple of days ago he asked me directly if I'd ever been with a woman. I gave him a direct answer. 'No, I have not, nor do I expect I ever will.' He gave me the kind of tirade I suspect we've all experienced at one time or another over one thing or another. Basically, he wanted me to grit my teeth and get on with it, marry, and get a child. I did not answer, which he took as consent. It was not."

He raised a brow before continuing. "How did you know? It isn't the kind of thing a man announces by the town crier. Theoretically I could hang for my preferences for bed sport."

"I guessed, but I assumed it was none of my business, so I did not ask you until just now."

Adolphus nodded as Benedict stepped toward him, but Adolphus merely patted his shoulder without looking at his brother. They were the sort of brothers who could communicate without words, unknowingly displaying their closeness by silent communication now.

"I suppose one of us must stay here, at least until our uncle is put to rights and the officials have arrived. What will we tell them?" Benedict said.

"The truth," Alex answered. "And nothing more."

"Yes, nothing more." Adolphus said. "There will be speculation. The magistrate and his associates will want to question everyone and trample over our privacy. The marquessate will be known for one thing only, unless we sort this out quickly."

"Sort it out?" his brother asked.

"Discover who is responsible for this," Adolphus said. He lifted his arm and gestured to the bed. Even now he had elegance, as if it was inborn. "Find the murderer and get him or her convicted and hanged. Anything less, anything that leaves matters open to speculation, will leave us vulnerable."

Cold common sense. Nothing more, but the words sent a chill through Alex, the first emotion he'd felt since he'd seen the body. Nevertheless, Adolphus was right. "Yes, we must." He paused. "It is just possible he could have done this himself."

The words fell like a stone into the silence.

Adolphus cleared his throat. "Yes. Men have cut their own throats. We should send for a doctor to view him and give his verdict. As soon as we can." He swallowed. "I'll stay here for a couple of hours to ensure nobody comes in who should not. You two should get some breakfast. I had something in my room earlier."

At his words, Benedict's stomach rumbled. He raised a shoulder in a half shrug. "The living are always hungry," he said, and led the way out of the room.

Alex thought he'd become accustomed to the smell of death, but the untainted air outside hit him in a rush.

Two burly footmen stood outside the door. Alex paused to speak to them. "Nobody is to enter without the permission of the Messrs. Fraser or myself. Clear?"

They bowed and murmured agreement. Alex paused to add another warning. "If anyone offers you a bribe to let them in and you accept, count your position lost. And you will not receive a character."

"Bribes?" Benedict said as they went down the stairs.

"You think they wouldn't?"

The aroma of bacon gave Alex's stomach a preparatory turn of hunger. Benedict was right. Life went on.

Except, when the footman threw the door open for them, they entered a scene of chaos.

The large round table held a number of half-finished meals, but nobody was paying any attention to them. Alex nearly turned and left, but he caught sight of Bianca standing by the window, her arms around a guest who was sobbing on her shoulder. Grabbing a napkin he made his way over to her, but his progress took longer than he wished, because everybody wanted to talk to him. "Oh dear, what shall we do?" one woman wailed. Another, stony-faced, stared into space, but caught his elbow as he passed. "Is it true?"

"Yes." He didn't ask her what she meant.

"How?" she asked.

He answered briefly. "Violently. I daresay you've heard that as well. We've sent for the magistrate."

"Oh God!" Lady Broome said. "The scandal!" She held her handkerchief to her mouth.

The thought of the scandal affected her more than the death of the marquess?

"Somebody murdered him?" a male voice said from behind him.

Before he could reply, the room erupted in gossip, shouts, and people trying to make themselves heard. Of course, when all were trying, nobody could be heard.

Alex moved to block the light from the window. He would appear as a dramatic silhouette against the ironically sunny day. Folding his arms, he waited. Five minutes later he was still waiting, so he tried his next tactic. He raised his voice.

Alex rarely shouted, even in anger, but he was capable of making his voice heard over the length of the weaving room. The trick was to pitch it right. He used that skill now. "If you want to know more, you should be quiet. You have five minutes."

The sound dropped as people heard his threat. Eventually only the sound of sniffs and blown noses remained. Alex took Lady Broome gently by her shoulders and urged her into the arms of her maid. Briefly he met Bianca's eyes. She nodded her thanks and sat in a nearby chair.

No breakfast for him, then.

Benedict went to stand by the door, so the cousins bracketed the room. About thirty people stood in the room, most of the guests. Good. He would not have to repeat everything over and over again.

He'd had enough time to gather his thoughts. "About an hour ago, Lord Stonyhurst's valet discovered the body of the Marquess of Stonyhurst." Gasps echoed around the room. As if they didn't know already. "He was in his bed, and he died violently." What should he say? Fortunately, someone asked him.

"How did he die?" Lord Colmondale asked. He was a tall man with a bristling military-style moustache.

"It's difficult to say."

A few ladies gave that faint half-scream that could stop a roomful of people. A wave of high-pitched sounds that could be heard for miles.

"Murdered?" Colmondale persisted.

"What else could it be?" someone else said.

"We don't know," Alex said, taking control before everyone decided to contribute their opinion. "We should wait. A physician has been sent for. He should be able to tell us soon enough."

"What do you think?"

"Murder or suicide," Alex said quickly. "Not natural. Not the result of a duel. Not accidental." That gained him a few quiet murmurs.

"And you're the heir."

Why did they keep saying that? "As matters stand."

"So are you assuming the title?" Lady Broome asked.

"That would be somewhat premature, would it not?" He hesitated and hedged his words. Instead of giving them all the information, he kept it to: "I understand that it is usual to wait awhile before taking that step."

Murmurs of assent followed. Perhaps they'd been expecting him to take a swift move, like a tyrant of old claiming the throne. This was no throne, but Alex was very much afraid he would inherit it anyway. The marchioness had better be pregnant with her late husband's child.

Thinking of the other heirs, he added, "Although the marquess was my uncle, our families have been estranged for some time, so I never knew him very well. I had expected to get to know him better, after the sad demise of his brother and nephews."

"Waterloo took a lot of lives," Worsley said, as solemn as Alex had ever seen him.

"And the fever took as many," he answered.

Worsley nodded. "The marquess kept his son at home, would not let him follow his cousins into the army. For all the good that did him."

While he spoke, Alex watched. Most people seemed shocked rather than distraught. Most knew the marquess at a distance. From what Alex had gleaned from his visit, the marquess liked to have people around him, but he preferred to keep his distance. He would arrange a play for his entertainment and then sit back.

A distant man. Alex suspected he'd never shared a bed with his wife. Certainly not literally, and he still had doubts that they had shared anything more intimate than a kiss. Though admittedly the marquess had with his first wife who had given him his beloved son. The only time Alex had seen true emotion in his uncle was that brief moment when he'd mourned Peter.

That gave him an insight into the late marquess's loneliness. Yes, he could understand why the man would want to kill himself. With an heir on the way, he might think his work was done.

But why would he do it when he did not know the sex of the baby, or even if his wife would bring it to term?

No, that would not do. He needed to talk this over with someone. He needed Bianca.

Chapter Sixteen

BIANCA ACHED TO go to Alex. How must he be feeling? She saw the one, agonized glance when he looked directly at her, but after that he did not meet her eyes again. She busied herself as best she could, soothing distressed matrons and sending them all to their rooms. Then she went to find the housekeeper. Nobody had been in to clear away the abandoned breakfast, and as she crossed the hall she noted the absence of the servants who usually bustled around at this time of day. Housemaids should be going upstairs to see to the bedrooms, footmen to their duties at the doors and to fetch and carry.

Only a single servant, a footman in livery, stood by the front door. Nobody else, not even a guest, occupied this vast hall with its display of antiquated weapons. Antiquated but lethal. Bianca narrowed her eyes and studied the displays. Swords set out like wheels, daggers in smaller wheels. She didn't pay much attention to the guns. The marquess hadn't been shot.

She couldn't see any gaps in the display, but perhaps she didn't know the display well enough. Perhaps someone could remove a weapon and then move another over to cover the space. But would it be sharp enough?

Bianca hurried across the hall to a servant's door, discreetly set into one of the wooden panels. Without hesitation, she went through.

A short set of stairs led down to a long stone passage with a rough strip of drugget laid down the center to muffle footsteps. Here all was bustle. Maids hurried down the passage, going into rooms on either side. Bianca glimpsed a dairy, a beer cellar, and a locked cage gleaming with silver. Nobody would be polishing that today.

At the end she found a large kitchen, fragrant with roasting meat. They were preparing dinner.

A woman dressed in a practical brown gown and spotless white apron and cap hurried up to her. "Did you lose your way, Your Grace?"

"No, I don't believe so." Determinedly Bianca moved into the room. "Since nobody else is thinking of doing it, I will talk to you all. Are most of the servants here?"

She glanced around. "No, Your Grace, but it won't take a moment to call most of them."

"Do it. Mrs . . .?"

"Foxgrove, Your Grace."

"Ma'am will do."

Mrs. Foxgrove, who must be the housekeeper, hurried off. Whether she was married or not, she would be known as *Mrs.* Foxgrove.

She returned with ten housemaids in tow. They filed in like a flock of blackbirds and ranged themselves along the back of the room, where the large cupboards holding kitchenware stood. Bianca regarded them all before she spoke.

"I am only a guest here, but I seem to be the only person who can think clearly right now. I only want to inform you that your master was discovered by his valet to have died sometime in the night. The officials have been sent for and will no doubt appreciate some refreshment when they arrive. It is up to Mrs. Foxgrove to direct you as she sees fit, but since the marchioness is prostrate with grief, and in no state to direct anything, if I can help, then I will."

Turning, she left. To her mind, if the servants knew what was happening, they could help to keep this huge household going. She had never seen such a huge number of household staff. Although the body servants of the guests would add even further to the number, most of them would be with their masters.

And Bianca wanted to see belowstairs. Beneath the ground lay a warren, an extensive set of rooms that would serve as another establishment. There must be a great deal she had not seen already, but she knew better than to linger.

"Your Grace—ma'am."

Bianca turned to see the housekeeper. "Yes, Mrs. Foxgrove?"

Like her, the lady was dry-eyed. Her dark, gray-streaked hair was smoothed back under her cap, not a strand out of place. Neat and organized. Bianca liked that. "Should I make a list of the guests? Many are ordering their carriages immediately."

"Yes, thank you Mrs. Foxgrove, that is a good idea. And I am not trying to take over, it's merely that, as a friend of the marchioness, I want to ensure the house is in good order for when she feels well enough to return."

"Thank you, ma'am. Your help is much appreciated. May I ask who the male servants should report to?"

"Ah, yes. For the time being, the three Messrs. Fraser are sharing duties. So any one of them would do."

Bianca went back upstairs. At least more footmen were standing in the hall now. So were a number of boxes and traveling trunks. People were leaving in a hurry.

Considering the marquess could have been murdered, Bianca thought it very unwise to let them go, but she had no authority here. She'd only gone downstairs to ensure the servants were not panicking and were doing their jobs. Which they were, as far as she could tell.

On her way upstairs she met Alex. His face was drawn, and he looked tired. Her heart went out to him. "There you are," he said.

"Yes, here I am."

He looked around. "Is there somewhere we can talk?"

She motioned to a door to their right. "In here?"

He opened the door and ushered her into the small sitting room she had discovered shortly after she arrived. The walls were lined with glass-fronted cabinets, which displayed precious porcelain pieces used to decorate the house and during dinner. The door was small so that it could be easily secured.

A sofa was set before the window, which was barred against thieves. They sat down.

Alex reached for her hand. "The doctor came. A good man, lives in Chesterfield, but was in the village on his rounds. He certified the death and said he thought it was murder."

Bianca gripped his hand tighter. "He's sure?"

"There will have to be an inquest to ratify his opinion, but he is sure." He paused, watching her. "How are you? Can you bear the details?"

He wanted to tell someone. She'd already learned that he liked to talk his problems through. She was flattered that he trusted her enough to confide in her. "I'll manage. Tell me."

"His throat was cut. One clean cut, the doctor said."

Bianca suppressed her shudder. The last thing he needed was a weak woman in tears. "Dear God."

"Indeed. His valet is currently cleaning him and laying him out. The man can hardly see, his eyes are so swollen, but he insists on doing the job himself."

"Well, at least somebody loved him."

He gazed bleakly at her. "Yes, I suppose so."

"Murder," she repeated, then recalled what she'd seen in the hall. "People are leaving. Do you think they should?"

"Eventually. They won't leave immediately."

She opened her hand. "How can you stop them?"

"My grooms are ensuring no horses are put to the carriages. I'll try to keep them here overnight, until we've had time to think. I doubt many will be happy about that."

"They'll accuse you of being a tyrant." She ventured a smile. "Although I know you are not."

"Are you sure?" But he was smiling, too. Very slightly, but it gladdened her to see it. He lifted her hand to his lips. "Obviously our plans must change. I can't go home now. Will you stay with me and see this through?"

She blinked, not sure she was hearing right. "You thought I'd abandon you? What kind of woman do you take me for? Of course I'll stay if you want me to."

"Bless you!"

"What about the Fraser brothers? Are they staying?"

He nodded. "So far, we're in tandem. Sharing duties, working hard to ensure everything is done properly." He got to his feet. "Much though I'd like to stay here, the magistrate will be arriving soon. No doubt he'll bring assistants. I want him in and out again so that we don't have to find a room for them, too. He will contact the coroner and start the process of an inquest."

"It's all so terrible. How can I help?"

"You are helping. But . . ." He paused.

"What?"

"Would you try to speak to the marchioness?"

"Maria?"

He was right. Somebody should speak to her. Not just her maid. She needed to make an appearance sometime soon, show herself as the grieving widow. That reminded her. "What about all the legal arrangements?"

"They can wait. But I daresay Villiers is ensuring they're in order."

A vague feeling of unease crept through her. "I would see him before the day is out if I were you. Make some time."

WAS IT REALLY only three o'clock? After a light meal in her room, Bianca changed from the pink gown to something more sober. Dark blue was the best she could do. Later on, when she got an hour to herself, she'd write to her mother and her sisters, letting them know what happened. Her mother might want to come down from Edinburgh, and Viola's husband would probably want to see her if she didn't assure him she was coping well. Indeed, she was coping better than she thought she would.

Repining over what she could not change had obsessed her for the last twelve months, but no more. She had done with that. It had happened, and she could do nothing to change it. Time to get on with her life.

Bolstered by those heartening thoughts, she made her way to the other side of the house—the respectable side, although to her mind the labels the guests had attached to each wing should be reversed now. Nobody on her side of the house had done anything worse than conduct an illicit affair. Most would have witnesses to that, if necessary.

Murder! She'd mulled the word along with her salad during her brief break. Suspects aplenty to be sure, but who had the time? And the nerve? Because getting close enough to cut someone's throat took more—more *everything* than a shot from across the room.

The marquess and marchioness's apartments were past the State Rooms, the magnificent and huge spaces where the greatest treasures were kept for people to process through them in state. Nobody actually slept in the State Bedroom, a magnificent chamber to be sure, with its delicately embroidered bed hangings and gleaming, formal furniture. It was not a friendly place to sleep.

The marchioness's suite was hard by the marquess's. Both were reached by double doors, before which two footmen stood stiffly, as if on guard duty at the palace. "I'm here to see the marchioness," she told them. "Would you let her know?"

When the footmen didn't immediately obey, she lifted her chin, and looked down on the shortest one. "Did you hear me?" she said in such a mild tone that the man scuttled off immediately-ly.

He returned in less than a minute. "Her ladyship says she would be pleased to see you."

Bianca had wanted Maria to send her away. She was a coward, she admitted it, but that wailing and weeping grated on the edge of her nerves. Perhaps Maria had calmed down a little.

No such luck.

She heard the weeping before the maid escorted her through the elegant sitting room, currently strewn with clothes, to the bedroom, which was relatively tidy. Only a dusting of powder on the dressing table and seriously disordered bedcovers. Maria was in pink, like the gown Bianca had recently discarded, but hers was a frilly wrapper.

Bianca could not help but feel sorry for her.

Maria and her maid were not the only occupants of the room. Walter Norris sat by the unlit fire staring at his hands. He looked up at Bianca's entrance. Fear etched his face. Walter Norris was a delicate creature, handsome and slender. Now he looked drawn, as if he had not slept for a week. If he'd been with Maria, perhaps that was true.

Maria looked little older than a child, bedraggled and woebegone. Her childlike prettiness, marred by a storm of tears, only added to that appearance.

"Oh, Bianca!" She sniffed and dabbed her nose. "What shall I do?"

"You must be the marchioness," Bianca said. "The household needs you."

"And I need Walter!"

She reached out a hand and immediately Norris was there, taking it between his own and chafing it warmly. "Maria, you cannot weep so much. You'll make yourself ill."

Bianca looked around and missed something. The tea tray. She lifted a finger. "Tea," she said without turning to face the maid. "And something to eat. Bread and butter would suffice."

"Your Grace, the kitchen is in uproar," the maid said.

That was not true, but all Bianca said was, "You may do it

yourself. You know how to make tea, do you not? And how to butter a few slices of bread? Do you need me to show you?"

She waited until the door closed behind the affronted maid. Then she went to the dressing table and opened the top drawer, where she found a stack of clean linen handkerchiefs. She took the whole stack and handed one to Maria. "For goodness' sake, Maria, compose yourself."

Norris's head went up, but he said nothing.

"But he's dead! Whatever shall I do?"

She related everything to herself. In this instance she had a point, but until now Bianca had not realized exactly how self-centered Maria was.

"I've been through something like your situation," Bianca said. "I know what it's like. My husband died in similarly shocking circumstances but in the full view of London society. When you married the marquess you accepted the position of marchioness." She rolled her eyes. "Behave like one, if you please."

Instead of bursting into fresh tears, Maria only sniffed and applied the handkerchief. It had been a risk, that brisk approach, but Bianca guessed Maria had been only indulged and comforted since she heard the news. But she also had a house to run and a position to keep up.

She added something else. "What would your mother say?"

Maria sniffed again. "I've asked her to come. Sent a letter by messenger."

Oh lord, and she would find Bianca here! If she hadn't promised she'd stay, she'd have packed her bags immediately and left on the next mail coach, dignity or no. Lady Rotherham had been their friend, or so they'd thought, but her every move had been calculated to place her daughters with high-ranking men. When the Burrells had taken society by storm, she'd been kind. When they had fallen into disgrace, she'd abandoned them.

Well, if she had to face her ladyship, then she would do it. No help for it.

She handed Maria another handkerchief but noticed that she

was not as distressed as before. Maria had always been a biddable girl, eager to please. Bianca had guessed that would be the best approach.

"Walter, how long have you been in Stonyhurst?"

Norris shrugged. "A few days. He sent me away and told me not to return, but how could I have obeyed that order when Maria sent me a message begging me to come back? I returned after the first week of the house party and found Maria in the utmost distress."

Something niggled at Bianca. Had he gone willingly? He didn't seem in the least upset about it. She let it lie for now.

"And you've been hiding in the house since you returned?"

He shrugged. "This is a large house."

But well managed, from what she'd seen. "It must have been difficult," was all she said, and received another shrug as her only answer.

"I know what the marquess required you to do." No time for modesty now. "He required me to do something similar."

That attracted Maria's attention. "He wanted you to bear a child for him?"

Bianca shook her head. "He wanted me to keep his heir busy. He didn't want the title to go to him. Mr. Fraser is good enough to tutor his heir, or to take care of his inheritance while the child is in his infancy, but not to hold the title himself."

Norris made a sound of disgust. "He said that? I always knew he was—" He broke off, biting his lip.

"You can say what you like here," Bianca told him. "Only we are present. And nobody will report back to the marquess anymore." She turned to face Norris directly. "That was it, wasn't it? He was the hub, the spider in his web, in total control here."

Maria hung her head, but Norris met Bianca's gaze directly. "Yes, he was. His house, his rules. Here, he was a tyrant. He controlled everything and everyone." He glanced at Maria, but she was calmer now. "That is why he retired to his estate after his son died. He wasn't just grief stricken—he was furious. Peter had disobeyed him, let him down by dying so inconveniently."

That fit with what Bianca was thinking. Her observations, the way everything was so perfect, so carefully arranged and displayed, the way he treated her, and, she now learned, the way he treated Walter Norris and the marchioness.

"Did he choose your clothes?"

Listlessly, Maria fingered one of the many ruffles on her gown. "He gave me advice. I don't have much of an eye for clothes."

At least Lady Rotherham had given her daughters free rein with their choice of clothes. She believed in them developing their own style, she'd told Bianca once. The late marquess had kept Maria in the style of a debutante, not a married woman. Bianca had assumed they were Maria's choice, merely that Maria had no taste. The pink did not suit her pale complexion, and the ruffles drowned her quiet prettiness.

Not her decision after all. And the pink was not appropriate now. "Do you have any blacks?"

"Oh!" With a helpless gesture, Maria turned to her maid, who had reentered the room. She had garments draped over her arm. "We have a few, my lady. We may dye some more, but we should order some."

"Yes, yes, of course." Maria waved at the maid, dismissing her once more.

Bianca stopped her for a word. "If the marchioness can bear it, she should go downstairs to dinner and speak to the guests."

"Oh no!" Tears in her eyes, Maria clapped her hand to her mouth. "I could not eat!"

"You must," Bianca told her firmly. "You need not come down to dinner tonight if you do not wish it, but you should make an appearance in the near future."

"Did you do that?"

Bianca nodded. "I was—am—a duchess. Certain things are expected of me, as they were not when I was Miss Burrell. That was why I went to my husband's inquest. I was called as a witness, but since I was not there when he died, I could have cleared that up beforehand." In George's case, the verdict was accidental death. It would not be so this time.

Surely Maria, the daughter of a prominent member of the ton, would understand that. She nodded, but Bianca didn't know if she was really listening. "You should make some kind of appearance, too, Mr. Norris. You can't hide away forever."

He gave her a brief nod. "We'll come down." If he could earn his place by ensuring Maria behaved as she should, then they could keep order even after a disaster like this.

BIANCA KEPT TO her dark clothing, but she did not have much of it. She spent the hour before dinner writing letters. The first was to her mother, then to her sister Viola, and then to her brother Frank in America, and Juliet on her way home with her husband. The last two would take some time getting there, but she felt better for having written them. As an afterthought, she wrote a brief note to the new Duke of Whiston. He would no doubt be kind enough to reply. Bianca liked him. He appeared mild-mannered, but he got things done with an efficiency she admired.

McMurdo worked on her hair with a concentration that told Bianca she wanted to speak. Bianca met her gaze in the mirror. "What is it?"

"Are we returning to Edinburgh soon, ma'am?"

Bianca shook her head. "I will stay to help the marchioness, until she feels able to continue."

"In that case, ma'am, we should think of our proper appearance."

"Could we have some of the gowns I brought with me dyed?"

"Aye, ma'am. I've been sorting through a few. Mrs. Foxgrove is planning to set aside a day to dye all the garments we need. The maids must be put in blacks, too. Unfortunately that will take some time."

"Yes indeed," she said, struck. "Is there mourning for the male servants?"

"Fortunately black armbands will serve for those."

"Can you make me some black armbands? Perhaps it would be wise."

McMurdo picked up a hairpin. "I've already made a few, ma'am. We have no black clothes ready, and if we choose to dye some, they will not be ready immediately. The day after tomorrow, I'm thinking at the earliest."

"Where is the nearest town?"

McMurdo stuck the pin in and reached for another one. "Chesterfield, ma'am. It's a large town, bound to have some dressmakers and milliners. We can easily travel there and back in a day."

That sounded more promising. "You may go there tomorrow. Buy a walking-dress, two day-gowns, an evening gown, and a bonnet. We should not need more than that, because I wrote to my mother. She will bring my mourning clothes down from Edinburgh. It does not have to be bombazine, but perhaps crepe would be wise." She grimaced. Crepe was dull black, no sheen, nothing. "And, of course, all the stockings, shoes, ribbons, gloves and so on and so forth."

"You do not want to select them yourself, ma'am?"

She would be too busy keeping Maria from weeping, and lending the Frasers what help she could. "No. You know the style I prefer."

"Indeed, ma'am."

"If the clothes are too dowdy, we may discard them when we have mine. I'll just wear black armbands when we visit my sister later in the summer." No doubt, the mourners at the funeral would receive mourning jewelry. She could wear that, too.

"Yes, ma'am. I should be there and back in a day. If we can acquire a few simple items, I will contrive to make them better."

She went down to dinner half an hour early, relieved that she was not in charge of these events. She'd help where she could, but she didn't even know how long Alex wanted her to stay. Dropping the letters in the mailbox in the hall, she realized there would be nobody to frank them. "Should I pay for these?" she asked a footman.

"No, Your Grace. Viscount Broome and the Earl of Colmondale have agreed to frank them promptly. They should leave on the mail in the morning."

"Ah, that is good." They were members of the House of Lords, so they could frank letters. Not that she minded paying her sixpence, but a franked letter would most likely get better treatment, which would mean her mother and sister would hear the news tomorrow, or the day after at the latest.

She went back upstairs and to the drawing room where many of the guests were gathered, including Alex.

Someone had been busy. Black cloth hung in swags from the ceiling to cover the upper part of the walls. The flower displays had gone, replaced by somber wreaths. Bianca appreciated Mrs. Foxgrove and her maids. Their efficiency was impressive.

Alex came forward to greet her, carrying her hand to his lips in a worryingly open fashion. Up to now they'd been very discreet. "Maria is coming down."

"Well done!" he murmured with his back to the guests. Most wore darker clothing rather than black. The crow look would come later.

As he spoke the door behind Bianca opened, and by the way the guests' attention immediately moved to it, she knew Maria had entered the room. Her simple black gown, a season out of date, was better than the more fashionable dark red McMurdo had unearthed for Bianca. Maria also wore a black veil, currently thrown back over her neatly dressed hair.

Walter Norris followed behind. He bowed to the company as Bianca said, "I'm sure most of you know Mr. Norris, his lordship's parliamentary secretary. He has been away on an errand for his lordship." A few guests murmured. None bowed.

"Yes, indeed so," Norris said in a small voice. He bowed low. "Such terrible news. I will do everything I can to help at this sad time."

Dinner was the most uncomfortable meal possible. Everyone wore dark clothing, except for the younger ladies who had resorted to white. They ate, discussed the weather, the latest fashions, everything except the terrible events that had turned everything upside down. One did not discuss such matters over dinner. After, they all drank a toast to his late lordship, proposed by the most senior ranking gentleman present, Lord Colmondale. He did not look in Bianca's direction.

After dinner was an entirely different matter.

The ladies gathered in the drawing room for tea, and the gentlemen stayed in the dining room. Usually the men joined the women fairly quickly.

It was all gossip. Bianca heard nothing of interest, until Lady Broome came to sit next to her. "There is confusion in the stables. I'm told there were too many horses ordered to be put to. And that a few animals had thrown sprains, or some such. Do you think, dear Duchess, that you could prevail upon the marquess to sort the matter out? After last night's unpleasant business, I am anxious to get my daughters home. They are distressed, as you might have noticed."

She had a point, but she had to correct her ladyship on one point. "There is no marquess yet."

Her ladyship raised her brows slightly. "Of course. The older of the Fraser cousins, I mean, Mr. Alexander Fraser. The heir presumptive. You seem to be close. And in any case, you worked miracles in the kitchen. Some of those dishes were actually hot! When I asked, the housekeeper told me you'd been downstairs."

She knew it was a mistake. Now they'd regard her as some kind of substitute for Maria. "The marchioness is my friend. It was she who invited me here, and it was as her representative that I visited the kitchens." Technically, at any rate. "I saw her earlier today to console her on her loss. She was obviously too distraught to complete her usual daily duties, so she asked me to help." It was only a little fib and unlikely to be contradicted.

"Oh." Her ladyship rallied. "The poor marchioness must be devastated."

"I tried to comfort her. She is overwhelmed, naturally."

Her ladyship flipped her fan open. "Ahh. Of course, you have suffered something similar."

"Except my husband wasn't murdered."

"Was the marquess murdered, then?"

She was wading further into the mire instead of climbing out of it. "It's either that or suicide. His valet is probably still laying his lordship out. No doubt we can all go and pay our respects tomorrow when he's decent."

That was more than George had.

The men interrupted them, entering the room with their usual noise and bustle. More than usual, as several of the men were engaging in a spirited discussion as they came in. Bianca took a moment to discern between the voices, something she found difficult when she was tired.

They were arguing about the murder, because whatever she'd told the women, Bianca believed it was murder. Several looked askance at Alex, not talking to him but about him. It wasn't surprising when Alex was first in line to a fortune and a prestigious title.

He didn't come to her, so Bianca walked over to talk to Adolphus.

That was how she heard it. "Razor," and then "monogrammed." Just a murmur.

Adolphus was sitting by himself, close to a sofa containing two gossiping ladies. No cards tonight, no music, but chatter enough to drown in. He spoke to her quietly, under the voices. "There are serious problems," he said. "Something was revealed after dinner. He will need your help."

No need to say who "he" was.

Half an hour later Bianca excused herself and went up to bed.

She undressed, sent McMurdo away, and waited.

Just when she was beginning to think he wasn't coming, Alex entered through the private door. He came to join her on the sofa by the window and took her hand.

He gazed at her for a moment in silence. "There's been a development," he said. "They found the weapon. A razor."

"So he did kill himself." She breathed a sigh of relief. If a man did not use a gun to kill himself, he would use a razor. She'd read of several occurrences.

But he shook his head. "With my razor?"

Chapter Seventeen

A LEX SAW NO withdrawal in Bianca's eyes, no sense of fear at being in the same room alone with a potential murderer. Perhaps she hadn't realized yet. "It has my monogram. My valet found it missing before dinner."

"How long has it been gone?"

"Since yesterday. I was in such a hurry this morning that I shaved myself with yesterday's razor, which was still on the washstand, so Fisher had no need to find the case with the others. The set was intact yesterday."

"Oh no!"

"It makes matters a little different, does it not? Someone killed him with my razor. I did not—"

She squeezed his hand. "You don't have to say that. I know you didn't do it."

A flood of gratitude filled him. And relief, for some unfathomable reason. "Thank you for that. But in theory I could have. I had time. I left your bed just before the servants rose."

"You'd have had to be damned quick. And avoid any servants who happened to be about."

At that she evoked a laugh from him. "There is not a shred of doubt in your heart, is there?"

She shook her head. "I know you. Besides, you do not want the title. You would certainly not kill for it. Everybody knows

196

that."

He wasn't so sure. "Do they? Perhaps that was a pretense on my part."

She frowned. "How can you speak like that? You know it's not true."

"I have to. Other people will think it."

"If you didn't do it—who did?"

"Ah." He turned her hand over and traced a pattern on the palm. "That is the question, is it not? It appears that my uncle was killed, probably in his sleep, by someone unknown. Although suicide is not completely out of the question, it seems totally out of contention to me. He would not have done it. Not then, not without securing the succession, not without leaving detailed instructions. There was no letter, no orders from beyond the grave."

He'd come to that conclusion easily. Having seen the body, both before and after it was cleaned up, he was sure his uncle had not killed himself. The cut was too deep, too sure for that. He paused, breathed deep. "And whoever did it wanted to ensure I was implicated."

"That brings up another problem. He was murdered by someone in this house. And yet the guests want to leave." She stared up at him, eyes wide. "They will gossip."

"That will happen whether we let them go or not."

Her jaw firmed. He could see she had something in her mind, but what was she planning? She refused to say, even though he used his best efforts to try to get her to tell him.

Although they shared the same bed, they only slept, wrapped up in each other's arms. He'd never been so exhausted, but he still woke up as the clock tinkled the hour at four o' clock. Silently, he left for his own room.

THE BREAKFAST PARLOR was so full the next morning that they had to bring extra tables and chairs in. Usually, many people preferred to eat in their rooms, but this morning everyone was there. When Alex entered, a silence fell before conversation immediately resumed. Instead of taking his place at the table, he stood at the head and waited.

Slowly, the conversation died down once more.

Alex began the most difficult speech of his life. "You know, of course, of the death of my uncle. The doctor and I are of the strong suspicion that he was murdered." He paused, while the shocked exclamations surged up and quickly died down. "The inquest will take place on Monday, here. I have asked that it be brought forward so there is no doubt of the outcome and we can see our way ahead. The coroner and his jury will be arriving on Monday morning and setting up in the Blue Drawing Room. I would request that you do not use it today to give the household staff time to prepare."

After that, there would be no stopping the gossip.

"I'm sure you understand that I must ask you not to leave until after the inquest."

Murmurs began to circulate as people speculated. Alex waited for the fuss to die down.

Lord Broome got to his feet. "I will be blunt. The marquess was killed with your razor in the middle of the night, and you have a lot to gain by his death. Surely that would imply your involvement in it?"

He was only saying what everyone was thinking. Alex had no choice but to reply. "I did not kill him. I do not know who did."

With a rustle of silk, Bianca stood. Everyone turned to look at her. "He could not have done it. He was with me. All night."

That did evince a strong response. A shout from Lord Broome, a nervous laugh elsewhere, and gasps from everyone. Someone said, "brazen," but he wasn't sure where that had come from. How could she do that? Why? To support him? And he'd left before the servants woke. He could, conceivably, have done it.

No. He would not allow her to throw herself in the breach like that. Should he deny it, or . . .

No, he had a better idea. Without allowing himself to analyze what he was about to do, he said, "I asked the duchess to become my wife. She accepted, and we sat up discussing our plans far too late." He directed his attention to her, and she smiled, although he read the shock in her eyes. Relief flooded him. She was going along with him, although he expected trouble later.

He would not allow her to wreck her reputation. If she did not want to marry him, they could let the betrothal fade away, or she could deny him if he was arrested for the crime he did not commit.

But he wanted to marry her. Very much, though he wouldn't force her to anything. Bianca deserved her freedom, if that was what she chose.

He quickly became the center of attention for the duration of the uncomfortable meal, though nobody talked to him. Afterward, he sought her out. "We need to talk," he said.

"Yes."

He led Bianca to a small anteroom close to the breakfast parlor. It didn't matter if they were seen going into a room together anymore. Steeds and stable doors came to mind. She clasped her hands together and went to the window.

"I understand why you did it, but really, my dear, it was too chivalrous," she said. "I will be fine. We must think about you now."

"I couldn't let you do it." He longed to go to her but dared not. If she rejected him now, he'd break. Everything else he could cope with, but not that. "I know how much you long to restore your reputation."

She gave a harsh laugh. "That is gone. They've been gossiping about me for days, no doubt sending letters to their friends. I will have to learn another way of living."

"By marrying me."

"No, not that! Not just to save face!" Spinning around, she would have left the room if he hadn't made the door first.

"Please, hear me out." Until now he had not realized how desperate he was to have her and keep her. He couldn't hide his feelings any longer.

"You don't want me. You can take your pick of anyone in society. Even if Maria is pregnant and bears a son, you'll be an important man, the child's guardian." She waved her hands expressively, her passion evident.

"I want you." How much did he want her! But he saw it, he felt it. Fear. She was afraid. Perhaps she was afraid of marrying again, or maybe she was still doubtful about him. "I cannot think of anyone I want more than you."

"Me?" She stared at him incredulously, more beautiful than ever. "I'm tainted, Alex. Labeled a hussy, a scandalous woman, and I can't even give you a child. You can do better, for the estate and for yourself."

"You are not to speak of yourself in those terms!" Anger rose, close to uncontrollable. Fury, more like. "You are not any of those things." He slashed his hand through the air. "Giving me a child? Why should I care about that when I never wanted the marquisate in the first place?"

"Nevertheless, I will manage on my own from now on. I did not ask for you to make that ridiculous statement. While I have enjoyed our association, sir, I fear it must now end. I will give what evidence I can on Monday, attend the funeral on Tuesday, and then take my leave. People will think what they like, but our betrothal is destined to be short-lived. You have my sympathy."

He would have added more, but she pushed past him.

Taken off guard by her shove, he stumbled, and that was enough for her to get to the door. She left, the door slamming behind her with a finality he wouldn't accept. Couldn't.

He wanted to strike out at something, smash the vase over the fireplace that was probably worth a fortune. He'd never wanted anything more than he wanted this woman.

⟫⟫⟫✦⟪⟪⟪

"TELL ME," ALEX said as he entered Villiers's office. "Legally, what does this mean? Precisely, please." After the interview with Bianca he was in no mood for prevarication or talk of ifs and buts. He wanted the truth with no bark on it.

He could not understand why she had done that, why she had refused him. Unless she didn't love him. He had determined to wait until she was sure before he made his declaration, but that would have to go by the board now. He would not have her become the subject of vicious gossip.

But as for Alex, he was sure.

Villiers, dressed in his usual sartorial splendor, but in deepest black, looked up from his desk. An alarming pile of papers rested on it, and a vellum scroll with several heavy wax seals dangling from the edge was spread carefully in front of him. The letters patent. He'd used a few items to weigh it down.

"I'm not sure what you mean."

"The inheritance," Alex said shortly. "I need to know how it stands."

"Sir. Legally, when a man dies with an heir presumptive instead of the heir apparent, several procedures are usual. The marchioness has assured me that she is with child, but there is no guarantee that she will bear the child to birth, or that the child will be a boy. Until she is delivered, you will remain the heir presumptive."

"She has definitely told you that she is pregnant?"

Villiers winced at the directness of Alex's tone, but Alex had no time for niceties. "The late marquess informed me. To answer your query, we wait until the birth of the child. Dates are carefully recorded, and witnesses brought in for the birth. If the child is a boy, he becomes the new marquess. If a girl, the title passes to the heir presumptive. Which in this case is you."

"I know that." So he would have to wait on tenterhooks for

six months or more? If the marchioness was newly pregnant, that would be nearer seven months than six. He couldn't live with that uncertainty.

"I will not accept any child not of my uncle's get. There will be no impostor taking the title."

"The marquess left instructions that any child the marchioness bears should be acknowledged as his."

Battle lines were being drawn. Villiers clearly did not want to see Alex as the marquess. Perhaps he shared his late master's opinion on Alex's birth.

"I understand that. However, if you wish for my support, you will respect my wishes on this."

Villiers bowed his head. "It is an interesting approach, sir."

"More than interesting. I have no wish for the title, but I will not allow my uncle to perpetuate a fraud on his heirs." He considered. "What happens if the child is a boy and was definitely fathered by my uncle?"

Villiers continued. "I can inform you that the marquess intended for you to be the guardian of the child, together with your cousin Benedict. Neither of you can legally act as trustees."

"Not Adolphus?"

"He did not like Mr. Adolphus and was afraid his extravagance would get the better of him. But Mr. Adolphus would act as mediator if there was a dispute, and he would have the final vote. You would be required to live at Stonyhurst and make the child's welfare your primary concern."

Alex glared at Villiers. "He cannot enforce that. I know enough law to be sure of that."

"Indeed he could not. It is a requirement of guardianship, though. And if you agree to do so, you will be in possession of a considerable allowance as compensation."

Thirty miles from his home? It could be done, but did he want to do it? The money was of no matter. Alex was well off enough to provide handsomely for his family.

He would think about it. His main motivation was the child.

A helpless baby, left in the arms of the law? He did not set much score by the child's watering pot of a mother.

"I drew up the new will two weeks ago and sent it to the lawyer. It is duly signed and witnessed. His lordship gave me permission to inform you of his decision. He wished you to be prepared for your new role, sir. I fear the late marquess had become quite obsessive about certain matters." He laid his pen down on the groove in the stand, stroked it into place.

"And what if there is no child at all?"

Villiers opened his eyes wide and stared at Alex. "I understood that the marchioness was most definitely expecting. She told my lord a few days ago, and stated that she had not wanted to tell him until she was sure."

"Answer my question."

"In that case, you would become the marquess immediately. The only way you can be omitted from the succession is by your own death."

Villiers was such a stickler for lineage that Alex had to wonder if he cared who had fathered the baby. "This is a delicate question, Villiers, but I do not think you are ignorant of the circumstances of the conception of this child."

"Ah." Villiers glanced at the pile of papers. "You do not have to explain further. I have explored Mr. Norris's lineage, and although he is of relatively humble origins, his family has a noble ancestry going back to the reign of King Henry VIII. Does that answer your question?" Lifting his chin, he stared down his nose at Alex.

"In a way," Alex replied. "But I am *told* that for the last few weeks, Norris has been absent." He paused. "I've also been told that he was not."

"Her ladyship was so distraught at the absence of her husband's secretary that I may have given a little aid in that direction."

Ah! So that was how Norris had managed to get into the house and hide undetected. Villiers appeared to know more than he should about the affair. So a cuckoo in the nest was more acceptable than a mongrel half-breed?

"He is her friend," Villiers went on. "And at a time like this, we must keep her ladyship calm and happy. Her tantr—distress disturbed his lordship greatly, especially when we heard her news."

"When did you hear that she was with child?"

Villiers smiled. "No more than a week ago. She wanted to be sure, she said, and I can understand that."

Alex answered his smile absently. "Indeed."

Villiers had the way events had unfolded laid out neatly, except they both knew it hadn't happened that way.

They'd sent Norris away so he couldn't be accused of being the father. That had not quite worked, but they would pretend it had. No doubt Villiers could present some handy records that could be slipped into one of those damned folders. Or a letter from his lordship, stating that he was the father of the child. Alex wouldn't be surprised in the least if that one surfaced.

"I doubt I can live here permanently, but of course I will look after the child, if required." Whether it was the marquess or not. "Perhaps he or she can come to live with me."

"In Sheffield?"

It was worth it to hear the outraged tones of the steward. "Yes, why not? Surely where the child is has no bearing on his birth." He warmed to his topic. "This is a showpiece of a house. Beautiful, but with no heart. I have no desire to live here. I have a home, a place where my family lives in comfort and happiness. If I have a child one day . . ." That phrase gave him pause. Yes, he wanted children. With a certain woman who was the jewel of his heart. "I would rather bring that child up in a place of joy rather than a lovely museum."

Mausoleum would be a better word. Especially today.

"We will discuss that in the fullness of time, sir," Villiers said. "I have no doubt about it."

"Neither do I," said Alex, foreseeing many hours ahead of

boredom and controversy in equal measure. "Now let us talk about the other possibility. What if I am convicted of murdering the marquess?"

Villiers got to his feet. "I have no opinion on that matter, sir."

"I'm asking about the succession, nothing more. I did not murder him, but innocent people have been hanged before."

"In that case, sir, barring a posthumous son from the marchioness, if you were tried, convicted and executed for murder, you would still inherit the title, but after your inevitable death, the title would go to your cousin Mr. Adolphus."

Of course it would.

Chapter Eighteen

THEY WOULD BURY the marquess next week, on Tuesday, after the inquest on Monday. Whatever the result, the marquess would be buried. Bianca would stay until then.

Several people made arrangements to leave, but she did not concern herself with that. Except to make lists of the guests here and put symbols of her own devising next to them to indicate the likelihood of them murdering the marquess.

She had spent last night alone, the door to the sitting room and the door to the corridor outside both firmly locked. She could only blame herself for pushing Alex away. Less than a day had passed and already she missed him terribly.

It was better this way. He had too much to cope with. He needed better than a disgraced duchess who could well be unable to bear children. And at the moment, he needed all his wits about him. She would support him, no doubt about that, and even keep up the pretense of a betrothal until any danger had passed, but that was all.

Her confession that she'd spent the night of the murder with him, effectively providing him with an alibi, was all she could do to help him. And for that, the betrothal must stand. For now.

But she had effectively confessed to being one of the scandalous set, a wicked widow. So that would be her new reputation, and she would have to cope with all that brought. The roués would flock to her. The other guests avoided her now. Not obviously, but none sought her out, and they did not stop to gossip with her, only with each other.

Until Lady Broome approached her. "My dear duchess." She offered an insincere smile, a mere tightening of her mouth. "I have not congratulated you on your betrothal, although to be sure you will be coming down in the world. But once a duchess, always a duchess."

Hearing the congratulations pierced Bianca's heart. But not the sentiment after. "Thank you, Lady Broome."

What did she want?

"I do not wish to expose my daughters to the rigors of a funeral. I understand the marquess is to be laid to rest after the inquest. I cannot believe that my girls are needed for that, so I wish to leave."

"Indeed, ma'am. I believe Mr. Fraser is making arrangements." For an orderly retreat, or a retrenchment. Bianca thought of her list. Lady Broome and her daughters featured very low on that scale. "The decision is not mine, so you would be better served speaking to him directly."

"I would rather not."

"Why not?"

"I recall his trick of using his provincial accent. He deceived us all, and it was a cruel thing to do."

"People tend to underestimate anyone with a regional accent. He had no way of knowing what he could expect here, since his uncle had cut his father off, so he came prepared."

"And why did he do that? Why did he not cut off Adolphus's and Benedict's father?"

"Because his youngest brother did as he was told. Alex's father had the effrontery to marry a woman the family considered inferior, and then the presumption to make a fortune of his own."

Considering the conversation at an end, she went downstairs.

In the breakfast parlor, she received the information that Alex had eaten early and gone out to the stables. The room was full of people, mostly in traveling clothes. And yes, the discussion was in equal parts about the marquess's demise and the accent Alex had used for most of his visit here. Both for and against. Bianca reflected how Alex would not care for their opinion, would probably smile and laugh about it. She did not, at least not to their faces. And a pang went through her when she recalled her current lack of the intimacy she'd enjoyed so much with him.

Most guests were declaring their intention to leave. Bianca took no part in the discussion except to repeat what she'd already said upstairs to Lady Broome.

Fortunately, she'd brought her list of guests with her, and she'd find him wherever he was. Dealing with their personal situation would come later, if there were any dealing left to be done.

She found a straw hat and went outside, disdaining gloves. If she got freckles, who cared? Not her, that was for sure.

As the sun bathed her face in glowing warmth, she lifted her face to it, enjoying its friendly blessing. She would be good to herself, she promised. In future she would take more time to savor those special moments that happened at random. They were the reality of life, not this damned treasure house and the people who squawked and flapped inside it.

She felt the gravel crunch under her feet, savored the faint scent coming from the rose garden as she walked past, enjoyed the sound of the trees rustling over her head as she got to the little wood.

A glimpse of dark brown moving among the trees showed her where Alex had got to. Not the stables, though she presumed he might make his way there eventually. Had he come here for some peace? As she turned to leave him to his solitude, he called her name. Softly, but her first name. "Bianca!" She went up to him, but not too close. "Did you want me?" he asked.

That was so full of double meaning that she didn't know how to reply.

He looked up. Had he been watching her all the time?

"I have a request from Lady Broome. I said I would talk to you about it."

"Let me guess. She wants to leave and take all her daughters with her. She's welcome to."

She smiled. "I thought you'd say that. I'll leave you to your peace."

"You don't disturb it." His soft voice took her back to nights soaked with passion. But she had finished that part, now. She shouldn't go back. "Stay awhile. It's so pleasant here."

Yes, it was, and he enhanced it. "The weather is improving."

"Hmm." He didn't seem inclined to discuss the weather but gazed up and around before his attention returned to her.

Hastily searching for something to say, she hit upon something as she moved closer. "I made a list."

"Oh?" His left eyebrow winged up.

"Of all the guests. I've been helping Mrs. Foxgrove. The marquess's death left the household in disarray, especially with the number of guests here. So I have a copy of her guest list, the bedrooms they slept in and so on. I listed the ones I thought were almost certainly not involved, and the ones that might be. So you could release the ones who aren't. It could make your task easier." She was aware of speaking too fast, but she couldn't help herself. She took a deep breath. This was the first time she'd really talked to him since she had told him her decision. The recommencing of—friendship. Going to bed with him had been a step too far. But she still liked him, respected him. She just had to get over her aching desire for him.

Bianca longed for Alex, wanted him to hold her, to touch her, to *look* at her. But that could not be.

"That's very helpful, thank you."

A cool response, but his next was not so cool. "Will you walk with me? Let's think of nothing, just enjoy the sunshine for a while."

That was the most seductive thing she'd heard in days. How could she refuse? But as she nodded and stepped forward, he cried out and lunged at her. They went down heavily on to the mossy ground still damp from the morning's dewfall. Alex rolled over her, pinning her down.

As they went down an unmistakable sound rent her ears.

The sound of a shot hurtled through the grove, followed by Alex's sharp cry of pain. He slumped over her, forcing the breath out of her body.

LIQUID WARMTH GUSHED over Bianca's right side. Hot and throbbing.

Alex's face contorted with agony for a bare moment, then he opened his eyes and stared into hers. "Are you all right?"

All she could do was nod. She couldn't breathe.

"A moment." He gritted his teeth, then pushed with his hands, rolling off her on to his back. Twigs and leaves cracked under his weight. He cried out again as his body hit the ground.

She gasped, painfully pulling breath back into her lungs. Then she lifted up, pressing her palms on the soft ground.

Her heart missed a beat. His coat was destroyed from the bullet that had seared into it, a blackened tear marking its passage. Most of the blood was coming from his right side. Was there a bullet inside him? She felt sick. Had it entered his heart? There was so much blood she couldn't tell anything clearly.

She kneeled over him, tearing at his clothes until she could see the wound, dragging off her ruined gloves to get a better grip. If she didn't stop the flow, he'd bleed to death. "Don't move. For God's sake, don't move." It all depended on where the bullet was. And he could shift it with an unguarded move.

Lifting her chin, she sucked in a deep breath of cool air and tore at the kerchief around her neck, dragging it off, thanking God that she'd chosen to dress quickly and just tucked a kerchief into her neckline instead of bothering with the more formal partlet. That wouldn't have been much good.

Wadding up the fine linen, she pressed it hard against his side. As she did that, trying to ignore Alex's cry of pain, the leaves rustled behind her.

A second of terror overwhelmed her. Was it someone come to finish the job? She turned her head to see the Fraser brothers. They both had hunting rifles in their hands. That did not help stop the fear clawing at her throat.

She moved so Alex's head was hidden by her body—an instinctively protective gesture. Only then did she notice that their shotguns were cracked, open and unloaded.

"Dear God!" Adolphus said, while his brother shouted, "Over here! Help!"

They dropped their shotguns on the ground and knelt by Alex's side. "What happened?" Adolphus demanded. "No, silly thing to say, ignore that." He tore away his perfectly tied neckcloth. "Use this." He tossed the fabric to her.

"It's gushing, not spurting," she muttered. "There's a lot of blood but we have a chance if we can stop the flow." She grabbed the length of cloth.

"We heard the shot," Adolphus said, "but it was the cry that brought us. 'That wasn't a rabbit,' Benedict said to me, and we ran."

"Wasn't it a shot from your guns?" she asked. When she'd seen the men holding the weapons, her immediate fear was they were about to kill her, too, but then they'd come to help her. She was in no state to refuse help, wherever it came from.

"No. We got a few rabbits, but we didn't reload our guns after the last two. We'd decided to go back to the house. Sent the servants ahead with our haul. But we heard the shot, a bit to the right of us." Benedict put his hand on top of hers, increasing the pressure on the wound. "We can't do anything else until we get him back into the house."

"Did you see anything?"

He grimaced. "We didn't look."

Alex groaned. Then he swore, quite comprehensively.

Benedict gave a low whistle. "Impressive." He glanced up. "I'll run to the house and get help."

He pushed past a woman moving into the clearing, no doubt alerted by the sound of the shot and ensuing commotion.

Lady Broome screamed. "Oh God! I think I'm going to faint!"

"Fall backwards, please," Bianca said. "If you fall over him, I'll kill you myself."

Lady Broome edged around the small clearing. Her feet shuffled around while she gasped and exclaimed. Nobody had the time to tell her to go.

Since Benedict had already gone for help, all they could do was staunch the bleeding until help arrived. Adolphus tore off his coat, then his waistcoat, so quickly that most of the buttons popped off. His shirt came next, the gold studs falling disregarded to the damp ground. The knife that was part of his hunting kit was put to use when he sliced the shirt, tearing it the rest of the way to provide extra wadding. The next strips he tied together into quick, firm knots. "If I lift him, can you get the end of this under him?"

She saw what he was about. They would have to transport him, but they needed to staunch the bleeding before they could do that.

Throwing Adolphus a darkling glare, Alex muttered, "I can do it."

"Best you don't, old chap. Using your admittedly impressive muscles would increase the flow. Let me."

Who would have thought the elegant, slender Adolphus was so replete with muscles that he could lift the bigger and heavier Alex? Which he did most impressively.

Another surprise came when Lady Broome knelt on the other side of Alex to Benedict. "I'll help," she said through gritted teeth. "Apologies, but I never could stand the sight of blood. And there's a lot of it." She shuddered. "But I can't stand by and do nothing."

Good for her.

Adolphus lifted, and Lady Broome supported. They helped to hold Alex up while Bianca wound the improvised bandage around the pads, pulling it as tight as she could.

Alex was still alive. He was alive and talking—mostly swearing now as Bianca tightened the bandage. Let him curse all he liked. The longer he stayed awake and alert, the less chance that this was a killing wound.

Bianca pushed her hair out of her eyes. Her bonnet lay somewhere behind her. "That's the best I can do."

Lady Broome, as disheveled as they were now, pulled off the ribbon tying her hat. It was a long, silk one. She offered the hat to Adolphus who ripped off the ribbons and provided Bianca with another tie to hold the makeshift bandage in place.

Bianca kept Alex's attention. "Please stay awake. Don't move. We need you to keep going until we get you into the house." She murmured to him, kept talking. "I'll do anything you want if you just do that."

He quirked a brow. "Anything?"

"Well, yes."

He winced and sucked in a shallow breath. "Best I don't talk," he said, but he kept his gaze on hers. "Don't go."

Shortly after, Benedict returned, with four footmen. They loaded Alex onto a door the footmen had taken off its hinges and lifted it. When he reached out, she was there to take his hand, and lay it gently on his stomach. "Don't go," he repeated, his voice thready now.

"That's for me to say to you. Don't go."

He held out his hand again and threaded his fingers through hers. "I promise," he said.

"Then so do I."

Chapter Nineteen

T HEY HAD AN audience waiting for them at the house. When Bianca turned to thank Lady Broome, the woman was already halfway up the stairs, her maid in attendance. The others stood around murmuring and watching as the footmen brought Alex in on the makeshift stretcher.

Adolphus took both her hands in his and faced her. "I'll be back as quickly as my valet will allow. He will no doubt have a breakdown when he sees what I've done."

His humor made her smile. In these circumstances she'd thought she would never smile again.

"I'll go with Alex." Her voice sounded rusty. It was full of unshed tears.

"Wait," he said. "Let his man do his work. Fisher was an orderly in the army. I've just ordered a doctor sent for. See to yourself, wash and change before you go back to him. You have to ensure your own health if you want to look after someone else."

He was right. "Yes. I'll go and change." She needed to look after herself while Alex was being cared for, otherwise she wouldn't be able to nurse him.

She longed for a bath, a luxurious wallow in hot water, but she didn't have the time for that. Instead, she stripped and let McMurdo wash the blood and mud off her, before putting on a gown in dark green. Unusually, she played no part in the dressing ritual, only urged McMurdo to hurry. The maid completed her task in silence, leaving Bianca with her thoughts.

Once restored to respectability, Bianca went to Alex's room. Two men not in livery stood outside and bowed to her. One of them opened the door for her. Wondering, she went inside and heard the door close behind her.

Only one man stood by the large bed containing Alex. Due to their positions, she couldn't see Alex until his valet stepped aside.

She gasped. Alex was sitting up in bed, dressed in a voluminous nightshirt, propped up by a mass of white pillows. Not a trace of blood remained on him. "What?" she said, dazed. She'd thought she'd find a gory scene of lifesaving, not this orderly room.

"You did well, if I may say so, Your Grace," Fisher said. "If not for you, he might have bled to death." He glanced at Alex and then back at her, far too cheerfully for her liking. "The wound was relatively minor but caused significant blood loss. It went across his right side, just below the lung. It missed his gut, thank God. Unfortunately, Mr. Fraser has cracked a rib, but I believe it will heal cleanly given rest and good food. I have tended to the wound, and I will dress it again tomorrow."

"Mr. Adolphus Fraser said you were in the military?"

"Before I came to Mr. Fraser's service, I was an orderly in the army. I learned how to deal with battle injuries wounds, wounds such as these." He sounded so calm.

"Oh, thank God!" She wanted to touch Alex, to convince herself he was in no danger. As she reached out, he took her hand. "Who are those men outside?"

"Two of my grooms," Alex said. His voice was soft but steady.

"What are they doing there?"

"They are guarding me." He reached his free hand out to her, but winced and pulled it back. "I do not know who I can trust in this house, so I'm using my own servants."

"He is weak, Your Grace, and needs rest, but I daresay he'll be much better in the morning." Fisher added.

Alex turned back to Bianca. "I have desired them to allow nobody but you in here." He produced a key. "This opens my side of the sitting room door. The servant's door is also secured."

"Why?" She was only just beginning to catch up. Her emotions had overwhelmed all other concerns.

Alex exchanged a glance with his valet. "Because somebody tried to kill me today. Now they know they failed, they could well try again."

Of course they had. Of course that was it. "I thought it might have been an accident."

"No, you didn't," he said softly. "That was no accident, and you know it."

Normally Bianca would have accused him of a vivid imagination, but not now, not today. It would be foolish to ignore what happened or put it down to an accident. One person in this house had been murdered, so why not another?

"We have to work out why, and what we will do about it. Until then, my servants are insisting on guarding me. And I rather agree, at least until I feel better."

Only an hour before he was bleeding to death, and now he was plotting. She had to wonder at that. Her head was still spinning, and her anxiety once more spiked to a high level.

"I'm relieved," he said as if he knew what she was thinking. "At first, I truly thought I was dying. Just in case, I have now sent several instructions to my business manager and a few others. Most importantly, after Fisher made fun of me for imagining I was at death's door, I dashed off a letter to my home, to let them know I am wounded, but recovering." He grimaced. "I wager that won't stop my mother hurrying to my bedside."

"A lot of people are planning to leave." She could hardly stop them. "A few are staying for the funeral. I'll ask for them to be prepared for new visitors."

He nodded. "In any case, we know where to find them if we

need them." He paused for a moment, then continued. "I've been thinking about what happened today," he said. "I have tried to recall everything."

"Go on," she said, trying not to let her voice quaver.

He laid back, resting his head against the stacked pillows. "I moved to talk to you, and that was when I saw it. A glint, that was all. Metal. Shouldn't have been there. So I moved, and as I pushed you I heard the click as the person cocked the hammer. I saw him, but only a brief glimpse. A man."

"I didn't even see that," she said softly.

"I only saw that he knew what he was about. This was no more accidental than the other."

His uncle's death.

"Somebody," said Bianca slowly, "is trying to get rid of the heirs to the estate."

"All the people standing between him and the inheritance," Alex added. "So it is a man."

"You thought it might be a woman?"

"I didn't discount it."

After all, a sharp razor was not a difficult weapon to use, and many women could fire guns. Including Bianca herself. But he'd seen a man.

She gasped, put her hand to her mouth. "Not Adolphus? He was so helpful!"

Alex groaned. "I remember. But we can't count him out. He and his brother are the immediate beneficiaries of the marquess-ate if I die. Or they might be in danger, too."

Bianca shuddered at the reminder. "I can't believe he did anything."

Alex continued. He was still lying on his back, half propped up by the pillows, staring at the bed canopy. "Neither can I. But he and his brother were carrying guns. Out hunting."

"They bought back some plump rabbits," Fisher added.

"But they do have to be under suspicion," Bianca agreed with Alex.

Alex sat bolt upright, eyes wide. "The marchioness!"

"Oh God!"

Bianca sprang to her feet. If Maria was pregnant with the heir to the estate, she was in danger, too.

Alex closed his eyes. "Oh God. I am so damned weak."

The valet moved to the door. "I'll see to it, sir."

"Take the two grooms outside and lock the door behind you," Alex said.

Bianca watched Fisher leave the room and heard the key turn in the lock. Still staring at the door, she murmured, "I don't like this."

"Who does?" he said. "Come here and talk to me instead."

She forced a smile as she turned around. The last thing he needed was for her weaken. "We'll find who did this," she promised.

"I know we will."

The image of him flashed through her mind as he was that morning, soaking the soft earth beneath him with his blood, his eyes closed, his breathing harsh and labored. Not this man seemingly at his ease, not a speck of blood on him, dressed in white, lying on white pillows. Beneath the nightshirt he was heavily bandaged. She could discern the lines of the linen wrappings.

"You pushed me down, away from the shot."

"Yes, I did. And I'd do it again."

"Chivalrous!"

"Not at all." He paused. "Come here. Climb up beside me. On my good side. Then I won't have to strain to see you. And I do like looking at you."

That touch of humor was back.

His bed was an old-fashioned high one, so she had to use the step at the side to climb up next to him. She smiled at him, lost in his eyes, as always. "Better?"

"Much. Now lie down with me."

If that was what he wanted, then she should do it. Humoring

a sick man, and all that. Careful not to get too close, she lay down, bending her elbow and resting her cheek on her hand, so he could look at her without strain.

She pulled the sheet and single blanket to cover over them both, all they needed in this mild weather. "You should sleep," she said.

"Are you going down to dinner?"

"I suppose I should. I'd prefer to have it up here. It seems a long time since breakfast."

He smiled. "That's your tension lowering and your appetite recovering. I'm glad."

"How about you?"

"Fisher made me eat some broth. But perhaps if you order your dinner served up here, you could sneak some solid food to me." He laughed then stopped abruptly. "God, that hurts!"

"You could have been killed," she said, as the realization slowly sank deeper into her being.

He ran his hand over her shoulder. "But I wasn't. I've told Fisher to tell anyone who asks that we'll know better how I am in the morning. I want time to rest and think."

"They will ask," she said. "And if I don't make an appearance, they'll ask about me, too."

"That's easy. Tell your maid to tell them that you're shocked, but unhurt, and you're resting."

"Hmm," she murmured. "Perhaps I should."

THEY WOKE AS Fisher was drawing the curtains closed. He smiled on them indulgently, before he said, "I ordered dinner sent up to the sitting room, Your Grace."

"Oh my goodness!" Bianca bolted up, rubbing her eyes. "I never meant to sleep!"

Sleepy, she was adorable, her hair in her eyes, smiling at him.

He badly wanted to kiss her, but he held back. She wasn't ready for that kind of affection yet, not with someone else present. But she would be. The way she looked at him in unguarded moments assured him that he'd made the right decision. He wanted her, and for the rest of his life.

"How long have we been asleep?" she asked.

"Not long. A few hours merely. Strain and shock will lead to fatigue and sleep, Your Grace," Fisher said. "I came across many men only mildly injured who could not stay awake. Sleep is a great healer."

"I wish it healed a wound completely," Alex grumbled. He eased himself a little, moved.

"Sir, if you will permit, I will contrive to help you up and into a robe. It will do you no good to stay in bed all evening."

Groaning, Alex eased up, forcing back his cry of pain as his rib sent a shot of pain through him. "I suppose you're right. Will you meet me next door?" That to Bianca, who was swinging her legs over the side of the bed. Fisher obligingly put the step under her feet.

"I should go down to dinner," she said. "But I won't."

"They'll bombard you with questions," he commented. "And we have not decided what to say yet."

She went through to her bedroom. The two men waited until they heard the bedroom door close. "You should have the certificate in a day or two, sir," Fisher said, as he crossed the room to the powder room. He came out bearing a blue banyan. Alex preferred to dress plainly, but his nightwear was different. The banyan displayed a flamboyance that made him smile, the pattern of summer leaves and vines vivid against the dark blue.

He cautiously edged along the bed, supporting himself on his hands as he sat up and swung his legs over the side. After ten minutes he did not want ever to remember, he was in the banyan and supported by Fisher as they shuffled across the room. "This is ridiculous," he muttered.

"You could use a Bath chair, sir."

Alex swore at him.

The sitting room was empty, the enticing scent of roast chicken filling the air. Slowly, they reached the armchair set before a table, and Alex lowered himself into it. "Lord!" He took a few breaths. Not too deep, because that hurt. Everything hurt. Fisher said he thought the rib was cracked rather than broken, and a few days' rest would see him well on the road to recovery. Alex didn't have a few days. He had to make himself mobile as quickly as possible. "We'll try your strapping technique later."

"If you have healed sufficiently."

"I thought you said it was just a graze." He glared at his valet indignantly.

Fisher continued, unperturbed. That glare could fell a foreman at twenty paces, and yet it had never affected Fisher. "It is, sir. The bullet carved a furrow over your side, cracked your rib in the process and went on its way. But it did not pierce any vital organs. You will be stiff and sore for a few days yet." He beamed at Alex. "You did magnificently, sir. I thought you would need the Bath chair."

"At least I'm spared that indignity."

Fisher stepped back. "Everything is within reach, sir. When you need me, ring the bell by your side."

"The inquest is on Monday," he said grimly. "I want to attend that."

Whatever came of all this, Alex's situation would change. One step closer to the marquessate meant he had to take his responsibilities seriously. Even more so now. The thought did not cheer him. But he was alive and had every chance of recovering from this injury. For the next few days he would be vulnerable, though. Much as he hated it, he would have to be guarded. And he wanted Bianca with him, because she needed guarding, too.

"Do you think the duchess is in danger?" he asked abruptly.

Fisher frowned. "If someone is trying to eliminate the heirs to the title, the duchess is safe. Unless you marry her, which you have told everyone present is your intention." Fisher straightened his jacket, tugging at the hem.

Everything in him revolted at that. While he knew Fisher was right, Alex did not want him to be. But if he married Bianca, any children they might have would be legitimate heirs to the title and would take precedence over his cousins. Who may or may not be guilty of anything. Damn, what a mess!

"So we have to find the killer, and do it right quick," he said. He would not have Bianca tainted by any accusation of immorality. He knew how much that hurt her. "This man wants the murder of the marquess pinned on me and then to have me conveniently silenced with an 'accident.'"

"That seems the logical conclusion," Fisher said.

Alex leaned back and then stopped as pain lanced through his side. He sat up again.

"Someone did not want the scandal of a murder trial," Alex said.

"Or the chance that you might be acquitted," Fisher said. "There is only the evidence of the razor, and anyone could have stolen it. When the duchess said that you were—with her all night, that weakened the case against you considerably."

"So whoever it was decided that I must die, and if she died with me, that was not unfortunate."

Fisher nodded. "Until we know who this person is, we cannot assume that she is entirely safe."

"Broughton," Alex said.

"Very well, sir. I will inform him. But you only brought six grooms with you."

"And yourself."

"Yes, sir."

The door to the other bedroom opened, and Bianca came back in. Her maid had restored her to respectability, but not to ducal grandeur, which Alex liked. Her hair was drawn back from her face softly, and her gown was a plain one. And not black, or a dark shade, but a pale apple green. "You look wonderful," he said.

"Thank you."

There, the duchess was back. But not for long, as she accepted the seat Fisher held for her with a smile, and then turned that smile on to Alex. He felt better for it.

"May I help you to your dinner, sir?"

Despite longing to be alone with Bianca, Alex was in no case to serve her—or himself for that matter. But the meal was simple, only four dishes graced the table, and after Fisher had efficiently portioned it out, he left them alone.

"An unusual valet," Bianca commented after her first mouthful of rabbit pie.

"Hmm. He came to me after being invalided out from the army. He was in the Rifles, a regiment that moved fast, sometimes in enemy territory. He had to think fast, too. He came from a family who knew my butler."

She raised a brow. "This Fraser family who lives so simply has a butler?"

He tried not to laugh because it hurt. "We're not savages."

Bianca laughed for both of them. She took a sip of the crisp, white wine before going back to her dinner. "I didn't think I'd ever be hungry again."

"Neither did I." He didn't think he'd live until dinnertime at one point. But Bianca, aided by Adolphus, had saved him.

He touched his napkin to his mouth. "Recent events, even before the marquess's death, have made me realize that my life must change. I will be appointed guardian to a baby worth a fortune, or I will inherit that fortune and status myself." He grimaced. "I will do what I must."

Bianca had her doubts. "In some ways the guardianship is a harder task, because nothing is as certain. And the marquess's death brings you one step closer to the title."

He sighed. "I know. Though I'm not sure what kind of mother the marchioness will make."

A bright thought entered the gloom. "Do you think she will marry Walter Norris now? He's a steady sort."

"We must pray that she does. I agree with you—he's likeable, intelligent, and quick-thinking. He also keeps the marchioness calm. I don't know if it's her condition or if she was always so volatile, but any agitation is bad for her at such a time."

"She's always been moody," Bianca said. "I'm beginning to think that the whole scheme to marry the marquess and keep Norris on was not her idea after all."

"Cynical." Alex began to lean back, then changed his mind. Instinctive actions were most definitely not advisable. He needed to recover his strength as quickly as possible. He couldn't afford to be laid up at a time like this. Fisher knew how to get men on their feet quickly after injury.

"Extremely so. But . . ." She shrugged.

He broached the subject nearest to his heart. "Bianca, I want you to continue our betrothal. In short, I want you to marry me."

"Oh!"

She seemed taken aback. "Even though I tried to finish our—association?"

"Even so. I'm certain of what I want, but the choice must be yours. Please, Bianca, think about it. I need you more than ever now." Remembering her doubts, he added, "If the marchioness is with child, then that takes some of the onus from you. From us."

"But you will still want children."

He couldn't deny that. But if he had to choose between Bianca and no children, or another woman, he knew without a doubt what he would sacrifice and what he would not.

Before he could tell her so, a knock came on the inner door from Bianca's side of the suite. When she called "Come!" her maid entered.

McMurdo was wringing her hands. "Ma'am, it's her ladyship. The marchioness, that is. She's very distressed and asking for you or Mr. Fraser."

Bianca exchanged an alarmed glance with Alex, then turned back to her maid. "Do you know what the problem is?"

"Apparently she objected to the footman Mr. Fraser sent. She said she would not be constrained in that way, and she wanted to see you at once."

"Did she now?"

Bianca got to her feet, tossing her napkin on the table. "I'll go."

"Not alone," Alex snapped, then calmed his tone at her raised brow. "I will become extremely agitated if you are wandering around the house unescorted, and that isn't good for me."

Bianca relaxed. She smiled. "Of course I'll take someone."

FISHER PROVIDED BIANCA with a groom called Moreton. Like the others, he was powerfully built and wore simple clothing rather than livery or anything fancy. Bianca thought of several people of her current acquaintance who would benefit from being a little less fancy as well.

He was obviously not trained in deportment or light stepping. As she walked to the other side of the house, he clumped behind her, making her feel like Jack from the fairytale being pursued by an angry giant. But if Moreton was angry, it was not with her. He stepped before her to open every door and accepted her smiles of thanks with a slight blush. Bianca found his reaction charming.

Tension tightened her stomach as they approached the wing containing the marquess and marchioness's apartments. She could smell death, mingled with the heavy scent of lavender furniture polish. The tops of the cupboards were festooned with clove-studded oranges, obviously put there to eliminate any lingering odor. Perhaps the smell wasn't there anymore, just lingering in her mind.

Only time would dull her memories and the clinging stink of death. The sooner she discovered what Maria wanted, the sooner she could get out of this part of the building. And back to Alex.

A maid waited outside Maria's door, together with another bulky manservant who nodded to Moreton. Another of Alex's grooms. He flung open the door.

The wailing hit her the moment the door was opened, only getting worse when Bianca went in. It sounded almost inhuman. Maria lay prostrate on the floor, drumming her clenched fists on the carpet, crying and screaming like a professional mourner. What had happened here?

She looked around. Norris wasn't there, which was a pity. Only a frazzled maid, cap askew, hair all over the place trying to lift her mistress from the floor.

Maria's face was puffy from crying, her complexion blotchy. Bianca hurried forward. "Oh, my dear girl! Get up, do!"

While she had no sympathy for the situation Maria found herself in, Bianca would have to be made of stone not to respond to this distress. "Come on." She helped Maria up, taking one arm while her maid took the other. Together they hauled the marchioness to her feet and on to a nearby chair. She sat there like an old doll, whose stuffing had become lumpy.

"I want to die!"

"No, you don't. You have everything to live for." What had thrown her into this fit of distress? It was not mourning for her husband. Neither was this tantrum brought on by her not liking a groom outside her door.

Wait . . . surely Maria had not killed the marquess? That would certainly explain her depressive decline. Fear, regret, terror at being found out. But if she had done it, then Norris must have been involved. Maria had been confined to her bedroom yesterday. Besides, she didn't have the wit to devise such a cold-blooded plot.

But was she involved? Did she know? And why? Could it be because the marquess had sent her lover away? Bianca supposed that would give her enough motive.

Sighing, Bianca handed her handkerchief to Maria. There was no doing anything while she was in this state.

Alex said he'd seen a man. But Maria could have dressed in men's clothing. Or—it could have been someone else. Norris. Oh,

God, this was terrible.

Bianca set herself to calming Maria down. Grabbing a cloth from the washstand, she waved it at the maid. The woman went to a tallboy set in the corner and found a pile of them. Fortunately the woman seemed more competent than her appearance would indicate, as she took a couple to the washstand and soaked them in the cool water. Her tousled hair, loose instead of being pinned back under a linen cap, told its own story.

While Bianca dabbed at the tears, she kept up a narrative, soothing, cajoling. "Now, Maria, you know you did not do too badly. You're the most high-ranking of all your sisters, after all. And you married a wealthy man. He even allowed your indulgences."

"He's gone!" The dramatic cry stopped Bianca. She reached out for a fresh cloth. The maid pressed one into her hand.

"I know, but that can't be helped. He left you well provided for." Perhaps, though she had not seen the will.

"No, not him, Walter!"

Bianca halted in her careful wiping. Maria's tears flowed anew. "He is the only man I have ever loved, and he is leaving!"

Suspicions crossed Bianca's mind. She lifted her hand, and behind her back beckoned for her guard. Taking a moment away from the sobbing woman, she turned her head. "Stop him," she murmured.

Moreton nodded and went out. Bianca had no doubt that he would do it.

Turning back to the marchioness, she managed to calm her down enough to speak coherently, although it took time and every one of the cloths in the stack.

Eventually she persuaded Maria to take a small glass of brandy and sip it slowly. Grasping the last of the cloths, Maria obeyed Bianca. When she'd poured the brandy, she'd noticed the decanter was more than half empty. Had Maria been tippling? She retired early most nights. Bianca had assumed she'd done it to be with her lover.

The woman needed a serious telling, and since there was nobody else to do it, Bianca took on the task.

"Maria, you are a fortunate woman," she began, softly enough.

"No, I'm not."

Bianca turned her attention to a fine French clock which adorned the mantelpiece, together with its matching porcelain vases. "You are surrounded by luxury. You have everything you could desire."

"No, I don't." Maria sniffed, but she'd turned from distress to sulkiness. "All this means nothing."

Bianca smiled wryly. She might have the superior rank, but not the wealth that should accompany that title. "It's not nothing. You have no conception of what nothing really means. Do you miss your husband?"

"God, no!"

The instinctive response was honest and direct. So there was a woman capable of telling the truth under all that fluff and self-delusion. "But he was your husband. Did he mean nothing to you?"

Her shoulders hunched, Maria dabbed her cheek with the cloth before she answered. "*I* only meant one thing to *him*. And when I failed, as he put it, he had no use for me. That's what he said. He said he would send Walter away for good."

Now Bianca wished she had not sent Moreton away. If Maria was about to confess, she wanted more than a lady's maid as her witness. "When was this?" she said softly, steadily.

"The night before—the night before it happened. He came to see me here. Said I must obey his commands. Only . . . only Walter came in."

"And he'd sent Walter away, had he not?"

Maria nodded, scrunched the cloth into a tight little ball. "He didn't know Walter had come back. So I told him I was expecting."

She'd told her husband she was pregnant in order to keep her lover? Infamous!

Maria grimaced and handed her empty glass to Bianca. "More, please."

Bianca ignored the request. That amount of brandy would have left her dizzy at the least. Maria did not appear affected at all. But she'd had enough strong spirits, especially with a child inside her. "I'll get you some tea and something to eat. You have to look after the baby."

"What baby?" Maria said. "Don't you understand? There is no baby! There never was! But I had to stop him sending Walter away. Don't tell anyone, Bianca. I want Walter back! He'll know what to do!"

Ten minutes later Bianca was storming back to her room. She went through into the sitting room. Empty. Without hesitation, she continued into Alex's bedroom.

He was sitting up in bed, studying a sheaf of papers. After taking one look at her face, he put them aside. "What is it?"

"Maria isn't pregnant."

Alex swallowed. The movement created shadows on his throat, cast by the single branch of candles beside the bed.

"So, my lord, you are the de facto Marquess of Stonyhurst."

She swept a deep, graceful curtsey.

Chapter Twenty

As if enough had not happened today. Now this. The information and its import sank slowly into his head. This would mean a new life, a new existence. He could not ignore the reality any longer, now the slim chance of the marchioness being pregnant with her husband's son had been snatched away from him. And from her, he reminded himself.

"Is that why she was so distressed? Has she lost the baby?"

"She was never pregnant. She said it to appease her husband when he found her with her lover. She'd already told Norris she was expecting his child. To keep him with her, she said. Because he would not abandon a child."

"It sounds as if he was leaving of his own accord."

"It does, doesn't it?" She still stood at the entrance. She glanced around. "I should not have rushed in like this. I should have let you rest."

She seemed abashed. But he'd rather know quickly. Like pulling teeth, quick and sure was the best way. "Not at all. Thank you for letting me know." He indicated the papers. "In any case, I wasn't resting."

Bianca took a step closer. "It could've waited. You're well-guarded, and you need to sleep. Where is Fisher?"

He waved to the powder room, his gesture more careful than usual. "I forced him to get some sleep, otherwise I'd have no peace, either." Using his good side, he pushed up to a sitting position. "Come closer. Will you lie down with me as you did before?"

She took another step closer, but shook her head. "Not tonight. I agree with Fisher. You need your rest."

"I sleep better when you are here." That was true.

"Not tonight." From that firm tone, he knew he wouldn't persuade her. He wanted to know why and feared he knew. He would spend the remainder of the night working out how to get her back. If he had to beg, he would, although he wasn't very good at it.

"Will you stay at Stonyhurst?"

"I will, until the inquest and the declaration of your inheritance."

"Until we find the murderer?" he pressed.

Bianca bit her lip. Nodded. "Yes."

"You know I want you to stay longer. That will never change. I will always want you, Bianca."

She didn't react, or at any rate he could not see his words reflected in her face. But then, she'd had practice at not revealing her inner thoughts. He wished she'd drop that barrier with him. At her most relaxed, her response was everything he could wish for. She wasn't ready yet, too skittish, too reluctant to admit what lay between them. If he declared himself too passionately, he could lose her forever. For now they were betrothed, even if it was only to save face.

"And you're sure about the baby? The marchioness isn't lying again?"

"Yes, I'm sure. I don't think she's lying. She wanted her lover back when he threatened to leave her, and she wanted to appease her husband." Bianca sighed. Knowing her as he did, Alex knew her own situation was in her mind. Maria would not have thought of it when she made her confession. Too concerned with herself to worry about anyone else.

"She may be the target of a killer, now that she is admitting the truth," he said. "Yes, that rings true. And in all honestly, I can't blame her for that. It puts Adolphus and Benedict in more danger as well."

"If they are not the perpetrators."

He nodded. "Yes, that." Closing his eyes, he let out a sigh. "Are the footmen back outside my room?"

"Yes. I put a footman from the household outside Maria's, since most people still think she is expecting."

He gave a shaky laugh, careful not to let it disturb the bound rib. Later he'd try an unaided turn around his room. "I'll do everything possible to get back on my feet."

"You should rest. You nearly died, Alex."

"At least I know you care." He laughed again and grimaced in pain.

"Take your time. You need to gather your strength. Promise me you won't force your recovery. A broken rib is not something to take lightly, and you lost so much blood . . ."

"Not so much," he said, trying to soothe her. He would achieve that so much better if she would come closer. "And Fisher thinks the rib is cracked rather than broken."

"Still . . ."

"Yes," he said. "But I feel better. The loss of blood was the main problem, and the danger of infection."

She paled. "I never thought of that."

He smiled, trying to reassure her. "Fisher did. He changes the dressings with monotonous regularity, but he says there is little danger of infection now." He heaved an exaggerated sigh. "Though he keeps changing the dressings."

She bit her lip. Was that worry over the danger of infection or something else?

There was only one way to find out. "What is it?"

"Oh." She came closer. "Well, you see, I had a thought. Several. Are you sure you're feeling all right?"

"I'll be worse if you don't tell me." He patted the bed.

She took another step to the bed, used the stool and climbed up to sit on the edge. "Well, could Maria have done it, or got Walter Norris to do it? Her husband, I mean, not you."

"So you're suggesting there are two murderers in this household."

"Possibly." She paused. "The second perhaps encouraged by the first one."

"Hmm. Why would she do it?"

Bianca met his gaze. "Because she was not with child."

Understanding crept into his mind on stealthy feet. "Yes, I see. We can't discount that, can we? But would she take a razor to him?"

She paused, frowned. "No. But Walter might."

"If he loved her."

Her mouth flattened. "He gave up a promising political career for her."

He nodded. "People change their minds." He picked up the piece of paper from the top of the pile on the bed and handed it to her. "This was delivered five minutes ago."

My dear Mr. Fraser,

You will be the next Marquess of Stonyhurst. I have done you great wrong, or tried to, and for that I apologize with my whole heart. I consoled myself with your reluctance to take the role, but that is not the point, is it?

I will relieve you of my presence and return to London.

Walter Norris

She looked up. "Ah. But he doesn't say that he does not love her."

"He does not. It was brave of him to admit that deception, but we cannot excuse him from suspicion. If the marchioness is complicit, he is too. I had Fisher send a groom to get him back. He can't have gone far."

"I sent Moreton after him, as well. Maria was in hysterics when I arrived at her rooms, but it wasn't because of her husband's death. It was over Norris leaving." She glanced at the note. "He must have written this before he went to see her. Probably had a horse waiting at the stables."

He nodded. "I want to know more. You solved one mystery

for me. The marchioness is not with child, was never in that condition. That explains the cryptic nature of his note." He waved it. "I couldn't make sense of it at first. Unless he was the killer, of course."

She frowned. "Although I wouldn't have thought it of Walter. He's a clever, quiet man."

He needed this woman. He had to woo her back. "We think alike, we are in accord."

She met his eyes, and he sent her all the warmth in his heart. "Oh."

"So what do we do about this problem? I want Norris back, not only to keep him under my eye, but to answer the questions about the marchioness, since I doubt we'll get a straight answer out of her."

"You think she lies?"

He nodded. "Indeed I do. I don't think she knows she's doing it, in a way. She gives the answer she thinks the questioner wants. But for what it's worth, while we cannot discount the possibility, I don't think she or Norris had anything to do with either murder. Their motives aren't strong enough."

She thought, biting her lower lip. "I see. Yes, I see. She might have murdered the marquess out of impulse or panic, but this murder could not have been done that way. Would she have been so afraid of him that she would kill him?" She raised her gaze to his. "Is that what you mean?"

"Exactly."

Bianca swallowed. "I see." She had never thought of getting rid of George like that. Not once, even when he was flaunting his latest mistress all over town. "What would drive a person to commit murder?"

"Jealousy, avarice, love . . ." He shook his head. "I would say the extremes of those emotions, but sometimes you can meet a person who you think would kill another without even thinking, if another person got in his way."

"Have you ever met someone like that?"

He nodded. "So have you." At her raised brow, he added,

"Adolphus."

"What?"

Asked to explain why, he had to think. Instinct had to be backed by reason. "He is the coolest I've ever seen in a crisis. He shows no emotion, ever."

"He has to conceal much of what he is."

She meant he preferred men in his bed. That had not even occurred to him as a reason, but it might explain the way he covered his inner self so carefully. "Yes, he does, but that's not what I mean." He made a sound of frustration. "I can't put my finger on it. I've met someone like him before, and once I remember who that was, I'll have it."

Her smile warmed him, but a wave of fatigue washed over him. "I'm tired, Bianca. I need to sleep now."

"Yes of course." She made to slide off the bed, but he tightened his grip on her hand.

"I'd love you to stay with me. I do sleep better with you near." And she would be guarded along with him. While there was no practical reason to guard her, he did not feel comfortable leaving her on her own.

"No, no I can't."

He took a moment to enjoy her. While her beauty had no bearing on the way he felt for her, not anymore, he couldn't deny that she was purely beautiful. "We are still betrothed, don't forget."

"We don't have to do that anymore."

"Yes we do," he said firmly. "I don't want you to become the talk of the town again for all the wrong reasons." There was only one way he wanted their betrothal to end, but these lesser concerns might ease her into continuing. "And while we are betrothed, it is not unacceptable for you to nurse me." He didn't need nursing, but in any case he was in no state to do anything other than sleep tonight.

She paused, frowned, pursed her lips in thought. "Would that help you?"

"Immeasurably."

More than he could say.

Chapter Twenty-One

"DARK DAYS," LADY Broome said at breakfast on Monday.

The Broome carriage stood outside, or rather, their line of carriages did. One for her and her husband, one for the daughters, and one for the luggage and their personal attendants. Each carriage was drawn by four horses, with outriders. Bianca had seen them from the window upstairs when she'd paid a quick visit to Maria, in a vain attempt to get her to eat something.

"Indeed," Bianca agreed. Unlike Maria, she was making a hearty breakfast. She would need it.

"If you wish us to stay, then of course we will, but I do not see how we can help. We'll only get in the way." She forked up a helping of scrambled eggs and took a deep drink of tea before she spoke again.

"It's not up to me," Bianca reminded her. "I am staying to give evidence to the inquest, if they wish it, and support the marchioness at this unfortunate time."

"And care for the marquess."

So the word had spread. Lady Broome would spread it further.

"Indeed."

"How is he?"

"Resting. He is recovering well." She'd left him with his valet. "Without your aid that might not be the case."

"I couldn't stand by and do nothing. However, when you return to town, you owe me a walking dress."

She'd have given her ladyship ten walking dresses if she'd wanted them. "With the greatest of pleasure."

Lady Broome smiled. Under that aristocratic, gossipy hide lay a practical, kind heart. "Mr. Fraser must take care, though. There is always the danger of infection. That has carried many people off." She sipped her tea. "I'm sure you will ensure his health. Do I congratulate you, even though you will be trading your title for a lesser one?"

Bianca had to work hard not to laugh. "Rank isn't everything."

"It is something, though. But I venture to suggest that the Marquessate of Stonyhurst has more potential than the Dukedom of Whiston. No doubt you'll have a full nursery to complete Mr. Fraser's happiness."

This was painful. What she wanted was not what was good for Alex. As it stood, he needed to produce that heir after all. Her heart broke, for him and for her. Especially after the last two nights when they lay together. That simple act of sleeping without making love had brought them closer together. They talked, shared childhood experiences, favorite foods, favorite colors. All the small things that made up real life.

Yet again, she made up her mind to let the betrothal die. But it was so hard to do! She must not allow him to declare himself for real. She knew he wanted to, and the foolish part of her longed for it. The romantic part of her, the part she'd killed when George had betrayed her with another woman.

Lady Broome leaned closer. "The marchioness appears stricken by her husband's death, but I understood the union was an arranged one. It seems somewhat strange to have her so affected by his sad demise."

"I expect the manner of his demise was one factor," Bianca said, but added, "However, your supposition isn't wrong. Poor Maria is dreadfully overset by so many things!"

"Ah yes, I thought so. Her mother had her eye on Langston, until your sister snatched him from right under her nose." Lady Broome smiled in a conspiratorial way. "That was not an arranged marriage, was it now?"

"Certainly not," Bianca said.

Her ladyship nodded. "They are returning to England soon, or so I heard."

"The treaty is done," she said, knowing that as far as her diplomat brother-in-law was concerned, he preferred discretion. The treaty was being trumpeted in the newspapers, though, so she was safe speaking of that much. "His future plans depend on the government." He was coming home, but she did not know how far that news had spread. Lady Broome could well be fishing for information.

Bianca would not have made a good diplomat's wife, but Juliet was a roaring success. Or a whispering one? Diplomats rarely roared. Either way, she was the perfect wife for him, where Maria would never have been.

As if she'd summoned the marchioness, Maria appeared in the breakfast room. "Appeared" was the right word. She was shrouded in black crepe, the non-reflective, heavy fabric that must be overheating her in this weather. She also wore one of the fashionable Tudor style hair ornaments, which had a heavy black veil pinned to it. As everyone turned to look, she lifted the veil.

A pale complexion and red-rimmed eyes, together with the headdress gave her the appearance of Mary, Queen of Scots. All she needed was the neck ruff. If someone suggested it, she would certainly adopt it, since the whole of her clothes shouted her state. But if she needed it in order to appear, Bianca would not begrudge her that.

"Ladies and gentlemen," she began in a thready, hoarse voice. "I am so sorry that I have not been much here for you for the past few days. But my husband . . ." She produced a black-edged white handkerchief, a lovely contrast to the black, and dabbed her eyes. "It was a shock. But you have sent me such touching messages, I felt obliged to thank you in person this morning."

Who had persuaded her to do this? It was the right thing to do, albeit with an extra helping of theatrical state, but when Bianca had seen her last she would not have believed Maria would leave her apartments this month. Maybe this year.

Bianca was answered when a familiar figure appeared in the doorway. Possibly the only person who could control Maria: her mother. Lady Rotherham nodded to Bianca but kept her attention on her daughter. Though they were not the best of friends when Bianca had last seen her, relief flooded her now.

"Dramatic!" Lady Broome murmured. Bianca was inclined to agree. She'd had no idea Lady Rotherham had arrived.

The gentlemen stood, and Lady Rotherham deigned to accept a place at Bianca's table. Her daughter sat next to her, and accepted a plate of food from a footman, although she did not attempt to eat it. Lady Broome greeted her contemporary with regret that they would meet so briefly. She was going to Chatsworth, where the Duke of Devonshire was holding a house party. "Do you go, Duchess?" Lady Rotherham asked Bianca.

"I have promised Mr. Fraser I will stay here and render what help I can."

"Her Grace has recently become betrothed to Mr. Fraser," Lady Broome told Lady Rotherham, who leveled her lorgnette at Bianca. She did not have to say anything. Condemnation was clear on her face. But her daughter spoke first.

"The marquess," Maria mumbled.

"I beg your pardon, my dear?" Lady Rotherham said frostily, turning her lorgnette on to her daughter.

"He is the new marquess," she repeated in a louder tone. Too loud.

"Yes, he is," her mother replied firmly, as if she was placating a child. "We must wait for the formalities to be concluded, but Mr. Fraser is the new marquess." She glanced at Bianca. "So your fall from grace will not be as precipitous, will it, dear Duchess?"

The last word sounded like an insult, and Bianca was sure it was meant to be so. If she knew Bianca did not intend to go through with the marriage, she'd be delighted. So she would not tell her. "I do not consider rank to be the ultimate definer of quality," Bianca said.

Lady Rotherham wagged a finger at her in such a parental attitude that Bianca was immediately offended. Her own mother did not treat her in that way, so why should somebody else's? "I never thought I'd hear a Burrell say that." She smiled in a patronizing way. "You came to London to trap a title, did you not?"

"No," said Bianca, thoroughly tired of this conversation. "We came to be presented at court and to meet a few gentlemen. That is all. Society did the rest." Nettled, she added, "Were we supposed to refuse anyone with a title?"

Lady Rotherham shrugged. "You were fortunate to attract so much attention in a quiet year."

Adolphus Fraser, who was sitting at a nearby table, came to Bianca's rescue. "Perhaps they recognized quality when they saw it."

Lady Rotherham heaved a sigh. "Of course," she said. But she had planted a few questions in the minds of the people present, who would then transmit it to the places they were visiting. The country house set might be more scattered than London, but news traveled fast. Her smile when she turned back to Bianca was sugary. "We must congratulate you on your good fortune, my dear. I have not heard of this Mr. Fraser."

"Yes, you have," Adolphus said. "He's the Midas of the North."

Her ladyship pursed her lips and for a brief, delirious moment, Bianca thought she was going to whistle. But no. Her eyes sparked interest. "And he is the marquess's heir? How extraordinary!"

"He is in effect the marquess," Bianca said softly. "But of course he will wait for the requisite amount of time."

Lord Severn, also sitting at the next table, sniggered. "When he arrived he used a distressing turn of speech. However, it seems that it was all a hum and he speaks like any other civilized man. A joke on all of us." He glanced at Bianca, as if to say, "except you," but he didn't voice the words. Bianca was grateful for that, at least. That was all the gossips here would need to propagate yet another misleading story about her.

"I assume then, that he is a gentleman."

"He appears in the clubs occasionally," Adolphus continued. "I do not think he has ever thrown himself on the mercy of the marriage mart. Now he doesn't have to."

Bianca hated this. Hated it. She'd wanted a quiet life, but by her reckless action when she'd stood up and said she had spent the night with Alex, her fate was set. She could not back away this early. And the last two nights when she'd slept next to him had consolidated her feelings about him. But it could not be.

"Where is your brother?" Lady Broome asked. "Does he not eat?"

"Gone to the stables," Adolphus said with a dismissive wave of his hand. "Try to keep him away. But he's adept at charming food out of the kitchens, so he probably ate early."

A few of the guests got to their feet. They were probably eager to be on their way. Chatsworth was not far away, and several people were heading there, the next house on the circuit.

Bianca had not received an invitation from the Duke of Devonshire. Not unless it had gone to Edinburgh.

Most, however, stayed put. They probably expected a show at the inquest.

THIS WAS NOT the first inquest Bianca had attended, but at least she would not be the center of attention. McMurdo returned from Sheffield the night before, even though, as she said, she was not accustomed to traveling on a Sunday. She brought what

Bianca needed to appear in mourning, and a few other items. McMurdo had done well to find items that would fit Bianca's tall figure, and for the inevitable shorter skirts, she added ruffles. "I bought some fabric and black lace, ma'am, so we can change the garments a little. I only bought three ready-made gowns, but if needed, I can make others."

"Impressive," Bianca said. McMurdo had taken Bianca's taste for simplicity into consideration. And her preference for fine materials. She had purchased everything Bianca would need for a week's deep mourning.

"I expect to leave off deep mourning quickly," Bianca said, "at least in private. I expect my mother will arrive soon with my mourning wardrobe, and more gowns." She paused, glancing at her reflection. "It would be unmannerly to appear at another house in deep mourning, so I will not require it when we visit my sister."

She watched McMurdo arrange a veil on her head, arranged over a large comb, Spanish style. "Put it back, please," she said. The maid drew the veil back, so that the spotted net fluffed over her hair. McMurdo's skill was impressive. She looked every inch the duchess. But under all the finery, she was still Bianca Burrell, the poor girl from Ireland.

Alex was to be the Marquess of Stonyhurst. He could take his pick of all the women society had to offer. Most would not care about his mother's origins, or his involvement in trade, not with the title and the wealth at his command. She could take nothing for granted. She must never forget that their betrothal was a temporary one, for convenience. But it was getting harder every day. She wanted him. She was close to using the word she privately swore she would never use again. Love.

Love was not for her. Not anymore.

INQUESTS HAD TO be held in public, so she had no idea if the locals would attend. She guessed they would. When she went down to the blue drawing room, she discovered she was right. They'd chosen that room because it was a good size and closest to the front door, which today was thrown wide open. People filed up the stairs, some stopping to admire the display of weapons in the hall. Several glanced up when Bianca appeared, and that murmur she was so used to hearing started up. It was like being back in London. She had not missed it.

She recognized one of the footmen showing her into the room. Alex had dressed his grooms in the Stonyhurst livery. A claim and a warning, she guessed. And to her, acceptance. He would be the marquess, and knowing him as she did, he would be determined to make a good job of it.

The gracious drawing room had been converted to a court. All the normal furniture had gone, replaced by plain desks and benches. The jury sat on a dozen kitchen chairs.

The coroner sat at a desk at the head of the room. She went forward and sat with Adolphus, who was similarly attired in black, but of the highest quality. A glance was enough to assure her of that. He leaned toward her. "I always carry at least one mourning outfit. Besides, gentlemen often wear black coats."

That was true.

"You look astonishingly beautiful in black," he added. "It's your color. Such a pity you can only wear it in situations like these. Perhaps you should contrive to always be in a place of death."

Bianca caught her breath. "At the expense of my happiness," she suggested.

"Some people would be delighted to be in the presence of death."

This was too close to what she was thinking about this house. One death, one near-death. Who was next?

Someone behind them cleared their throat as if to warn them. Adolphus slanted an eyebrow. "I thought I'd left school years ago."

That was exactly what it felt like.

Another murmur set up and this time she could discern words. "Marquess," "Fraser," and even "Sheffield" rippled through the crowd. And one murmur of, "I thought he was at death's door." Alex took notice of none of it, but let them look as he walked to sit next to Bianca. If that was not a public demonstration of attachment, she didn't know what was. Since she'd agreed to continue with the betrothal, she supposed she should have expected it, but it made her uncomfortable.

Alex looked every inch the gentleman. His black coat was closely fitted to his powerful frame, his neckcloth, black for this occasion, perfectly tied. He wore pantaloons and Hessians, a sign of the changing times. He crossed his legs and stared ahead, but he touched her hand, just grazed it, before resting it on his knee. That touch was enough to acknowledge their connection. Heat warmed Bianca's cheeks. That was a public acknowledgment.

Then the widow entered, suitably shrouded in black, a heavy veil covering her face. She leaned on the arm of her mother, who was also dressed in a black shroud.

"You're looking remarkably well, sir, considering the . . . circumstances," Lady Rotherham commented to Alex as they took their seats. "Are you sure you are strong enough for this ordeal?"

He gave her a bland smile. "Perfectly, madam."

But this meeting was not about Alex or Maria.

The coroner, one Mr. Sidebotham, banged his gavel on the table. At least it wasn't one of the French ones from the music room. The thought crossed her mind in the few minutes it took the room to quieten down.

He started the preamble. She'd heard it before, only with different names. Her emotions shot straight back to the previous time, her sense of guilt because she had not been there, her confusion, the public excoriation and exoneration, both at the same time. She'd borne it all with as much dignity as she could muster, and now she found herself in a similar situation.

This coroner stared at his documents rather than at the audience, until he'd droned his way through. He managed to make a shocking, violent death sound boring. Quite a gift, for a coroner.

At last he looked up. "I call the first witness. Maria, Marchioness of Stonyhurst, please take the stand."

Bianca would say this for Maria: she knew how to behave like a marchioness when it suited her. Supported by her mother, she sat on the chair provided for the witnesses, and let her mother lift her veil. She was completely white, the only color in her face in her pale blue eyes and pink button mouth. She drew a breath and folded her hands in her lap.

Her evidence was clear and short, duly recorded by a man scribbling notes on the other side of the coroner. She had not been there at the time of her death. At the question "Do you have a separate bedroom?" Bianca had to admire the lifted brow and response, "Of course I do. Doesn't everybody?"

The coroner tried again. "Is your bedroom close to the late marquess's chamber?"

"Fairly close, yes."

"Did you hear anything?"

"No."

That more or less concluded the evidence from Maria. But her story was now a matter of record. Naturally, she did not mention Norris, and the coroner seemed not to have heard of the convenient arrangement.

The marquess's valet was called. At least he wasn't sobbing into his handkerchief. He did describe the way he discovered the body in lurid terms, which gave the spectators an agreeable shudder or two.

To her shock, the coroner called her name.

Alex stood and helped Bianca to her feet, going with her to the witness's chair and standing close. He couldn't have made his attachment to her more obvious. The coroner balanced a pair of gold spectacles on the bridge of his nose. "Your Grace, you are a guest in this house?"

"I am." She already knew from her previous experience not to volunteer information.

"A guest of the marchioness?"

"Yes."

"On the day of the marquess's death, you went to his chamber and witnessed the body?"

"I did." Resolutely she put her mind away from the vision in her mind. She would never forget that sight.

"What did you see?"

"The marquess was lying on his bed. There was a lot of blood."

"What did you conclude?"

"That he was dead."

A ripple of laughter, quickly suppressed, passed over the spectators.

"Anything else?"

"I was shocked and distressed."

The coroner fixed his attention on her. Bianca stared at a spot just above his head. "Is that all?"

"Yes."

"You are betrothed to Mr. Alexander Fraser, who is next in line for the marquessate?"

Ah. So that was to be written down as well. "I am."

"Interesting that you were one of the first people to see the body."

The insinuation was obvious. Alex took a step toward her, but she held up a hand to stop him. "Are you implying anything by that remark?"

Mr. Sidebotham reddened. "It is for me to ask the questions."

"I beg your pardon, sir. So it is. But you did not ask a question."

Let him say it now. Let him accuse her of something—anything. "You are excused, Your Grace. You may stand down."

She stood down.

OUTSIDE HER BEDROOM, he paused, turned to face her.

His eyes were sparking with the anger he felt too. "All that for a verdict that was so obvious," Alex fumed. "What a waste of time."

The verdict had been Murder by Person or Persons Unknown. As Alex said, obvious.

"Procedure," Bianca said.

He gazed at her, gave a wry smile. "Of course. You've been through this before. I'm sorry, I should have remembered."

She pushed open the door. "Come in." She didn't want to stand talking to him in the corridor, where anyone could hear.

The room was empty. Immediately the intimacy of their situation struck her, but she did her best to ignore it. During the past few days she'd felt safe with him, but now, when it was obvious he was recovering quickly, awareness rippled through her.

He showed no recognition of this, but strolled in after her and chose to sit on the daybed set at the bottom of the main bed. He did not cross his legs this time. "Does it hurt still?" she asked.

"A little, but I have a new appreciation for ladies who wear stays. Fisher trussed me up like a chicken."

"Not quite," she said, the vision of a trussed-up chicken inevitably making its way into her mind, superimposed on a picture of her lover. She went to the chest of drawers and lifted the stopper of one of the decanters. He shook his head, refusing the proffered brandy, so she replaced it and went to join him.

Since the attack on him until today Alex had worn nightwear, or more casual and comfortable daywear, not this formidable formal black. With new eyes, she surveyed him. "You're every inch the marquess," she said.

He grimaced and rolled his eyes. "Please. Not yet."

"You have to get used to it sometime."

"I know. But not here, not now. It's been a difficult day for both of us." He took her hand.

That action was becoming a habit for both of them. The reassurance of a warm presence had come to mean everything to her. She loathed the idea of trying to live without it.

"Should we make a list? Do you want us to look for the murderer?"

Another grimace. "I fear we have to. Otherwise the marquessate will be overshadowed by the accusation that the heir was responsible for the murder." He shook his head when she opened her mouth to protest. "Mere proof won't do, I'm afraid. Once a rumor starts, it grows legs of its own."

Sadly, he was right. She had all too much evidence of that herself.

A knock came on the door. After exchanging a glance with Alex, Bianca went to open it. She widened the opening when she saw who was outside. One of the suspects entered, namely Adolphus Fraser.

He bowed to them both, then at Bianca's bidding, pulled up the chair from her dressing table to sit on. Unlike Alex he crossed his legs, ankle over knee. Since they showed no inclination to speak, he did. "You are in effect the marquess, and I am the heir. That is enough for us to work together instead of separately. And once you discover more about me, I'll go to the top of your suspect list. Despite the fact that in this at least, I'm completely innocent."

"More about you?" Bianca prompted. "You mean your— preferences?"

"No, no not that." The amused, slightly sly smile Adolphus usually used was completely absent. Bianca had never seen him so grave, and it added an extra facet to his character. Intrigued, she listened to him. "I am independently wealthy, thanks to a maiden aunt, my mother's sister. Although "maiden" was not the right way to describe her. Remind me to tell you about her sometime. But not today. Today is all about the murder of our uncle, and my role, or rather, my non-role in the affair." He took a moment, sucked in a deep breath. "For some time now I've been working with some shady characters in government. Sometimes my services are required, my very special services. Unfortunately, I was recruited by foul means rather than fair. The threat of blackmail, to be precise, to make my private life public."

"That's iniquitous!" Bianca cried. Alex murmured his agreement.

"I agree. I am in the process of extricating myself. I do not object to the work I do, but I will no longer undertake it under duress."

A thought insinuated itself into Bianca's head. "Have you worked with my brother-in-law?" Lord Langston worked for the Foreign Office, and before his posting to the United States, he had been involved in some murky areas of government work.

Adolphus shook his head. "Not directly. Now and again we have come into contact with each other. He worked mainly in code breaking. My area of expertise is, shall we say, darker." He paused. "No time for euphemisms." Another pause. "I'm an assassin."

Bianca felt as if all the air had been sucked out of the room. Alex gripped her hand.

"And as you have cause to know, I am in no state to defend myself," Alex said steadily.

Adolphus met his gaze directly, blue against brown. "No, you are not, and that should warn you to stay on your guard. But I have no designs on the title. Ever." The last word had an emphasis that demonstrated the truth of what he said. "I have no need of it, and should I inherit, undue attention will fall on me. It is the last thing I want." He spread his hands. "But I have no proof I did not contrive to end your existence except for the word of my brother. None, except that I worked hard to save your life, not to end it." His smile appeared again, ever so slightly. "By the time you had pushed the duchess behind you, I would have had this in your neck." Opening his hand, he revealed a slim, lethal-looking knife. It barely had a handle.

Bianca had not seen his hand move. "How did you do that?"

Adolphus put the knife by his side. "I had it in my hand all the time." He patted the blade fondly. "I do not usually carry such items in this company, but I had it today because of the inquest. Anyone could have come in."

"That's true," Alex said. "I had my men watching Bianca all the time."

"Watching is not always enough," Adolphus said. "But that particular danger is over now. Do you believe that I mean you no harm?"

"Unless you're the theatrical type who prefers to announce his intentions beforehand, I don't think you're here to kill us," Alex said.

"Not my style," Adolphus said. The smile was back. "I told you so that you would not find out another way. My soon-to-be ex-masters could use this affair as another lever to compel me to do their bidding, if the true murderer is not found. Therefore I decided to come to you and offer my services." His smile broadened. "Oh, not in the main part of my craft. But in the covert aspect."

"Answer me something," Bianca said suddenly.

Adolphus turned his attention to her and crooked a brow. "Ask away, dear lady, though I cannot promise to answer."

"Were you involved in the deaths of the last Duke of Whiston?"

Adolphus closed his eyes. Then opened them again. His gaze met Bianca's directly. "You mean the carriage accident that caused the sad demise of your husband's successor? I really cannot say, Your Grace, though you will recall the circumstances."

Bianca nodded. "I remember. No clear evidence."

"Indeed."

"I can say no more."

But that solved a mystery for Bianca. She'd always wondered

about that carriage accident. The man who had succeeded her husband to the title, a cousin, had not treated her or anyone else well. He had been strongly suspected of working for the enemy, though no absolute proof had been found. Justice had been done, though not in the most conventional way. That, more than anything, persuaded her to trust Adolphus. Besides, what proof did they have? And if Adolphus was the government assassin he claimed to be, they were unlikely to find any.

"You did not kill the marquess, or try to kill Alex, then?"

"I did not." Adolphus glanced from one to the other. A clear denial, unlike her question about the carriage accident. "But I went out that morning with my brother to do some rabbit shooting. The gamekeeper suggested it, said that the rabbits were outnumbering the pheasants he was rearing. And had the attempt on your life been successful, it would have set us up to be the main suspects, would it not? We are the heirs, and if my little hobby were to become known, I fear it would drop the lid on my coffin."

His little hobby?

"So we are both invested in discovering the murderer," Alex said.

Adolphus nodded. "I trust nobody outside this room unless you can vouch unequivocally for them. Even then I reserve the right to make my own decisions."

"Understood." Alex considered. "You may trust my man, Fisher."

"Ah yes. Excellent man." He paused. "Do you have a list of people you suspect?"

Alex sighed. "Yes, I do. But it is far too long for my liking. And people are leaving. After the funeral tomorrow even more will leave."

"Do you believe the same person committed both crimes?" Bianca asked. "Could they be separate incidents?"

Both Adolphus and Alex shook their heads. "It is worth asking the question, but in this case I think they are one and the same.

Or one person and their minions."

The two men watched each other. "I never suspected it of you," Alex said eventually.

"And yet . . ." Adolphus tilted his head to one side. "Working together, I have no doubt we will catch the villain. I recommend that you keep your doors locked until we do." He got to his feet. "I would also recommend that you think very hard about when you were shot. While it is still fresh in your mind. Go through every step, every second. Because you will have seen something or recollect something you have not remembered until now." He bowed to Bianca. "You too, Duchess. I think the key to a swift discovery lies there."

"Why did you tell us?" she asked him abruptly. "You did not have to."

He paused at the door. "I had to tell somebody. Don't forget to lock the door after me."

Chapter Twenty-Two

THERE WAS NO question of where they were going to sleep. They shared the same bed again, this time in Bianca's room. All the doors were locked tight.

"He was right about that," Alex said, as he turned the key in the lock and left it there, half-turned.

"Why did you do that?"

"What, this?" He touched the key. "If anyone has a duplicate, they won't be able to use it."

"Good Lord." She sat up in bed, her night rail a shroud of linen around her. "I would never have thought of that."

"Schoolboy trick," he said, crossing the room to join her. "I never thought it would come in useful." He climbed into bed. "I prefer this bed. Not as high as mine, nor as hard. We should use this one."

She lay down, and as if they'd been doing it for years, his arm came around her waist and he moved closer. She could not have rejected him if she'd tried. For one thing, she was sure he would have worried about her, and he needed his rest.

Although she'd happily gone without any kind of intimate contact for two years without missing it, she had to admit that she would miss it now.

➵➵➵❮❮❮❮

ALEX SAT BOLT upright. Pain shot through him, but he ignored it. As Bianca stirred beside him, he said, "I must go."

"What?" Sleepily, Bianca rubbed her eyes. He adored her like that, but even she couldn't distract him now.

He turned to smile at her. "Go back to sleep," and bent to kiss her. Life, despite its problems, was sweet. "I'll see you later."

She rolled on to her back. Never had he been more tempted to forget everything. "Do you have to go?"

"It's eight o' clock, sweetheart."

"What?" Her heavenly blue eyes opened wide.

"We locked the doors, remember? Nobody can come in. Though I confess, I did oversleep. It's too easy when I'm with you."

"How do you feel?" She touched his arm.

"Better." He smiled. "So much better." Desire stirred. He must be getting stronger. He felt much less like a weak kitten and far more like himself. Fisher had told him it would take a while to replenish the blood he'd lost, and he was right. But thanks to the swift action of the woman next to him and his cousins, he'd lost far less than he might have.

Ignoring the sharp pain that shot through him when he moved was getting easier, too. He knew what to expect. So he barely winced when he rolled to take her in his arms.

"Oh!" She opened her eyes wide when she recognized what was happening. "That seems a bit early."

"Love conquers all," he murmured against her lips. "I've missed you."

"I've been here."

He tried to prop himself up on his elbows, but the pain was too much. Sighing, he turned on to his back. "Most of me is willing."

"Oh." Fully awake now, she lifted over him. Then sat up, her body pressing against his.

He groaned. "This is perfect. You're perfect."

She unfastened the little pearl button on the cuff of her night rail, but she didn't take her gaze from his, watching him as he devoured the sight of her. He reached for her other wrist, but she pulled it away. "Tsk, tsk." She touched her lower lip with her tongue, then touched her wrist, deftly undoing the other button. "You're an invalid. You mustn't overtire yourself."

"Perhaps not," he agreed, and dropped his hand. "You're in charge."

He loved this. She took her time pulling the tapes at her neck free, then crossed her arms and grabbed a handful of material, dragging the garment over her head. He saw her body first, that delectable, mouthwatering collection of curves and delicate shades. From the deep rose of her nipples to the soft fair hair at her groin, everything about Bianca was perfect. The scent of her arousal reached him as she tossed the garment away. Her hair fell out of its loose braids, too silky for mere ribbon to hold it. "Dear God," he murmured.

"No," she said. "Just me." Smiling, taking her time, she proceeded to drive him insane.

She pulled at his nightshirt, and helped him remove it, her breasts grazing his lips as he tugged it over his head. White linen swathed his middle, but she took no notice of that, other than to pull her knee down a little so there was no chance of her touching the wound. "Nothing but pleasure," she murmured.

"For both of us," he answered.

She stroked him, explored him, circling his nipples, bending her head to taste, sending tingles through every part of him. "Have you missed me?"

"I've missed this," she confessed. "With you."

That last part meant more to him than he could ever say.

She kissed every part of him that wasn't covered with bandage. Who knew that ankles and toes could be so sensitive? All Alex could do was hold on, while she came back up and traced the length of his erection with the tips of her fingers. Desperately he wanted her to take hold, a proper grip. "Touch it properly," he said, through gritted teeth. "Hold it."

"Oh no." She came all the way up, straddling him, thighs wide. The sight of her, open to him, boldly displaying herself made him groan out his desire for her. "If I did that, you might not last."

"I need you, Bianca. Please." He was not too proud to beg.

"Yes." Her voice was little more than a whisper as she lifted up, hovered over him. Her heat scorched him, seared through to his very soul.

Then she joined them, pressing down, enclosing him in warm, wet heaven.

"Oh that feels so good!" He reached for her and this time she let him touch, grasping her waist to support her and help her move, but not to guide her. Bianca knew what she was doing, and he gloried in it as she rose and sank, each plunge driving him higher toward the inevitable peak of delight.

He had no words as they worked together. She leaned over him, bracing her upper body on her palms either side of his head, gazing into his eyes. Neither looked away or closed their lids, as their bodies heated, their concentration unbroken and mutual as they climbed the peak.

And fell off the edge, tumbling free and unfettered, trust and love combining, making them truly one.

THE CLOCK CHIMED again, but Alex did not pay attention to the time, only to Bianca as they kissed and kissed again, locked together still. He didn't want to leave her, so when she slid to one side he went with her. Even now she was careful not to touch his wound. He'd forgotten that completely as they'd made love. Only now did the familiar soreness and splinters of pain return to him. He didn't care.

His lips left hers long enough for him to murmur, "I love you."

He hadn't meant to say it like this, from impulse, but what better time was there?

Her eyes opened, stared into his. He kept his gaze steady, letting her see everything he was, all he had to give her.

"Oh." She swallowed. "I love you too."

Overjoyed, he held her tight, wouldn't let her go. "Marry me."

"I—I can't. You know it's impossible." Tears glistened in her eyes.

Alex kissed them away. "Don't cry, not now. I want you, Bianca, forever. Not just as a lover, but as my partner in life, my love, and my companion."

"But you're the marquess."

"I don't care. I am Alexander Fraser, and I will always be so. Why should I give you up for a useless title that I never wanted? You would sacrifice our happiness for that?" If she'd said she was uncertain, worried because of her previous unhappy marriage, he'd have given her time. He still would, if she asked, whatever that cost him. But not that. Not the idiotic title.

"I might not be able to have children," she reminded him.

"There's Adolphus, and after him, Benedict. After that, probably more, though we'll have to go back a generation or two. If I could give it all away, then I would, but I can't do this without you."

"You can." She smiled. "Of course you can."

"But I don't want to. It will be a chore without you. Would you condemn me to that?" To remind her of what was at the heart of this discussion, he kissed her again. And also because he wanted to.

"N-no," she said, uncertain.

"Just say yes. I adore you, Bianca, I love you to the bottom of my soul. Marry me. Make this betrothal real. Spend your life with me, let me adore you to the end of our days."

He waited, forcing himself to breathe.

"Give me time." She touched her fingers to his mouth when he would have answered. "Not long. Until the end of the week?"

He could see in her eyes that he'd pushed her as far as she would go. For now.

He kissed her, longing and loving and passion combined in one symbol of his love. Their lips parted slowly. "Never forget the single truth, the only one that matters," he murmured against her mouth. "I love you."

Chapter Twenty-Three

S HE WOULD ACCEPT him. How could she not? He didn't consider himself irresistible. If anything could persuade him that she wouldn't accept him, that would. But he'd seen it in her eyes, the responding love, the acceptance she was not ready to verbally give to him.

But she'd told him she loved him. That was the first time.

Whatever happened next, he would hold that in his heart. Smiling, he went to his room, and put up with Fisher poking and prodding. "It doesn't feel as bad today," he remarked as his valet unwound the bandages. He glanced down. "That looks dreadful."

"It's the bruising," Fisher said. "It's going into the black and blue stage. It's a good sign." He touched something and Alex winced. "That's good, sir. You could not bear for that to be touched yesterday. You are becoming more tolerant of the pain, that is true, but it's also a sign that you are mending. The wound is healing well. It will be stiff for a while, but bearable."

"I thought of making it known that the wound was worse, or that I took infection and I'm seriously ill."

Fisher stopped probing the wound, which was a relief. "Why, sir?"

"To draw out whoever was responsible for this. They might try again, you see, especially when I'm weak. Is it too late for me to succumb to my injuries?"

Fisher grunted. "Only if I were neglecting to care for the wound. It could fester then. But you would be noticing something by now. The poison could go deeper, I suppose." He picked up a rolled strip of linen. "If I did not take care." Carefully, he wound the linen around Alex's body, choosing to walk around rather than try to encircle his body.

"Then don't tell anyone how carefully you're looking after me," Alex said. "Leave that possibility open. I want to find who did this sooner rather than later, and I want all options left open until I close them."

"Yes, sir." He finished winding and tied the bandage off. "There. A little lighter today, sir."

As he crossed the room to fetch Alex's shirt, Alex gave a wry grin. "It's not really that bad, is it, Fisher?"

Fisher paused before he turned around. "Sometimes the slightest wounds hurt the most. You can't always tell, either."

A slight wound. Well, that put him in his place. Alex grinned at his valet. "I believe my mother will arrive today. When she arrives, make sure she is cared for, will you?"

"Of course, sir."

"Thank you, Fisher."

Alex enjoyed the way Fisher turned him out as a gentleman with a minimum of fuss. By the time they'd finished discussing Alex's wound and then his mourning wear, Fisher had him shaved, dressed, and ready to go. Fisher even tied the black neckcloth for him, because he knew without asking that Alex was finding lifting his arm and holding it steady awkward. But with such a *slight wound*, he would recover from that soon enough.

He left his room and stopped dead. A thought crossed his mind, the realization of something that had been niggling at him for some time. He couldn't be sure, but a closer look would help. So would consulting someone else.

The funeral was at two this afternoon. He had plenty of time.

He made his way to another room and rapped on the door.

What if Adolphus had a guest for the night? That only occurred to him now. He decided he did not care. He called out. "Adolphus, it's me!"

After a sleepy murmur from inside, the valet reluctantly let Alex in.

Adolphus was alone. He sat up in bed, his hair rumpled, looking as normal as he ever did. He waved his valet away.

He listened to Alex's suspicion. "I'll go to the office and verify it," Alex said. "But it could be tedious work."

Adolphus nodded. "We need proof."

"We still don't have any." Alex paced off his pent-up energy. "I saw him in the woods, but that isn't proof. I didn't even remember at the time. I dreamed it last night."

Adolphus grunted. "It happens like that sometimes. I don't doubt you."

Alex turned, watched the sunlight gild his cousin's sharply-drawn face. "What do we do if we can't find the proof? We can't let him get away with this."

Adolphus offered him a knowing smile. "I could use my old arts." He waited for Alex to catch him up. It took less than a second. "But I'd rather see him in court."

"If you do that, we'll never be free of doubt and whispers. This must be without question," Alex said. "I want the man brought to trial and hanged, if he is found guilty. I do not want suspicion hanging over my head for the rest of my life."

"Or the duchess's."

Alex met his cousin's guileless gaze. "Precisely."

Adolphus sighed. "I will see if I can find him, have a quiet conversation. Perhaps I can lure him into telling me more. It should not be difficult."

Despite his vaunted talents, Alex felt apprehensive. "Be careful."

"I'm always careful. If I weren't, I'd be dead."

WHEN ALEX HAD gone to his own room, locking the connecting door behind him, Bianca touched her lips. They felt the same, if a little swollen, but with his words she'd become somebody else. All her fears, all her worries had melted away. For how long she couldn't tell. Perhaps forever.

But she needed that time to let the reality sink in. With Alex, she could return to society, but not the same as before. She'd have great houses to manage again, this time with ample funds. She might even bear children, though she had set her heart and expectations against that, too afraid to let it be a possibility.

Inside, she felt Alex's certainty and knew her own, but disbelief still echoed through her mind—a lack of confidence, perhaps. Alex did not know about that part of her married life. Perhaps he would understand if she told him.

Someone tapped on the inner servant's door. Grabbing her robe, she went to answer it, and in came her maid with a breakfast tray and a bright smile. "Your lady mother has arrived, ma'am. And the new marquess's mother, too."

Bianca clapped her hand to her mouth. Lord, what would they make of each other? "Then I'd better go downstairs as soon as possible."

"I've ordered a bath for you, ma'am, but you need to let them in to fill it. If I put the tray next door, we may lock the connecting door and let them into this room."

A bath sounded heavenly.

And so it was done. It was worth making her mother wait, although Bianca half expected her to push her way in while she was luxuriating in the tub. However, she bathed alone and dressed alone. Only then, when McMurdo brought out a new fresh black bombazine gown did Bianca recall what day it was.

It was the day of the marquess's funeral.

By the time she'd done it was ten o'clock. They would be serving breakfast.

If she really cared for the late marquess, she'd be fasting, as she had for her father, but she was hungry, and four hours was a long time to wait with an empty stomach. She would not be attending the funeral—women rarely did—but she would be sitting quietly in a room with her Bible in her lap and her prayer book by her side.

Downstairs she found the breakfast parlor full of people, mainly women.

But she had eyes for nobody except her mother who stood to greet her, hands extended. Heedless of the other people in the room, Bianca embraced her. "Oh Mama, so much has happened! When did you arrive?"

"About an hour ago. I stayed overnight in Sheffield and started out first thing this morning. I had to come as soon as I saw the news. I've brought your mourning clothes, and some others. We may go straight to Viola's if you wish, or back to Edinburgh if you prefer."

Bianca hesitated. This day should be devoted to the marquess. Her mother saw something and drew back. "Have you eaten?"

That was so like her mother, who had cared for three daughters on her own for such a long time. Bianca almost smiled. "Yes, bread and butter in my room."

"We should go and talk," Mrs. Burrell said firmly. "But first, would you like to meet the new marquess's mother? I've been introduced, so I may introduce you."

Startled, Bianca looked around, and saw her immediately. Mrs. Fraser's complexion was a shade darker than her son's, but those glittering dark eyes were exactly the same. And her hair was the same rich, dark brown—all but black—the glossy length drawn back in an intricate swathe of braids and smooth locks, not a hair out of place. She was sitting at the table, gracefully disposed in a way that appeared natural but was far from it, her long fingers draped over the arm of her chair, her head tilted as she listened to whatever Lady Colmondale was telling her. She seemed perfectly at ease, but when she looked up, Bianca recognized the look in her eyes. It was the same kind of uncertainty she herself felt so often. Did everyone feel that way? Was Bianca fooling herself to think that everyone but herself knew who they were and where they belonged?

When Bianca approached with her mother, Mrs. Fraser stood. Her curtsey put Bianca to shame, and she thought she'd mastered the art. But when Mrs. Fraser curtseyed, it was less an obeisance, more a graceful display. "You know my son," she said in a deep, musical voice.

"Yes, I'm pleased to say that I do." How much had Alex told her? Would she accept Bianca into her family? So many questions raced through her head. Together with Alex's unsettling declaration of passion, Bianca did not know what to think.

Oh, she believed he'd fallen in love with her, and she had fallen deeply for him, but was that enough? It hadn't been so before.

"He has written to me." Mrs. Fraser's speculative eyes told Bianca what her son had said. "He mentioned you, and I see he was not exaggerating."

"Thank you."

"And now he is to become the marquess, or so he tells me."

Bianca nodded. "Yes indeed, after the required period has passed. It is merely a matter of respect now, since the marchioness has indicated she is not in a delicate state."

"It will be interesting to see how he copes with this change in his fortunes. I expect him to excel. He always does."

ALEX WENT STRAIGHT down to the offices. Like the family part of the house, they overlooked the gardens at the back, if overlook was the right word. The offices were partially underground, part of the old part of the house, half-buried over time. Villiers's office lay here, and the armaments room. They were all part of the old monastery that had once stood on this site. Worn out carvings in the ancient stone, unrecognizable now, marked his way. He knew them all now, familiar as his own office at the factory, if damper, colder, and not as convenient.

Alex unlocked Villiers's office. It had been modernized somewhat, paneling lining the walls and a few prints and pictures hanging there. A few stacks of paper were set on tables and by the door. Unusual for the meticulous Villiers, but perhaps he was having a clear-out. Narrow windows at the top of the room gave access to some natural light and fresh air, if one was good with the window-pole that hooked into a loop at the top of the window to pull it open. Alex didn't bother.

He went to the diagram of the family tree hung on the wall. It was not like the elaborate one hung in one of the corridors upstairs for the edification of the guests, but a simpler affair, one compiled by Villiers himself. Lines ruled on the paper instead of fanciful boughs, plainly written names instead of elaborate script.

He let his mind settle as he stared at his ancestry. He traced his own branch, all neatly written, and went back to his grandfather, and then to his great-grandfather. That gentleman had been so prolific that Alex was sure they could trace more heirs from that line if they were forced to do it. This line ended with himself, Adolphus, and Benedict.

"Hmm." He went to the desk and the huge account books he'd last been working on. Then he went to the bookcase and selected a few.

They were so heavy that opening them gave him a twinge in his side, which he largely ignored. "Aha!" He found what he wanted, closed the ones he didn't need, and stacked them at the side of the desk.

Someone cleared his throat.

Expecting to see Villiers, Alex slipped his hand around the butt of the pistol he'd stowed in his pocket as he looked up.

Adolphus stood in the doorway, leaning against the jamb, elegant in black.

Alarm coursed through Alex, instinctive and unbidden. Adolphus, the man who stood most to gain by his death, who'd been conveniently to hand when a bullet had ripped through Alex's side. The trained killer. He was wrong, but that instinct had given him an idea of how Adolphus's victims might have felt.

A smile quirked Adolphus's mouth and he deliberately turned his attention to Alex's movements. "Really? You still think I mean you harm?"

"No, of course not," Alex said. The air between them tightened with tension.

Adolphus strolled into the room. "You should at least close the door, and probably lock it behind you. If I'd wanted to, I could have killed you before you knew I was here."

He was right. Alex was sure of him, but his research had made him jumpy. It could easily have been someone else.

Adolphus strolled into the room, but when he touched the door handle, Alex held up a hand, palm out. "Don't close it."

Adolphus looked quizzically at the door and then back at Alex. "You don't like closed doors?"

Alex shook his head. "Not in this room." He indicated the windows, high up and narrow. The desk faced the door. "This room is damp, smelly, and it feels like a gaol cell."

"Hmm. Known many of those, have you?"

"Have you?"

Adolphus's smile disappeared. "Once or twice. Not in this country." He pushed the door not quite closed.

"I don't particularly want the title, you know," Alex confessed. "I told our uncle to pass it to you, before he had Villiers explain the rules of entail to me."

Adolphus stopped dead, eyes wide. "You didn't know about entails?"

"No. My father refused to have anything to do with his previous life. I knew how the laws of inheritance worked. Entails never entered my life until I walked through the front door of this house."

"Good Lord." Adolphus stared at him. "Why did you come?"

Alex thought through his reasons before he answered. "Because I wanted the matter cleared up. I thought I could persuade my uncle to pass over me in the inheritance if I behaved like an uneducated person."

"Hence the accent."

"Aye."

The thread of a smile passed over Adolphus's lips. "And you were right. If he could have rid himself of you, he would have done it in an instant."

Alex went on. "So the marquess set me to learning. I let him because it occurred to me that the marchioness could get with child. While I don't care about the title, I don't like to think about a babe in arms and his mother being exploited."

"Chivalrous of you." Adolphus strolled to the old, glass-fronted cabinet holding some of the estate records. He opened a door and touched a ledger. "Did you find what you wanted?"

Alex glanced at the ledger before him. "Oh yes."

His cousin turned back to him. "Let me guess. There are two sets of books, are there not?"

Alex shouldn't have been surprised that Adolphus had worked it out. "I'm sure of it. When our uncle sent me here, I noted how detailed and precise Villiers kept the records. But something was wrong. I couldn't work out what it was at first."

Adolphus perched on the corner of the desk and tilted one of the ledgers toward himself. He flipped the page, flipped another then went back to the first one. "I see. I'm not an expert at figures and bookkeeping, but I know a duplicated signature when I see one."

Something so small it had taken Alex some time to work it out. "I was concentrating on the figures, but something niggled at me. Nobody has precisely the same signature twice. It won't even be exactly the same when they just use their initials. Not even if they're in fine copperplate."

He'd found the original ledgers, the ones the marquess had actually signed. "He didn't even hide the second set of books.

They're all bound the same way, in that green cloth. That must have made it easier for him to compile his fraud, having them to hand."

Because that was what he'd done. The true numbers were in the unmarked ledger, the one Villiers had put away after getting them signed by the marquess. For the books he'd presented to the man of business, he'd forged the marquess's signature, and inflated the figures a shade. Just a shade, but with such a large estate, it added up to a lot of money.

Adolphus glanced at the cabinet. "You have a key."

"I do. But even a novice like myself could pick the cabinet lock."

His cousin laughed. "True enough. I think he was getting overconfident. I wonder what he did with all that money," Adolphus said.

"You'll never know," a voice said from the doorway. Slowly, the door swung open.

Adolphus cursed.

Alex got to his feet, snatching the pistol out of his pocket. Adolphus spun around, seemingly weaponless, but Alex knew better.

Villiers, immaculate in unrelieved black held a pistol of his own in one hand. In the other heavily gloved hand, he held fire. It stank.

The kitchens used dried dung as fuel. Mixed with straw it was explosively combustible.

Villiers had obviously seen stage villains lose the battle when they paused for explanations, because he wasted no time. He tossed the flaming bundle in the room and slammed the door. The key turned in the lock as Adolphus's thrown blade hit the wood.

"Jesus!" Key in hand, Alex leaped through the flames to the door. A moment was all it took to discover they couldn't get out. "He half-turned the key. I can't get it. And there are bolts on the outside of the door. No getting out."

Adolphus had his coat off and was beating at the flames. That only served to feed the fire, so he threw the coat into the flames. One side of the room caught in no time, the draped cloths on the tables feeding the stacks of paper. Adolphus choked and staggered back.

Trying to unlock the door was useless. Alex's eyes smarted. He could barely see.

"Come over here!" Adolphus yelled. Glass smashed and the flames soared higher. Taking a chance, Alex plunged across the room. Heat seared him. At the command, "Coat!" Alex didn't hesitate. He ripped off his coat, thankful he didn't wear skintight ones, and tossed it away, heedless of the sharp pain from his rib.

"This is taking hold really fast," he said when he reached Adolphus, who had smashed one of the windows with the window pole. His hand was bleeding, but not badly.

"He prepared the room. He was always going to do this," Adolphus said. "Finding us in here was a bonus." He dragged the chair over. "Can you get through that?" He pointed at the window.

"Not a chance," Alex said. "You go. Get help."

Adolphus looked him up and down. "It's our only chance." A sheet of flame separated them from the door now. No way through it now. "Keep low."

Heat seared Alex's throat as he watched Adolphus climb on the chair. After a moment, he dropped back down. "Bars," he said briefly. "In tight."

Damn. They both sank to the floor. The air was almost breathable here. But it wouldn't be for much longer. "He seeded the place," Alex said. "I wondered. All those piles of papers. He's metic—meticulous." Bending his head, he coughed. "Helpless. Stupid."

"Both of us," Adolphus managed. He lowered his head, managed to tear his neckcloth free.

Alex did the same, and they stared at each other. "We can't give up now."

All they could do was pray that help reached them in time. Flame roared over their heads.

Chapter Twenty-Four

AFTER BREAKFAST, BIANCA and her mother left the room. Subdued gossip followed them. "We have much to discuss," her mother said.

"We do. I know a place where we won't be disturbed."

Not her room or the sitting room—the maids would be busy tidying and cleaning at this hour. But there was a small room at the end of that corridor, plainly furnished, by the staircase leading down to the offices in the family wing.

Bianca felt as if a band in her chest had relaxed, seeing her mother. "You look well," she said to her mother as they walked toward the little room. Despite the unrelieved black.

"I've slept, eaten, attended more musicales than I care to remember, and read your letters," Mrs. Burrell said.

"I tried to write every day, but I've been busy."

"So I read."

That laconic remark was enough to tell Bianca her mother had also inferred something. Bianca had barely mentioned Alex at all in her letters, or so she thought. But by the tone of her mother's remarks, she was not just talking about the marquess's murder.

"You know this house very well," her mother remarked, seemingly casually.

"I've been here a while."

Bianca stopped at the end of the corridor. "What can you smell?"

Her mother sniffed. "Cloves, orange . . ." she turned to Bianca, urgency tightening her features. "Burning. Something is on fire."

They raced down the stairs, barely skimming the drugget covering the bare stone. As they descended, the smell grew stronger, the harshness of burning wood stinging their throats.

Neither spoke. There were no words.

When they arrived downstairs, the narrow corridor leading to the offices was in chaos. Maids, footmen, and others carried buckets, water spilling over the edges.

Until a voice yelled, "Silence!"

Bianca had never heard Benedict use that commanding tone before. Without hesitation, they shoved through the crowd to reach him. He spared them a glance. "The offices are on fire. Adolphus and Alex are in there."

Numb shock filled her. No, not again. Was fire about to take this man from her, too?

An instant later, she rallied. No, it was not. This time she was here, she could make a difference, maybe the difference that would save him. "What can we do?"

Benedict did not look at her as he said, "Get them to form a line. I ordered all the sand buckets brought down here."

"Are they alive?" her mother asked, anxiety pitching her voice high.

"I heard them shout," Benedict said. "I was coming back from the stables—"

Bianca displayed her hidden power. She shoved two fingers into her mouth and whistled.

Such a blast stopped the chaos dead. The servants stood still, jaws agape.

Mrs. Burrell stepped in, "Make a line!" she bellowed. "Come on, sort yourselves out!" A touch of the Irish accent she'd worked so hard to suppress tinged her words, but now they startled the servants into action. Quickly, they did as they were told, and before a minute was gone, they had the order sorted.

They passed pails of water down the line, hand to hand, while the footman at the front, aided by Benedict, hurled the contents into the flames.

Bianca yelled through the door. "Alex!"

A faint cry answered her. They were alive. Relief flooded through her, but only temporarily, as every minute counted. Every second. The center of the room was a sheet of flame; they couldn't see beyond that, except for the narrow windows ahead which were smashed open, feeding the flames but also, with any luck, providing air to breathe.

She beckoned to the chain of fire fighters, urging them on.

The sand arrived. That made more of a difference. While the water kept the fire from spreading, the sand was more efficient and actually started to smother it. Eventually they could see through the flames.

The two men inside had upended the large desk that dominated the room. On its side, it served to shelter them, if they crouched behind it. Someone stood. Alex, it was Alex! Crouching again, the desk seemed to explode as both men kicked what was left of it away. It collided with the remnants of a cabinet, glass smashing as both men hurled themselves through the room, and the place where the fire was thinnest, through the door. Bianca beat at the flames that licked up Alex's coat and someone threw a bucket of water over him.

He was laughing as he seized Bianca and in front of everyone else, pressed a smacking kiss on her lips. "Proud of you," he said.

Only then did she recall that she was afraid of fire. But she was more afraid of losing Alex.

ALEX WOULDN'T LET Bianca out of his sight as his valet stripped him, washed him, examined his existing wounds and the new ones, and patched him up. She was anxious to see how much the fire had added to his injuries, so she was glad to stay. The new wounds were superficial: a few burns, none serious, all painful. Of course. But time was of the essence now. The funeral was in an hour.

While Fisher tutted around him, Alex shot her a private grin. "What I don't understand is why now," he said as Fisher helped him into a fresh shirt. "Well, not precisely. I suppose the marquess discovered Villiers was keeping two sets of accounts."

"What?" She had not known that.

"Oh yes."

He smiled at her wide-eyed reaction. "I was looking for figures, but I was looking in the wrong place. He'd been very careful to inflate his accounts only slightly. The kind of numbers that someone might charge a lord, with a little extra added on. But the answer was in the signatures. My uncle signed the accounts and inventories every month, and initialed every page, as most good masters do. They were identical. Precise."

"Too precise," she said. "Yes?"

He nodded. "Villiers was a precise man, but without imagination."

He turned as a knock came on the door. Bianca didn't move as Fisher went to answer it. He admitted Benedict and Adolphus, both back in mourning clothes. Benedict was grinning. "I got him," he said.

"You did?"

They nodded to Bianca, and she returned the informal greeting with amusement. "You did?" she said, repeating Alex's words.

"That's what I wanted to tell you. He's bound and guarded in one of the anterooms downstairs—the butler's safe."

The butler's safe was a fortified room where the silver was kept when not needed. It amused Alex to think that Villiers was where he could look at treasures that had escaped his notice. "Why did you lock him up?"

Benedict shrugged. "I was with Hon—." He blushed red.

His brother provided a helpful prompt. "Honoria," he supplied. "Along with all the other things happening here, my brother has finally discovered the woman he wants to spend the rest of his life with."

"Adolphus!"

"I'm sure the new marquess will not refuse his permission," Adolphus said smoothly, but the smile he gave his brother held true affection. "I'm very happy for you both, brother. Are Lord and Lady Colmondale content?"

"We haven't told them yet."

"Congratulations," Bianca said, to which Alex added his mite.

"So how did you get him?" he asked Benedict. "And why?"

"He was creating a damn—dreadful fuss," Benedict continued, ameliorating his words to spare Bianca's sensibilities, she assumed. "Wanted a horse immediately. Told the grooms to put the carriage to. Seemed agitated. So I told him to calm down and he tried to hit me. Well, I won't have anybody behaving that way in front of Hon—"

"Honoria," his brother prompted.

"Exactly. So I told him to calm down. He seemed to, but then the shout of 'Fire!' went up from the house. One of the grooms came in the yard, shouting, and that seemed to work Villiers up again. So I decided to help him calm down. He fought back, so I marched him into the house and put him in the butler's safe. Tied to a chair. Told the servants to leave him there. He was still there when I checked again five minutes ago." Another grin. "Cursing up a storm."

Alex crossed the room and clapped his cousin on the shoulder. "Magnificent! Well done, Benedict! And don't worry about Honoria's mother. I'll bring her around. I'll tell her that her daughter is marrying the heir to the marquess, a man with a fine future rearing bloodstock."

Benedict blinked. "I wouldn't go that far. I mean, I'm fairly warm, but it takes a lot of money to go into that line."

"Lucrative, though, if it's done right. Who else would I entrust the task to?"

"Oh, you mean you were planning to invest in horse breeding?"

Not if Bianca knew him, but she wasn't about to stick an obstacle in the way. Benedict and Honoria would be blissfully happy. "Yes, of course," Alex said, turning so Fisher could fold his neckcloth for him. He couldn't lift his arms high enough to do that yet. A black neckcloth, naturally.

"We'll see to Villiers after the funeral," Alex said. He turned around and presented himself to Bianca. "Will I do?"

As the marquess's heir, Alex was chief mourner. The cousins were pallbearers.

"You look perfect," she told him, and meant it. They exchanged a long, lingering look.

"Are you all right?" he asked her.

He remembered. His concern warmed her, and she knew she would deny him nothing. The threat of losing him had taken every fear away from her. If she could have saved him that way, she'd have run through the flames to him. Losing him would not just hurt her, it would damage her. Permanently.

With a jerk of his head he dismissed everyone. Bianca heard doors close but she didn't look away. She went into his arms and lifted her head for his kiss.

He eased her, he thrilled her and aroused her with the first caress of her lips. Not long and luscious, not a precursor to lovemaking, more an acknowledgment of what lay between them. Everything she wanted lay here in his arms.

He raised his head. Already he was smiling. "Are you ready to answer my question?"

"Yes," she said. "It's yes."

His smile broadened, and they lost themselves in another kiss. "I love you," she murmured against his lips. This was real and lifelong.

"I love you too. You have no idea how happy you've just

made me."

When he released her, she stepped back reluctantly. "We'll have to wait."

"Until Friday, maybe." Lifting his head he checked his appearance in the mirror hung on the wall behind them. Then, as if drawn back, he returned his attention to her. He bathed her in love. "I sent a man to London before the accident in the woods," he reminded her. "He's bringing a special license back, among other things. I expect him here by the end of the week. No longer, love. It would not be seemly for us to marry with all the pomp of an elaborate service and wedding breakfast, so we will do it quietly and privately."

His uncle's death meant they would marry sooner rather than later. Sad though the circumstances were, she could not be sorry.

"I must go. May I escort you down to the drawing room?"

She sighed. "If you must."

"I'll be back in an hour or so. We have to walk to the village and attend the service so that his tenants can pay their respects. Then we walk back. I have to admit I feel happier doing it without wondering if someone is about to make another attempt on my life." He crooked his arm, and she tucked her hand through it. "Fisher informs me that my mother has arrived. Have you met her?"

"Briefly at breakfast. She is so lovely."

He lifted her hand to his lips and kissed it before tucking it back under his arm. "Not as lovely as you. But I'm glad. I will have a quiet word with her before I go."

"She left your sisters at home, she said."

"Good. They have no place in this. After we marry, I'd like to take you home and introduce you to them."

"I'd like that too." From the little she'd heard of his sisters, they intrigued Bianca. She wanted to know more.

Before he went to the church, Alex formally introduced Bianca to his mother as his betrothed wife. Mrs. Fraser took the news in her stride. "I thought as much," she commented, then cordially welcomed Bianca to the family.

Alex expected nothing less from his formidable mother.

The walk to the village gave him time to think. Putting on a suitable expression of grave concern, he led the cortege, stopping at the lychgate, where they took the coffin off the gun carriage and lifted it onto the shoulders of the pallbearers.

Everything went smoothly. The service was read, the solemn words emphasizing the nature of death, however it was sustained. The vicar, thank all the powers that be, kept his sermon short, a mere twenty minutes eulogizing the late marquess. He did not welcome the new one, since the announcement of Alex's succession had not been made, but outside the church, when Alex paused to shake hands with the cleric, he called Alex "my lord."

Alex worked hard not to wince. He would have to get used to it, he supposed. Leaning close, he asked, "Are you free on Friday? I have a favor to ask you."

"Indeed, my lord." There it was again. "Should I attend you at the house?" It was quite a euphemism to call Stonyhurst "the house." Alex wondered if he would have to permanently locate here. He would do his best not to. Perhaps there was a way. He would ask Bianca which she preferred.

His heart swelled with love when he thought of her. Oh, he was completely, irrevocably in love with her. A man should not be this happy at a funeral. He kept his expression suitably mournful by thinking of Villiers and what he would do to him when he got back. Most of his fantasies would not come to pass, especially the more imaginative ones.

When he arrived at the butler's safe, he found four sturdy menservants and his cousins outside the strengthened metal door. The magistrate, a man he'd met after his uncle's death, was also with them. They shook hands, a greeting Alex was more used to than bowing.

"Well, Mr. Barnsfather, here we are again."

"Aye, my lord."

He supposed he'd get used to it sometime. "Do we have a strategy?"

Adolphus nodded. "We thought we'd let you ask. Do we have a good case without a confession?"

"I think so. Only the most recent inventories and accounts were kept here. The rest are with the estate's man of business in London. As long as he did not start this practice recently, we have the motive for the crime."

Adolphus grimaced. "It's not enough. We need a confession, written or verbal."

Alex wondered if Adolphus had personal experience of getting a confession but decided not to ask. "You may lead this. You have more experience in this field."

"I won't complicate matters unless I have to," Adolphus said.

"What does 'complicate' mean?"

Adolphus smiled, but there was no humor in it. "Let's leave that for later, shall we?"

The footmen unlocked the door, and they went in.

Like the offices above, this part of the building must have been part of the old monastery. The stone walls oozed age. While the office had paneled walls concealing the stone ones, these were bare. Glass-fronted cabinets held gleaming silverware, and the two safes in either corner indicated other vessels and gold plate. Alex was profoundly glad *that* had never been brought out.

A tray holding cloths and some other silver items stood on a simple table just inside the door. It seemed the butler had not quite finished polishing.

In the center of the small space left was a chair holding the prisoner. His hands were tightly bound to the spokes, and his legs were secured together at the ankle.

At a nod from Alex, Adolphus put his slim blade to use, slicing through the rough rope. He stepped back, staring over Villiers's head. "Anything to say?"

Silence fell, which Adolphus chose not to break. Alex counted silently. At ten, Villiers spoke. "You should release me."

"This is as far as you go. Then to gaol, then to the gallows," Alex told him.

"You have nothing to send me there." That supercilious smirk was asking for a slap. Alex folded his arms.

Adolphus smiled again. "We have a charge of attempted murder."

"Do you? I did not see you in the office."

Adolphus raised a brow. "And you're guilty of arson. Which you just admitted to." Arson alone could hang him, but Alex wanted more, and by the sound of it, so did Adolphus. Benedict said nothing, but the grim set of his features said it all. Adolphus continued. "We both saw you, and you looked straight at us."

"And the embezzlement?" Alex asked. "What about that?"

Villiers's smirk spread in a sneer. "What embezzlement? Where is your evidence?"

"With the marquess's man of business. And no doubt we will discover what happened to the money you stole. Did the marquess discover your deception?"

"What deception? I am a true servant to Stonyhurst. I would never steal from the estate." He sounded sincere. Perhaps he even believed it.

"So that means you have the money tucked away somewhere, waiting for this mythical true heir."

Villiers looked directly at Alex, then at Adolphus. "Not you, nor you." He turned his attention to Benedict. "You are the true heir, sir. I have always believed so."

Benedict gave a short laugh. "Third in line."

"Second," his brother gently corrected him.

Villiers remained silent, but Alex got his meaning. "My heritage?" he said softly. "Is that it?"

"A mongrel," Villiers said. "Neither one thing nor the other. Impure blood." He turned to Adolphus. "And you sir, you are a sodomite. Deny it if you dare."

Adolphus shrugged. How long had it taken him to appear so insouciant? Alex had reason to understand him. Adolphus's preferences were no more sinful than Alex's birth. Neither of them had a choice—they were what they were. But while Alex might be gossiped about and even shunned, Adolphus could be hanged for his differences.

He would support and defend his cousin with every drop of his blood.

"So now we have the motive. You tried to kill me once, and then when I was with Adolphus." It took his deepest concentration to keep his voice steady.

"Two birds with one stone," Villiers said, his lip still curled in a sneer. "It was irresistible." He wasn't even trying to deny it. He lifted his chin. "You are not worthy of the great title. You were even planning to marry that whore."

Alex slapped the man, backhanding him so hard he felt the man's teeth rattle.

Villiers yelped and put his hand up. He spat blood and what looked like a tooth into his hand.

Adolphus smiled. "If you'd punched him he wouldn't be able to speak. I'd rather like to see that." He turned his back on the man. "Not worth our time," he said.

"I agree," Alex said. He'd barely kept his fist from clenching.

"I accept your challenge," Villiers managed to mumble. "Pistols at dawn." Only he had an unfortunate lisp now.

Alex did not even bother to reply. He left the room, his companions following him. The magistrate locked the door to the safe and pocketed the key. "I will have him out of this house in an hour, my lord," he said.

"Thank you." Slowly, Alex was simmering down. Villiers could insult him all he wanted, but not Bianca.

Chapter Twenty-Five

H ER SECOND WEDDING day. Bianca let McMurdo finish her hair, adding the diamond pins that Alex had sent her. They were all the more precious because they were new, a personal gift from him, nothing to do with titles.

They'd had to wait an extra day for his messenger to arrive from London with the special license. When she suggested they could have the banns read in the regular way, he'd laughed her to scorn. "Not an extra hour, not an extra minute," he'd said.

Now everybody called him by his title. Nobody had declared him the marquess, but people were assuming it. So she would be "my lady" after today. She had no intention of using her previous title. That belonged to one person now, the gentle woman married to the current duke. Bianca would gladly abandon it.

Her fear of fire seemed to have gone. When her maid had suggested lighting the fire while Bianca bathed, she'd agreed, not giving the matter a thought. Perhaps love did conquer all. At least, true love did.

They had not spent a night apart, and they were ordering the family apartments to suit their preferences. As they'd surveyed the bedroom the last marquess had occupied, they decided to change the whole suite. And next week she would visit Alex's house near Sheffield.

Her bedroom door opened. She saw the entrants in the mirror and sprang up. "Viola! Juliet! When did you get here?"

Her joy was complete. She embraced her sisters, first one by one, and then in a great huddle. Just like the old days, the three of them and their mother against the world.

"We arrived back in London last week," Juliet said, laughing. "The treaty is signed, and we are home for now." She paused. "Except we have the opportunity to return for a longer stay."

"Isn't the United States a barbarous country?" Bianca said. She had read some startling things about this young country.

"It's beautiful," Juliet said. "And it's exciting. There are so many opportunities, and there is so much to explore! But we would not see you again for years." Her mouth turned down at the corners. "It is a major consideration, I have to admit."

"You should not think of that," Bianca said. "Follow your heart. That is what I've done this time."

"So you have," Viola agreed. "As did I. We must never be afraid. If Mama taught us anything, it is that."

Laughing, Bianca linked her hands with her sisters. "And look where that got us!"

"Blissfully happy, married to the men we love, and with a wonderful future ahead of us," Juliet said. "Less a haven, more the start of new adventures."

"Of course," Bianca said. "We only have what we deserve."

And she went out to meet the man she would love for the rest of her life.

A SPECIAL LICENSE meant they could marry in a place of their choosing, so they had selected the chapel at Stonyhurst. The few guests that remained from the house party were there, as were the people who meant most to Bianca: her family. Lords Langston and Knowsley came forward to take their beloved wives to their places and Bianca was left alone. She needed nobody to give her away. She would do that herself.

Alex was standing at the altar, gazing at her, his love clear for all to see. But before she began the short walk to meet him, she paused. The spoiled, beautiful image of her first husband appeared in her mind, and he was smiling. Finally free of his demons. As she was free of hers.

Goodbye George, she said to the vision. It melted away, leaving her vision clear at last.

As she walked up the small aisle, she had eyes only for the man she had chosen with all her heart. Before the vicar started the service, she made her vow. "I will love you for all my days," she said.

"And I you." He folded her hand in his and side by side they began the service.

About the Author

I write stories, and I always have. And I love a happy ending, especially a well-deserved one.

I'm an award-winning, best-selling author of historical romance. I fell in love with the eighteenth century when I was nine years old, and it's my dream job to write about the people who lived and loved back then.

I used to work in marketing, and I have more letters after my name than in it, but I don't use them much anymore.

I live in the UK with my family, including my muse, Frankie the Nonsense, a ragdoll with no decorum. I love traveling, and I get over to the States at least once a year.

My website is at lynneconnolly.com. SItwitters @lynneconnolly and my Facebook page is here: facebook.com/lynneconnollyuk. My blog is at lynneconnolly.blogspot.com.

I also have a newsletter. If you'd like to join it, email me on lynneconnollyuk@yahoo.co.uk or fill in the form on my website.